DORIS LANGLEY
MY CARAVAGGIO

Doris Elizabeth Langley Moore (*née* Levy) was born on 23 July 1902 in Liverpool. She moved with her family to South Africa when she was eight. She received no formal education, but read widely, under the influence of her father.

Moore moved to London in the early 1920s, and wrote prolifically and diversely, including Greek translation, and an etiquette manual. In 1926 she married Robert Moore, and they had one daughter, Pandora, before divorcing in 1942.

She published six romantic novels between 1932 and 1959, in addition to several books on household management and an influential biography of E. Nesbit.

Moore was passionately interested in clothes, and her own clothes formed the basis of a collection of costumes, to which she added important historical pieces. Her fashion museum was opened in 1955, eventually finding a permanent home in Bath in 1963.

In addition to books, she also wrote a ballet, *The Quest*, first performed at Sadler's Wells in 1943. Moore also worked as a costume designer for the theatre and films, and designed Katharine Hepburn's dresses for *The African Queen* (1951).

Doris Langley Moore continued to write books, with a particular emphasis on Lord Byron. Her last novel, *My Caravaggio Style* (1959), about the forgery of the lost Byron memoirs, was followed by three scholarly works on the poet.

Doris Langley Moore was appointed OBE in 1971. She died in London in 1989.

TITLES BY DORIS LANGLEY MOORE

Fiction

A Winter's Passion (1932)
The Unknown Eros (1935)
A Game of Snakes and Ladders (1938, 1955)* **
Not at Home (1948)*
All Done by Kindness (1951)*
My Caravaggio Style (1959)*

* available from Dean Street Press and Furrowed Middlebrow

Selected Non-fiction

The Technique of the Love Affair (1928, reprinted 1999)
E. Nesbit: A Biography (1933, expanded edition 1966)
The Vulgar Heart: An Enquiry into the Sentimental Tendencies of Public Opinion (1945)
The Woman in Fashion (1949)
The Child in Fashion (1953)
Pleasure: A Discursive Guide Book (1953)
The Late Lord Byron: Posthumous Dramas (1961)
Marie & the Duke of H: The Daydream Love Affair of Marie Bashkirtseff (1966)
Fashion Through Fashion Plates, 1771-1970 (1971)
Lord Byron: Accounts Rendered (1974)
Ada, Countess of Lovelace: Byron's Legitimate Daughter (1977)

** Published in 1938 under the title *They Knew Her When: A Game of Snakes and Ladders*. Revised and reprinted in 1955 as *A Game of Snakes and Ladders*. Dean Street Press has used the text of the 1955 edition for its new edition.

DORIS LANGLEY MOORE

MY CARAVAGGIO STYLE

With an introduction by
Sir Roy Strong

DEAN STREET PRESS

A Furrowed Middlebrow Book
FM42

Published by Dean Street Press 2020

Copyright © 1959 Doris Langley Moore

Introduction © 2020 Roy Strong

All Rights Reserved

The right of Doris Langley Moore to be identified as the Author of the Work has been asserted by her estate in accordance with the Copyright, Designs and Patents Act 1988.

First published in 1959 by Cassell & Co.

Cover by DSP

ISBN 978 1 913054 61 8

www.deanstreetpress.co.uk

To

JOHN GREY MURRAY

with gratitude
and
without prejudice

INTRODUCTION
BY SIR ROY STRONG

"I WAS the first writer to take the reader through the bedroom door". That announcement to me by Doris Langley Moore (1902-1989) has always stuck in my mind. I only came to know her late in her life, in the mid 1960s when I was involved in establishing The Costume Society. I already knew her work for I was early on fascinated by the history of dress and consumed her pioneer volumes *The Woman in Fashion* (1949) and *The Child in Fashion* (1953) while I was still at school. I had also travelled down to Eridge Castle in 1953 where Doris opened the first version of her Museum of Costume which was to find its resting place in Bath some ten years later in what is now called The Fashion Museum.

She later became a friend, a formidable one making me quickly grasp why she had gained a reputation for being difficult. She was. But any encounter with her tended to be memorable providing fragments of a larger mosaic of a life which had been for a period at the creative centre of things. Later encounters were remarkable like the one when she took me out to lunch at The Ivy so that I could sign her passport photograph as a true likeness when transparently it had been taken through a gauze! This was the occasion when she suddenly volunteered that she had been the handsome Director of the National Gallery Sir Philip Hendy's (1900-1980) mistress.

If the material existed Doris would be a good example of the new emancipated woman who burst on the scene in the 1920s flaunting convention. She, of course, rightly takes her place in the *New Oxford Dictionary of National Biography* but what we read there raises more questions than it answers. Here was the Liverpool born daughter of a newspaper editor who, having passed most of her childhood in South Africa, suddenly arrives on the scene with a translation from the Greek of *Anacreon: 29 Odes* (1926). Two years later came the even more startling

The Technique of the Love Affair (1928) under a pseudonym 'a gentlewoman' of which Dorothy Parker wrote that her whole love life would have been different if she had had the good fortune to have read this first. It has apparently stood the test of time and was reprinted in 1999. Two years before Doris had married and, although she did not divorce her husband until 1942, one would conclude that that marriage rapidly went on the rocks. Indeed I recall being told that her husband had gone off with the nanny of her only child, a daughter called Pandora. She never married again.

Doris was an extraordinarily multi-talented woman who moved with ease within the creative art set of the era. She was closely involved in those who were to become the Royal Ballet and, in 1943, wrote the scenario for a patriotic ballet *The Quest* to get the future Sir Frederick Ashton out of army. The music was by William Walton and the designs by John Piper, and Margot Fonteyn and Robert Helpmann dance in it. Again I recall her telling me that the members of what were to become our Royal Ballet at the opening of the war were all up in her house in Harrogate. And, after I married the designer Julia Trevelyan Oman, she took us out to dinner with William Chappell, the designer of Ashton's *Les Patineurs*. Then there were connexions with the Redgrave family who appear dressed in Regency and Victorian costume in her books. Vivien Leigh also figures in these books, again Doris remarking disparagingly of Olivier's part in the famous break up.

Between 1932 and 1959 she wrote six romantic novels, appreciated today by a readership which scours the Net for copies. All of this sat alongside a sharp academic mind which she applied in particular to a life long obsession with Lord Byron. Again I recall her opening a lecture on him describing how she had fended off a young man trying to kiss her at her first ball by drawing back and saying "Have you read *Childe Harold*?" Her first book *The Late Lord Byron* (1961) revolutionised Byron studies and two more of equal importance followed, *Lord Byron, Accounts Rendered* (1974) and *Ada, Countess of Lovelace* (1977).

But her greatest legacy must be The Museum of Fashion in Bath. Doris was obsessed by fashion and details of dress. I remember her noticing the way that I followed in town the correct gentleman's etiquette of wearing one glove on the hand which held the other. She herself followed fashion and indeed her hats were the subject of a Sotheby's sale. Why was her contribution in this area so important? Doris was the first person who moved the study of dress out of the antiquary's study into the land of the living. When it came to wheeler dealing with historic dress she had no equal. To her dress was vivid visual evidence of the attitudes and aspirations of a whole society. In that she ranks as an original enabling others to follow in the path that she blazed. She began collecting in 1928 and was to campaign for a museum for some twenty five years until at last it came to rest in the Assembly Rooms in Bath. And, typical of Doris, it embraced the new from the outset inaugurating the annual Dress of the Year Event which took off with a Mary Quant mini-dress. But then we can still see her in action for we can go on line and watch her in the first ever BBC colour television programmes from 1957 on the madness and marvel of clothes.

Roy Strong

Chapter One

Everything written, Byron said, is written for the purpose of being read, however much many writings may fail in arriving at that object. And so I must be writing for a reader; but who he may be or why I'm doing it, I'm fairly at a loss to explain. This won't be the kind of story I can publish with disguised names as a novel—not the kind of story I can publish at all if it comes to that. Yet here I am, pen in hand, compelled in spite of myself to set the whole business down.

I suppose hardly anyone has ever been in the antiquarian book trade without having some dream of finding an important collector's piece which only he has the wits to recognise, and cashing in on a big scale. The curious thing is that, if there was ever an exception to that rule it was myself. I'd taken the job at Rossiter's because it seemed likely not to interfere too drastically with my literary work, and I was entirely preoccupied with that. . . . I mean, as preoccupied as a man can be who's got himself involved with a kind of goddess. If I had a recurring daydream it was of striking some vein that would be congenial both to me and to a public big enough to pay for my taking possession of the goddess, a girl who was accustomed to trailing mink coats along the floor after her.

So far, my tastes and those of the public had never come anywhere near to coinciding, and, as a matter of fact, that very day—the day that begins the story—I had received a cheque for royalties which amounted to £4 13s. 2d.

The figures are engraved on my memory. Sales for the six months preceding April 1956—fourteen copies of *Washington Irving in England* at a royalty of fifteen per cent and a few sold overseas for the miserable reduced price which always makes it so astonishing that publishers bother to send books overseas at all; nine copies of my small Ravenna anthology, which was about to be remaindered; and for *The Follies of William Beckford* a debit account. The book hadn't earned its modest advance.

I sat in the little back room lined with Rossiter's all too unmoving stock and asked myself, not just rhetorically, whether it was going to be a luxury beyond my means to write my book on Byron. Of course, Byron was a much bigger gun than Beckford, but for that very reason, the ground about him was well trodden. I had only to look round to get some reminder of how well trodden it was, for in the back room was part of our biographical section, and I confess I'd been guilty, for the sake of my researches, of not pressing the sale of books on this particular topic. It was handy to have them there on the shelves beside me.

The question had been gnawing at me from the first—whether I ought to refrain from writing about Byron because there were so many others doing it, or set about it with a will because the theme was so popular. But now, with the advance on *Beckford* still unearned eighteen months after publication, the problem had developed an acute aspect. After the losses they must have made on me, would my publishers take another biographical work of mine? Would even Byron go down with them if there were no new material, no stimulating discovery?

I don't want to give a retrospective dramatic colouring to events which happened quite undramatically, but I really believe that when the American walked in I was meditating on the rich good luck in the way of fresh evidence that almost every recent writer on Byron seemed to have enjoyed—the English love letters first brought out by Peter Quennell, the Italian love letters in Iris Origo's book, the suppressed bits of Hobhouse's diary that Michael Joyce and others had been able to use, and in America Leslie Marchand who'd accumulated all sorts of stuff with dollars galore, no doubt, at the back of him. Now if only somebody would subsidise *my* researches ...

That was my line of thought more or less when the American's shadow fell across the trapeze of sunlight quivering on the linoleum near the shop door on a July afternoon.

It had been a quiet day at Rossiter's. No one at all since lunch-time except a woman who'd bought a fashion print for three-and-six, a runner inquiring for a set of Dickens, which we didn't happen to have in stock, and two young men who'd giggled rapturously over some scrapbooks without the intention, as I could see at a glance, of buying anything. My commission on sales was going to be a serious consideration with Jocasta's birthday looming up. I prepared to become active.

'Mind if I take a look round?' called the American in bright, eager American tones.

'Do!'

I remained seated the better to reassure him, but my eyes followed him closely as he moved among the shelves occasionally reaching for a volume with a hand that seemed to know what it wanted. After ten minutes or so, he came to the doorway between the outer shop and my lair and held up a leather-bound quarto.

'Pope's *Iliad*. First edition but incomplete. Do you have the missing volume?'

I admitted we hadn't.

'Pity! It would have made a handsome set.'

'Yes. What wouldn't a poet give to have his works printed with so much lavishness today?'

'That's right,' he said, not with our nonchalant downward inflexion, but on quite an ardent note. 'They don't print books like this any more.'

He wandered off again, disappeared behind a tall bookcase, and presently returned with an early Victorian music book.

'Pretty binding. How much is this?'

'Isn't the price inside?'

'Yes, but I'm not sure I understand it.' He handed me the book.

'It's three pounds ten,' I said.

'Not three guineas ten?'

'There's no such reckoning.'

'I'm glad to know it.' His smile, like his diction, was emphatic. 'Florins, half-crowns, sixpenny bits, I can just about grapple with, but to count in guineas when they don't exist any more—that gets me down.'

'Is this your first visit?' I asked politely.

'The first since 1945. I was very young then, and in the army, so I wasn't worried overly much about counting guineas.'

He must indeed have been young then, I thought, for he looked less than my own age, thirty. But I found later that he was four years older. His slight stature and springy movements, and a smile that seemed like a deliberate effort to be disarming, combined to give him a perpetual air of youthfulness.

He laid the music book on my desk asking me to set it aside while he went on with his foraging, and soon he put another volume on top of it, a little Treasury of Tennyson in watered silk with spangled embroidery.

'I've got a very nice miniature set of Tennyson,' I said, 'complete in eight volumes if that would be of any interest to you.'

'Not the kind of thing I can sell,' he answered briskly.

My spirits, damped by the £4 13s. 2d., rose a little. American dealers didn't often come our way, and one who was virtually on his first visit and, judging by his innocence about our currency, at an early stage of it, might prove quite a windfall.

I've mentioned the antiquarian book trade, but to be exact, Rossiter's was only a rather good second-hand shop—a better one, I may say, than it had been when I came to it. Mrs. Rossiter was a resolutely thrifty buyer and would seldom spend anything substantial except when a quick profit was assured. In consequence, though she was too shrewd to let the stock fall below a certain level, it was by no means distinguished. Lately, however, I'd gained her confidence sufficiently to be allowed to do some of the buying myself, and, having made a first-rate deal over a private library and one or two lucky bids in the sale rooms, I was gradually winning her over to my policy of raising the standard even at the risk of a delayed return. Still, we were very far from being on the foreign dealers' beat. Our geographical position alone pretty well ensured that; it was a side street with no associations and leading to nothing in particular. I determined to make the best of a rare opportunity, and threw out a candid feeler.

'Are bindings your line?'

'Not specially. But I can always sell nice copies like these—suitable for gifts, you know. At least, I think I can.' He laughed. 'I haven't been in business long.'

Better and better! I prepared to lay on the charm. Perhaps I ought to mention that I *have* charm. (This strange story will convey the truth whether it reflects creditably or discreditably upon me.) The principle of all charm is, to my thinking, flattery, whether by look, word, or deed. Flattery had got me my job with Mrs. Rossiter, and a publisher for my books though they were produced at a loss, and Jocasta's beauty—what I'd had of it—and all the other privileges which, in my rash way, I'd squandered. I was surely equal to flattering this confiding young bookseller into making a purchase that would redeem the day.

Leaning on the bookcase he was now investigating, I looked benevolently down upon him—I was a head taller—and remarked: 'I was sure I didn't know your face, and yet . . . might I ask who told you about us?'

'Not a soul! Do I have to have a recommendation?'

'No . . . only we don't often get Americans unless they've been put on to us by a collector or a friend in the trade. Practically none ever come here casually.'

There's nothing an American likes more than being told he's doing something or seeing something other Americans don't know about. Mine looked pleased and interested.

'*I* got here casually all right. I simply took a wrong turning on the way to Hodgson's Sale Rooms, and seeing a book-shop I walked into it.'

'But there's no sale at Hodgson's today.'

'There's a pre-view, though, of some manuscript items I'd like to get my hands on.'

'They'll fetch a good deal of money,' I said. I'd studied the catalogue.

'Think so? But I'm not going for the big stuff. Not this trip anyway.'

'Manuscripts are up your street, are they?'

'I'm hoping to make them my specialty.'

I cast around vigorously for something in our stock that might appeal to him. He could hardly have flung a more unacceptable challenge. All I could think of was one holograph letter by Marie

Corelli which had been pasted into a copy of *The Master Christian*. I preferred not to mention it.

Instead I directed his attention to the scrap-books which I thought I had a good chance of selling to him. I was right too, but in his amiable and emphatic way he drove a hard bargain and seemed to enjoy it. To add to my sense of frustration, while I was warming up to some better feat of salesmanship, an aged gentleman came in and tried to off-load a family Bible which he reiterantly informed me was 'more than a hundred years old'—a span always supposed by lay people to have some magical significance. As a rule, I'm sensitive about disillusioning the unfortunates who've been counting on the value of a family treasure, but my patience began to wear a little thin when I saw my customer making an apparently final summation of his purchases at my desk while this persistent dodderer continued to buttonhole me. I was disposed to snatch away his Bible and batter him with it, but it was by suavity at last that I steered him into the street.

'I'll give you the address for delivery,' said the American, taking a cheque-book from his pocket. 'My name's Darrow. *Earl* Darrow. Does that embarrass you?'

'Not in the least!'

'Well, it does me—here among the British anyhow. They look at me as if I was trying to get away with something.'

I murmured a disclaimer almost at random, for my wits were grappling with the urgent problem of how to detain a buyer who could doubtless as easily spend seventy pounds as the seven he was now writing a cheque for. Once gone, it was unlikely that he would ever return. Hodgson's next sale had some exceptional stuff in it; Sotheby's latest catalogue was distinctly tempting; and then there were all the allurements of the top reaches of the retail trade in Mayfair, not to speak of the call of Bloomsbury and the Charing Cross Road. Rossiter's could never compete— not when the novice had become initiated.

Mentally I was ransacking the stock to the last corner of the basement in search of some item that might appeal to a manuscript hunter, and it reflects a gleam of credit on my resourcefulness that, at the same time, I could hit on a means of at least arresting his attention.

'Did you say you were going *to*, or coming *from*, Hodgson's?'

'Going *to*—and I'd better be on my way. They close at five-thirty.'

'You've plenty of time. It's only three or four minutes from here. I wonder if I could ask you—I admit I oughtn't to—if you're after those Gissing letters.'

'Why? Are you?' He smiled very directly at me.

'Not if you are. I can't compete against dollars.' I pretended to be concealing chagrin. 'So there are Gissing addicts in America too?'

'A few, and those letters are of considerable American interest, judging by the extracts in the catalogue. He spent an impressionable period of his life there after all.'

It was because I knew this that I had so sagaciously singled out the Gissing lots as his likeliest quarry. 'At any rate,' I said, 'Gissing's fairly safe as yet from the attentions of forgers.'

'You'd think it'd hardly be worth their while, but it's amazing what trouble they'll take to turn a dishonest penny. The Shelley forgeries began long before Shelley letters fetched big prices. I'll bet a dozen people are busy right now practising Dylan Thomas's handwriting.'

The mention of Shelley put something into my head, and it was positively without ulterior motive that I went off at a tangent. 'You don't happen to have any Byron items within the purchasing power of an Englishman?'

It was I who asked it! I actually had a sudden lunatic idea that, among the shoals of major and minor Byron documents that had made their way across the Atlantic, there might be something that had slipped through the nets of librarians in California, Texas, New Jersey and New York, something—even the littlest piece—that would fit into the jigsaw puzzle of the notes I'd made for my as yet unventured work. The literary man had got the better of the bookseller in me. It was a moment of not having my feet on the ground.

'Byron items!' Earl Darrow raised his eyebrows. 'You mean *in manuscript*! You must be mistaking me for the Rosenbach set-up. I don't know how it may be here, but in the States Byron's on the up-and-up. Your Englishman will need a pretty good bankroll to go looking for Byroniana in America.'

In a quite illogical way, I slightly resented that. Perhaps I was annoyed by the instant pricking of my foolish little bubble.

'I wasn't aiming at the manuscript of *Don Juan*,' I said, and I was going to beat a retreat from the subject when he closed in on me with the words: 'The Morgan Library has that.'

'Not all of it.' The shade of resentment became more defined. 'We still own a few trifling relics here, you know.'

'So you should, having such a long start. But we've been cleaning up everything that's come on the market for a long while now.'

It was wholly contrary to my interests as a bookseller, and not even in keeping with my personal views, to take umbrage at this: I have never regarded it as a calamity for a certain proportion of our treasures to be sent to a country which has so lavish a regard for them. But the stealthy export of Byron papers had been a nagging inconvenience to me. Many things had gone which no English enthusiast had been given an opportunity to bid for or even to examine, and the position about obtaining microfilm or any other kind of copies was—for me at least— all but hopeless. I had no dollars, no transatlantic friends, no reputation as yet to plead favours for me as a Byron scholar. In making my card index I had sometimes been obliged to rely on incomplete published extracts from letters which students of fledgling American universities could read in their entirety.

Darrow's complacent remark had enough truth in it to sting me into protesting: 'There are a great many things that *don't* come on the market.'

'Sure, I know . . . the collection at 50, Albemarle Street.' He said it—or so it seemed to my already jarred ear—as if he were humouring me.

'You ought certainly to try and get an opportunity of seeing that if you're keen on holograph stuff. It isn't only Byron. There are letters—'

Genially he interrupted me. 'Sure, sure. It's wonderful! Out of this world! I was there this morning.'

I don't believe, in the light of my later knowledge of him, that he was even faintly conscious of having deflated me. It was his brightness and eagerness that made him flip back ripostes like counters in a game of tiddlywinks. This one fell into the cup with a very irritating percussion, but I returned smoothly enough: 'Good going! You know the Murrays?'

'I wrote to Sir John before I came over. They were most helpful there—showed me almost more than I could really take in. It was a great experience'—he became disarmingly expansive—'just being there in those rooms where so many famous people have talked and planned about the thing that mattered to them most, I guess, being writers and artists. And to see all those portraits on the walls and that identical fireplace where they burned Byron's Memoirs a hundred and thirty odd years ago . . . though I must say that incident is something of a blot on the history of the house.'

'Did they show you what was left of them?'

'Left of them? I thought nothing was left of them!'

'Oh, there's an exercise book which had part of the copy in it. The binding wasn't the kind that would burn easily, so they tore the pages out: but there's a fragment still clinging with the end of one word on it. It's the most tantalising empty shell I've ever seen.'

'I can imagine! My goodness, what would that book be worth with its pages intact!'

'It wasn't, of course, in Byron's handwriting.'

'No?' He stared at me blankly.

'No. This was the copy that Thomas Moore had made in Paris.'

'I didn't realise there'd been a copy.'

'Yes, there was a Dr. Williams who worked on it because Moore was afraid the original would get worn out with too much handling. Moore was living in France to avoid being arrested for a debt, and passing the Memoirs round among all the fashionable English visitors. Williams didn't get on fast enough with the job, and Moore gave them to a Frenchman named Dumoulin. Dumoulin died after a few months, and then as Byron had sent another batch of sheets, a continuation, they were put into the hands of one more copyist, a paid one. You can find the particulars in Moore's Diary.'

'That's a book I haven't read. There's too much of it.'

'Most of Byron's biographers seem to agree with you, judging by the mistakes they make about the Memoirs.'

'Then they weren't really secret?'

'Hardly. A lot of people read them, and they were definitely copied.'

No doubt it was satisfying to me to have flipped back a counter or two of my own to subdue his bumptiousness, but to do myself justice, I was pleased to be talking on a subject I felt thoroughly engrossed in. That he should be responsive to it followed naturally from where he had been and what he had seen that morning, and I was not unmindful that, as long as I could hold his interest, there was a chance of improving my professional footing with him—though how that was to be done I couldn't precisely envisage.

'No question, I suppose, the copy *was* destroyed?'

'None. It's mentioned in the account Hobhouse wrote immediately afterwards.'

'You don't think Hobhouse could have slipped up a little on that occasion?' His eyes mirrored with wistful self-mockery the bookseller's daydream I've spoken of—the glorious dream of buried treasure.

'In my opinion, Hobhouse slipped up on that occasion in every possible way except the one we could have forgiven him. The copy was destroyed all right. As a matter of fact, another copy had been destroyed while Byron was still alive.'

'*Another?*'

'Yes, of the first portion, anyhow. It was written by Lady Burghersh, one of the friends in high life that Moore took such a delight in playing up to. It must have needed a bit of courage to tell her she'd gone too far and make her promise to burn it.'

'Did she, I wonder?' He sighed. 'Yes, of course she did, otherwise it would have come to light by now. Can you beat it though? All that copying, and nothing survives except the end of a word! Even in someone else's handwriting, an authentic transcript of those Memoirs would surely be a fabulous discovery.'

'Fabulous. More so than Byron's own generation could possibly have recognised. Those who sanctioned the burning had to make out a case afterwards that the loss wasn't an important one, but letters published since show that he worked on them for a long while and put a great deal into them. They contained a minute record of his married life and separation.'

'That alone would be a fairly meaty slice of scandal.'

'On the contrary'—I had to pause to take the edge off my voice—'he believed it would justify him in the eyes of posterity. He was extremely anxious for his wife to read it, and he gave her a solemn pledge that if she could detect anything in it that was false, her comments would be allowed to stand.'

'That so? Then why did his friends burn it?'

'It was destroyed,' I said concisely, 'in the presence of seven people. Only two of them had read it, and those were the ones who tried to save it from being burned. Scandal wasn't the primary reason for the stampede to get rid of that book.'

Darrow, who had glanced at his wrist-watch, was edging towards the door, with his head politely inclined upwards me as if to signify that time was pulling him away against his will. 'You've evidently made quite a study of the Noble Poet.' His tone was valedictory. 'A fascinating topic. If I get over this way again you must tell me more.'

He was two steps from the threshold and was about, I apprehended, to devote some last remark to the dispatch of his purchases. I was determined to forestall him, and now it was rather because I had set myself a little challenge than out of regard to my prospects as a salesman. To get my own way had become a kind of game.

'I have a special concern with the Memoirs,' I said, 'because Dr. Williams, who did so much of the copying, was an ancestor of mine.'

'You don't say?' He paused, his hand on the knob of the open door.

'He left,' I went on, 'some papers.'

Darrow stood still, listening, receptive.

'I believe I'm the only member of the family who's ever had the smallest vestige of interest in them, but that's because I'm the only one who's bothered to dig up the facts about his friendship with Tom Moore in Paris.'

'You're not going to tell me'—his inflexion was sardonic, but in the manner of one who braces himself against too willing credulity—'that this Dr. Williams made an extra copy of the Memoirs?'

'It may not have been very ethical of him, but I'd be almost prepared to swear he did.'

It was amusing to see Darrow trying to remain casual.

'You mean—it's in existence now?'

'I hope so. I admit I haven't seen it for a few years.'

'A few *years*!' He wheeled round, the pretence of detachment gone. 'You've known about this copy for years and not done anything about it?'

'Strangely enough, when I first lit upon it, I didn't realise what it was. Even now I don't go further than to say I'm *almost* prepared to swear.'

'But how can you stop yourself from making sure?' So far did he surpass himself in emphasis that every word of the question was a small explosion.

'I intend to.'

'When?'

'In a month or two.'

'Well, talk about British phlegm! Now I understand what they mean by it. Unless,' he added searchingly, 'you're taking me for a ride.'

'Why should I?' I treated him to what Jocasta had called my nice frank smile. 'I'm not trying to sell you anything. Far from it.'

'I shouldn't mind if you were, on that level.'

'If this came on to the market, the price would be steep. There'd be a lot of competition for it.'

'I don't say I could buy it on my own account—'

'Not being,' I reminded him, 'the Rosenbach set-up.'

'But one has ways and means.' He flicked over the pages of a book without, I divined, a notion of what was printed on them. I was silent, glad of a moment to meditate my next communication.

'Is this manuscript—whatever it may be—at your own disposal?'

'It probably will be.'

'And why—just why do you have to wait all that time to look at it again?'

'Because I work for my living in London and my family is'—I stopped abruptly and ended with deliberate caution—'elsewhere. Besides, I don't want to start up any excitement prematurely.'

'Prematurely! After—what did you say?—several years! It's natural that you should be cagey with me, but I can't figure why you should be willing to remain in uncertainty yourself about a thing that's obviously so important to you.'

'I'm not in much uncertainty.'

'But look!—maybe I'm stepping in where angels would fear to tread—if you once establish this document for what you believe it to be, then working for your living is something you can forget about for a while.'

'Only if I should sell it. I don't think I would.'

He turned on me a baffled, reproachful frown. 'To a simple American dealer in books, this is all somewhat incomprehensible. You're in the trade too, and presumably you don't count it as an act of vandalism to sell things. This isn't the original manuscript anyway. Its value is largely what a publisher will pay for the right to print it.'

'Exactly. That's the problem.'

The entrance of a woman with a brisk inquiry for some school text-books I was able to supply gave me a pretext for breaking off a conversation which had taken a turn equally astonishing, I fancy, to both participants. I was now more anxious to get Earl Darrow off the premises than five minutes before I had been to detain him, and as he seemed disposed to linger, I took the initiative in ensuring his departure by offering to show him the best way to Hodgson's and stepping at once out into the street, where he was obliged to follow me.

'When you're passing again,' I suggested blandly, 'you must look in. I'll clear up the mystery for you if you like.'

'*"If I like"* is good!'

'Would you mind in the meantime not mentioning it?'

He glanced back at the shop front as if to memorise its appearance. 'Your name Rossiter?'

'No, it's Williams. Quentin Williams.'

'Are you here every day?'

'Most days—except Saturday.'

'Well then, I'll be seeing you. . . . But I still can't help feeling you're up to some kind of joke.'

Looking back I see it as almost pathetic, his struggle not to snatch too greedily at the radiant prize that might turn out to be a snare, but at the time it grated on me. 'You give me credit for an odd sense of humour,' I said stiffly.

'Some Englishmen do have an odd sense of humour.'

'I'm a Welshman. Now if you'll forgive me'—I turned to go indoors—'I can't afford to lose a customer.'

'With Byron's Memoirs up your sleeve, I'd say you could afford to lose the shop.'

I could have wished by now that the idea, so impulsively conceived, might be stillborn, but like the hero of the Arabian tale, I was to learn that it is much easier to conjure a geni out of a bottle than to get him to go in again.

Chapter Two

I was seeing very little of Jocasta at that time because July is the month when a number of London fashion houses present what they call their collections, and she was in demand as a model. Nevertheless, I was completely in her ambiance since her grandparents were allowing me to occupy her room. The journeys between South Brockford on the outermost fringe of London and the W.1 district where she worked were a strain during a season of daily engagements at irregular hours, and she had taken the opportunity of sharing a flat in the Marylebone High Street with a friend whose husband had gone abroad for a time. Mr. and Mrs. Leverett, partly out of their great kindness for me, and partly because my contribution to the household expenses was welcome, had accepted me as a lodger.

Their home was an inconvenient distance from Rossiter's but I went by tube and spent the time reading whatever book I had in hand relating to Byron and noting the passages to be transferred to my card index, so I didn't feel it was wasted. That day, however—the day of Earl Darrow's advent—I couldn't bring myself to open the bound volume of *Quarterly Review* notices that I was carrying. My researches seemed futile. The contemplation of my literary prospects was filling me with an increasingly embittered reluctance.

My books had cost me so much labour to write, had been received on the whole with favour by the critics, were, I was sure, informative and accurate; but never yet had they brought me within even vaguely measurable distance of earning my living from them. And here I was engaged to a girl whom I wanted ardently, and who in her turn wanted, with all the obstinate concentrated longing of a child, to wear in everyday life the dazzling robes and trappings in which, as a mannequin, she served at the altars of her simple faith. Of course she knew I couldn't give her these things, but in the optimism of her twenty-three years, and her belief in our respective careers, she supposed that sooner or later we could, between us, at least furnish some not contemptible share of them. What would happen to us if I persisted in writing biographical studies which tumbled straight between the two schools of prevailing taste?

They were neither huge investigations covering every inch of the ground with painstaking thoroughness and, if sometimes dull, still assured of a steady future as works of reference, nor mere entertaining performances, slyly mingling fact with conjecture, full of unverifiable guesswork about thoughts and motives, and depending for their liveliness on their amusing irreverence for the great. My subjects moreover were not popular. I had hoped in Byron to profit by a theme on which many good, bad, and indifferent writers had handsomely cashed in, but lately, as I've already said, I'd been afflicted with doubts, and my conversation with the American dealer had extended their area.

Until today, I'd only worried about the large number who'd explored the same territory, but that evening I went back to South Brockford realising that I was under another handicap. Darrow's remark about the 'meaty slice of scandal' had belatedly woken me up to it. Scandal was what the world demanded. The attitude to Byron hadn't changed—people wanted him to shock them.

It was my misfortune that I liked and admired the man. I had no desire to expose his foibles or reprehend his morals. I actually hoped—incredible as it may seem in the light of what is to follow—I actually hoped to show how well in the face of all the odds he had behaved, and how absurd it was to talk smugly of his having 'redeemed himself' in Greece, as if to have lived the life, the only life, in which the seeds of his major work could have germinated were a crime requiring the gloomiest of expiations.

Mine was not the spirit in which the most successful books about Byron had been written. Naturally, there'd been a few authors, and even in recent years, who'd anticipated my view, but from the first, disparagement, open or disguised as objectiveness, had paid far better. Darrow's palpable bias in favour of the scandalous aspects of the subject had confirmed me in the depression with which, at the moment more or less of his arrival, I'd been surveying the task before me.

At first my personal literary problem gave me more concern than the hoax I'd so impetuously indulged in that afternoon. Then, on the walk between the Underground Station and the Leveretts' house, I started to consider that hoax with a measure of uneasiness. My purpose, in so far as I could now unravel it, had been compounded of a straightforward love of making an effect, one of the boyish weaknesses I've never quite outgrown, a wish to inveigle a promising customer back to the shop, and a temptation to tease him by dangling fruits of Tantalus before his eyes. There was also an element of sheer—how shall I put it?— sheer high spirits in my little piece of fantasy, an appreciation of my own skill at make-believe which, in my schooldays when I could go on for hours with a perfectly straight face elaborating my inventions, had often got me into scrapes.

The idea about the Memoirs had come to me when, meeting Dr. Williams's name somewhere in Moore's Diary, I'd wondered whether by any chance he could have been an ancestor of mine, and wished in an idle fairy-tale sort of way that he had been, and that he might be found to have taken an additional copy which I could have the glory of bringing to light. It was as a man of letters and not as a bookseller that I envisaged this triumph, and I'd been playing with the theme as, at my prep school, I played with daydreams of being a pirate king or rescuing the sarcastic games-master from a burning building. I'd even worked out, relaxing over long spells with my index cards, just how the wonderful discovery might come about.

So when I started that game of mine with a young man who seemed to need what he himself would probably have called a come-uppance, the lie—if I must give it so harsh a name— was ready, as it were, to leap to my tongue almost of its own volition. And up to a point I'd enjoyed it—the point when I'd seen that the game mightn't end precisely when I wanted it to. That had been the trouble at school—carrying my play-acting a fatal move too far; getting carried away, in fact, myself. That was why they'd expelled me from Queenswick. Expelled me quietly and discreetly, so that I wasn't stigmatised, but it had upset my father very much and spoiled a good many things for me, and it always gave me a nasty turn to find my adult self still capable of getting up to the same kind of mischiefs.

And yet, if there was a measure of uneasiness, there was a measure of exhilaration too. It was a good story. I'd put conviction into it and Darrow, for all his attempted scepticism, had been unmistakably impressed. I feared but at the same time hoped he'd come along for more. To excuse my hope, I told myself that he'd be finding it diplomatic to make further purchases at Rossiter's whilst I, in the certainty of a customer, could get hold of items that would make it really worth his while, and in the long run no harm would be done: but I knew in my heart—at any rate, I know now—that I was fascinated with my own ingenuity. I wanted to see how far I could go without having to produce the manuscript.

I suppose I must have begun there and then to think out the 'plot' as a novelist thinks out the plot of a book, because I can remember that as I approached Brockford Lodge, I was puzzling over the identity of Moore's friend Williams with a view to investigating who, if any, his descendants might be. Where could I set about looking him up? Or need I, at this stage, go to the trouble? Williams was among the commonest of Welsh names: in the thirteen and a half decades that had elapsed since those precious folio sheets had been handed over for copying, thousands of Williamses had begotten thousands upon thousands of Williamses who were scattered all over the earth—in Australia, New Zealand, South Africa, Canada, the United States; even, I'd heard, a little outcrop of them in Patagonia where the Welsh had settled as sheep-breeders. Unless it could be shown that Moore's Williams had been both childless and without near kin, a claim to some sort of descent from his stock would be hard to disprove.

Perhaps if I'd been spending that evening with Jocasta, I should have been distracted from my seductive fiction, and my enthusiasm for it would have cooled, but she was doing a fashion show at the Dorchester and there was no alternative amusement. I'd asked Mrs. Leverett, who was out with her husband at a parish meeting, to leave sandwiches on a tray in my room—Jocasta's room—so that I could settle down to a long session of index card entries, but when I got the little cabinet set out on the work-table, instead of extracting the *Don Juan* cards to continue where I'd left off, I went irresistibly to the batch marked, over various sub-headings, MEMOIRS.

I had a pretty comprehensive catalogue of what was known about them because I was anxious to discredit the idea, persisted in by some biographers, that the loss hadn't been of much consequence. Any such work by Byron would have a claim to preservation merely for the excellence and wit of his prose style, but the data I'd collected showed that, though Moore had to play it down, once having been induced to countenance the destruction, what had been burned amounted to something much more than 'Memoranda' of the first twenty-eight years of the poet's life, as well as loosely-connected records, undoubtedly tending to bawdiness, of two or three subsequent years. Byron himself, it was true, claimed that he had been obliged to omit a great deal 'out of regard to the living', and had compared the narrative to *Hamlet* without the prince: but then he was communicative to so extraordinary a degree that the necessity of any form of suppression would fret him into exaggerating his reticence. The dozen or so of passages which Moore cited from his own and others' recollections formed in themselves a proof of the intimate and highly personal nature of the material. Byron had called it his 'Life and Adventures' and had joked in connection with the financial arrangements about his resemblance to the Spartan in selling his 'life' as dearly as possible.

The financial arrangements . . . I couldn't help thinking of those. John Murray had paid Moore two thousand guineas for the right to publish after Byron's death, and at the time, Byron being thirty-three, it must have seemed a very long-term investment. That was in 1821; the equivalent sum today would be, I calculated, easily six times as much—twelve thousand guineas at the lowest estimate. But now the monetary value would be still greater for Byron's fame, always flamboyant, had been blazing away for much more than a century and had become worldwide in a sense unrealisable in his own time, while, contrary to the prophecies of friends and enemies alike, curiosity about his private life had never diminished.

How immense would be the market for those long-lost reminiscences! The sales of books formed out of the rich find of Boswell papers must have been vast, but Boswell was a national, Byron an international figure, one who had inspired novels, odes, dramas, essays, biographies, literary criticisms, political disquisitions from pens all over the Western World. Italians, Greeks, Germans, Frenchmen, and Russians would be jostling one another for the translation rights. With its 'long and minute account' of his domestic relations and certainly some excursions into his amatory affairs, the book would have the combined allurements of a detective novel, an historical romance, and an erotic 'true confession', all raised to the level of literature. No wonder the attempts at forgery had been so feeble and half-hearted! The man who could make a convincing job of forging Byron's Memoirs would need such talents that he would be famous in his own right.

Or would he? Wasn't that as much as to say that to give an imitation of a great actor in a certain role, one would need to be a great actor oneself? The real requirements of mimicry are accurate observation, a sense of proportion in selecting salient features, and knowledge of one's subject. A great actor must be a good mimic, but a good mimic need not be a great actor. As for imitation in literature, brilliant creative power might only be a hindrance. . . .

Had the time come to admit that I was lacking in brilliant creative power?

I should like to be able to write that I pulled myself up at this point, horrified at the trend of my meditations, but the truth is I was drifting into known danger without a struggle, drawn on and on by the recognition of the qualifications I unmistakably possessed, qualifications—yes, I took dispassionate stock of them—to commit this forgery. What if I *did* produce a manuscript?

I was in a mood of irony, and I derived a sort of bitter relish from deliberately facing the collapse of all my literary pretensions into this, that I might successfully pass off a work of my own as Byron's. And the reward (the quintessence of the irony was here) would be more than, at my present rate of pay, I had any prospect of making in the whole of my writing life.

But in a moment or two, I reflected that my literary pretensions, so far from collapsing, might on the contrary receive salutary benefits: I could go on producing the books I wanted to produce irrespective of royalty cheques for £4 13 s. 2d. I might have it both ways, using my gains to purchase the leisure that would enable me to build up my own career as an author. And it went without saying that I could marry Jocasta, could take possession of all her beauty, all her delightfulness.

That was prize enough, but it wasn't the least attractive part of the vision that I would be able to put over my conclusions about Byron with an authority no other biographer had enjoyed since an early eighteenth century charlatan had got away with the 'autobiography' of Benvenuto Cellini—a shoddy job too when one looked into it which I felt I could distinctly improve on.

Unlike that forger, who must have been among the first to trade on the enjoyment people take in believing a great artist can be a dreary scoundrel (and whose methods had been particularly favoured by the manufacturers of false Byroniana), I should embark on my enterprise with the firm intention of doing justice to my subject, and showing up some of his traducers. There would be no need to make capital out of delinquencies because, the holocaust of the Memoirs being one of the most celebrated follies in literary history, their resuscitation would be proportionately sensational, and for once invention would not have to get its effects by evoking delicious disapproval.

There must be ribaldry, to be sure, otherwise the thing would not be in character, ribaldry and venom, and even an occasional touch of angry scurrility—No! on second thoughts that wouldn't be wanted. Byron's aim had been to answer his accusers; he would have been stepping warily.

I turned over my cards, and found the appropriate reference in MEMOIRS, *Moore's Remarks on*:

> The charm, indeed of that narrative, was the melancholy playfulness—melancholy, from the wounded feeling so visible through its pleasantry—with which events unimportant and persons uninteresting in almost every respect but their connection with such a man's destiny, were detailed and described in it. Frank, as usual, throughout, in the avowal of his own errors, and gener-

ally just towards her who was his fellow sufferer in the strife, the impression his recital left on the minds of all who perused it was, to say the least, favourable to him.

...

Melancholy playfulness—that was the note to strike. The indecency didn't come in till the later portions, written more than a year after the first. It was not in the script confided to Williams, nor even Dumoulin, the second copyist, whose death had just taken place when Moore was alluding bleakly in his Diary to a change of tone:

> I see that Byron in his continuation says, that I advised him to go into the details of his loves more fully; but if I recollect right, it was only his adventures in the East I alluded to, as in recounting these there could be but little harm done to any one.

'Very coarse things' he said there were in the continuation, and Lord John Russell spoke of 'three or four pages that were too gross and indelicate for publication', while Lord Rancliffe had been shocked by their hopelessly immoral tendency. But none of this would be my concern. The first and most important part, the record of his infancy and schooldays, his earliest and most ardent love affairs, his first taste of fame, his reckless doings as a young man about town, his doomed marriage with a searching account of its crash into ruin, the explosion of public indignation, and the beginnings of his exile—these were the ingredients of the work as it stood when he committed it, in Venice, to the guardian destined to fail him.

I'd already acquired a substantial amount of the knowledge needed to recount these matters without coming a cropper over dates and social background; but what of the skill to reproduce that deceptively easy style, compact yet discursive, slapdash yet always, so to speak, falling on its feet, vivid, intimate, good-natured, and suddenly ferocious? It was a formidable challenge, and there would be a kind of silent glory in meeting it. If I could.

I pulled myself up. This reverie was after all the merest fatuity, what Darrow would probably describe as a pipe dream. If I were to contemplate the colossal imposture seriously, I should need to master another handwriting, to use paper that would stand up to the most exhaustive chemical tests, to learn the secret of making ink look faded. I'd never forged anything except a letter from my father undertaking to be responsible for my account with a Savile Row tailor when I was very young, and the results of that little essay had proved a most effective deterrent.

Then there would be the question of provenance. I'd have to have an absolutely watertight story as to how this manuscript had been acquired, something that would bear the most microscopic scrutiny and stand up to a floodlight of publicity. And there was another snag. Several people knew that I'd been studying Byron documents. I'd been to the firm of John Murray to consult their collection: I'd had access to Sir Harold Nicolson's copy of Moore's biography with Hobhouse's marginal comments. I'd exchanged a couple of letters with Professor Marchand and a few words with Peter Quennell. When Angus Wilson was at the British Museum he'd often come to my aid in tracking down elusive items, and there might be someone in the Manuscript Room who knew me by name. There was my publisher—

No, come to think of it, there wasn't my publisher: I'd put off talking to him originally in the hope that my *Follies of William Beckford* might have sales that would improve my position with him, and later, when that didn't by any means happen, I'd felt the topic of my next book was one to be broached rather delicately. I didn't want to be the first to mention it—not until I had something in hand more substantial than a card index. That seemed somehow providential. I said to myself, wondering why I found the fact so impressive: 'I've never discussed my Byron book with any publisher.'

When inclination and prudence are trying to come to an agreement, the brain has a mysterious double way of thinking. Inclination reasons faster than prudence, and what it had so rapidly worked out in this case was that, whereas to have made an arrangement with a publisher or even to have talked to one in business-like terms about a work on Byron might be a suspicious circumstance should I afterwards appear as the discoverer of his Memoirs, there was no insuperable difficulty in any other quarter. I could always claim that I'd really been seeking information in order to check my text against known data, and that until I'd established its genuineness, I had preferred to camouflage what I was about. I should be asked, of course, why I hadn't taken some Byron scholar into my confidence, but there'd be time enough to face such minor problems as this when I came to them.

I've spoken of being like a novelist getting to grips with a plot. There's a stage, the pleasantest stage and unfortunately seldom of long duration, when one can't leave it alone, when the difficulties are positively captivating: and I was in that incandescent heat of creativeness now. To carry ideas into execution is labour, but to conceive them is happiness, and I will dare to admit that I was happy as I reviewed the various obstacles I had set before myself, and one by one demolished them.

How I demolished them will be shown hereafter, but I may as well say at once it was the tangible part of the equipment that turned out, in practice, the least troublesome. It happened that recently I'd bought a small private library on terms very advantageous for Rossiter's. The vendor was a factory foreman who'd inherited it from his mother, formerly a housekeeper. The elderly and childless widow for whom she had worked had left her the house and its contents, which included a thousand or so of books accumulated by some relative a long while before. The widow had apparently placed no special value on them for the housekeeper had received them with the furniture, and it was a furniture-dealer who gave me a friendly tip about them—in consideration of a rake-off—when the son was selling up after his mother's death. In the second-hand book trade such windfalls are not infrequent, though on the whole ignorance tends to work the other way, sadly over-estimating possessions that are not understood.

I felt entitled to a trifling perquisite or two after doing such a good deed for Mrs. Rossiter, and I extracted a few very modest items for my own use before she took delivery—nothing of monetary worth because that's the kind of thing I'm squeamish about. But besides some beautifully printed classical texts and certain five-volume novels in French, for which we had no demand whatever, there was a pair of un-used exercise books which attracted me by the quality of their thick cream-laid leaves and sumptuous marbled end-papers. The leather bindings were in a fair way to being perished, and as Mrs. Rossiter could have derived small financial benefit from them, I hope no reader (if ever I have a reader) will be so priggish as to condemn me for taking them. I had a notion that it would be a luxurious sensation, when I began my work on Byron, to feel under my pen the sort of paper he himself might have used, as a change from the synthetic bodiless stuff we modern authors are obliged to put up with.

On the evening of this crucial day, the day when I'd sprung the surprise on myself and Earl Darrow, I naturally recalled the existence of these volumes, which were in a small deed box under my bed. To tell the truth, as I always shall in these pages whatever I may have done elsewhere, some recognition of how serviceable they might be to anyone perpetrating a literary hoax had not escaped me at the time when I lighted on them, and an instinct had warned me from the first to keep them out of sight.

Now I made a bargain with myself. If they were, as I believed them to be, of a date approximately correct, I'd try one or two experiments, not committing myself—I was determined to play very safe—but simply practising handwritings and seeing what I could do in the way of Byronic composition, which I might or might not ultimately transcribe. If on the other hand, they were decidedly earlier than 1820, the year when Williams did his copying (a year later would of course rule them out completely), I should renounce the project once and for all, however many tempting materials might be handy. In fact, I'd take it as an omen that, discouraged or not discouraged, I was to get down to the serious and respectable work I'd planned.

I was prepared for a long job finding out about that paper because if the watermark was undated it might be tricky, since experts were nevertheless capable of ascertaining the date; but the matter was settled in little more than the five minutes it took me to unlock my box and hold the open pages against the light. They bore the watermark of the Basted Mill, and the year appeared plainly on every eighth leaf, 1816.

It would have been better, certainly, Dr. Williams having been resident in Paris, if the paper had been from a French mill, but failing that, which was too much to hope, the books were as good as could possibly be found for my purpose. One alone would hold as much as Williams could have copied, that is to say a substantial portion of the seventy-eight large loose folio sheets, each consisting of four pages, which Byron had personally handed to Moore—who had exclaimed in short-lived gratitude that they would be a legacy for his son and would astonish the latter years of the nineteenth century. Provided the contents were pithy enough, one volume would suffice to make the sensation I predicted, and the second would be a valuable standby in case I blundered over the first.

Though there was still a stretch of dangerous ground to cover which I haven't so far mentioned, by the time Mrs. Leverett came home and invited me to share their bedtime pot of tea, I was feeling an absolute eagerness to try my hand at least at the literary side of the adventure. Devoted as I was to the Leveretts and grateful for the homeliness of my footing in their house, it was as much as I could do to break off my enthralling sequence of calculations and go down to spend half an hour with them. I speak of calculations, but I should like to assure that stern phantasm, my reader, they were very far from being chiefly mercenary. The more I turned the idea over in my mind, the more I saw its potentialities for setting my subject in precisely the light in which I wanted him to be seen.

I had theories about his boyhood and his married life which were new and original, and I'd anticipated with some dismay, not being much of a controversialist, the incredulity and even scorn with which they'd be greeted. But if I were to write in the guise of Byron himself, what an immeasurable difference—assuming I could pull it off—that would make! Events and characters could then be given the interpretation I believed to be the right one without my having to bear the brunt of any criticism or the exacerbations of any controversy. I would willingly forgo (so I then decided) the credit of my deductions if only I could see them accepted without having to battle for their validity. The harvest of money would be a most gratifying compensation for having to present my best and cleverest work under a screen, but it was not my primary object.

It may have been easier for me to renounce personal kudos because, as an author, and doubtless in that role only, I've always been of a somewhat recessive temperament. I am deficient in what Byron himself so conspicuously had—the asset known in the theatre as star mentality. Not that I'm lacking in the desire or for that matter the power to make myself felt, but as a man, not, alas! as an artist. My career would have been far more successful had it been otherwise.

I was never, for instance, able to inform casual acquaintances that I was an author: it went against my grain even with friends to bring forward that aspect of my existence, vital though it was to me, and few of them bothered to read my work since I didn't impose any obligation on them to do so. This indifference hurt me, but I was under an inward compulsion not to show it. Jocasta was flatteringly attentive to my literary activities, but then, as her grandfather had been my tutor after my public school debacle and as both he and his wife had the greatest faith in my talents, she may be said to have been brought up on me. Besides, she was, under her air of softness and casualness, a dutiful girl, and didn't need the women's magazines she read so assiduously to tell her that she should strive to share the interests of the man she was to marry and encourage his ambitions.

And this brings me to the 'dangerous ground' I touched upon a page or two ago. It was, of course, Jocasta—Jocasta who knew all about my preliminary studies for a book on Byron and who was the last person in the world to enter into the spirit of any hoax, however difficult and daring, which she would regard—though it wasn't the word she would have used—as unethical. As, directly or indirectly, she's of immense importance to all I have to tell, I think I've reached the point where I ought to say something more about her.

Chapter Three

I'VE ALREADY let fall that Jocasta was twenty-three years old, a professional mannequin, and beautiful. I won't describe her beauty beyond saying that it wasn't, any more than the beauty of a rose or a spray of blossom, confined to the eye of specified beholders. She belonged to that rare group whose attributes, whether they arouse desire or not, are undisputed and who, if they were transported to Ethiopia, to Formosa, or to Lapland, would be recognised at once by the most untravelled inhabitant as creatures precious and lovely of their kind. She was not voluptuous, but combined a spring-like freshness, which had always been natural to her, with the elegance and restraint which she had learned.

There was something quaintly incongruous in the surroundings in which these qualities had flowered. The child of a spectacularly unhappy marriage, she had been brought up from the age of six or seven by her father's parents, a retired clergyman and his wife in very reduced circumstances. Mr. Leverett had formerly been the vicar of South Brockford, a parish which, in his early years there, had been almost rural, but which was now caught up in the tentacles of Greater London. Ill-health had compelled him to give up his work, but the ecclesiastical authorities allowed him to go on living, on no very secure tenure, in the old vicarage, a less unmanageable dwelling having been provided for his successor.

The old vicarage, renamed Brockford Lodge, had been built in the days when servants were in the habit of carrying coals and hot water to bedrooms, when kitchens were stone-floored, bathrooms scarce and Spartan, and perpetual stair-climbing taken for granted. Apart from the installation of electric light, the house had never been modernised, nor could any amount of good housekeeping disguise the worn and shabby condition of appointments that, even in their pristine state, must have announced the modest resources of their owner. The vicar had no private means; his stipend had always been unequal to the demands on it, and his pension, increased by what he could earn from coaching examination students, hardly sufficed for maintaining a visibly threadbare gentility. Ever since I could remember they had been making a struggle against difficulties which they could not conceal, but for which they never sought acknowledgment or sympathy.

Mr. Leverett was a classical scholar, his wife a woman of wide reading and a mind that retained, after years of drudgery and even tragedy, its lively capacity for interest and high freedom from prejudice. Jocasta did not inherit their intellectuality, and it was only by a fortunate chance that she had been favoured with the means of cultivating her gift of beauty, and becoming the mixture of innocence and sophistication, domesticity and worldliness, I and everyone else found so engaging; a girl who knew the price of a pair of kippers and also what to look for in buying a diamond necklace—though she'd not as yet had that experience.

What this chance was I'd better explain. Her grandmother was a kinswoman of the rich and fashionable Bentham-Lyalls, but by marrying a penniless clergyman whose first living was in Huddersfield, had vanished from their orbit as long ago as the reign of Edward VII. A new generation of this socially preoccupied family had grown up barely knowing of Mrs. Leverett's existence. The eldest Mrs. Bentham-Lyall, however, who was her contemporary, had felt some compunction on reading in the newspaper of the death of her first cousin's only son (Jocasta's father), and had written a very tactful letter of condolence, which led to a slight and occasional renewal of contact. It had thus come about that Mrs. Leverett's pretty grandchild had been seen by this worldly lady and had, as a result, been invited thenceforward to Christmas and birthday parties among the children of the clan, the invitation being invariably accompanied by the gift of a suitable dress, sent with gracious and disarming words.

Not that Mrs. Leverett had a trace of defensiveness in her attitude towards relatives whose kind of life she had renounced of her own free will, and against whom she had never felt any sense of injury. It would no more have occurred to her to deprive the little girl of enjoyment for the sake of sustaining pride than to make a deliberate plan of securing social advantages for her. But social advantages to some extent accrued.

Certainly because she was captivating, but also perhaps in some degree because she touched their compassion—for her father had committed suicide—Jocasta was taken up, in their casual and irresponsible way, by some of her distant cousins. She shared many treats with the children of Lady Tandon and Lady Nunheaton, Mrs. Bentham-Lyall's daughters; she wore good clothes that they sometimes passed on to her. She was admitted to a dancing class held weekly at the Nunheatons' house, and in her early teens took lessons for two or three terms with one of Lady Tandon's daughters who needed a pace-setter.

With the emergence from the schoolroom, her situation developed its discomforts. She could not mix on an easy footing with companions whose privileged life cut them off from any realistic conception of her own circumstances, and whose hospitality always let her in for some awkwardness, if it was only having to slip away from a party at its height because she dared not miss the last bus or train to South Brockford.

'I'm sure the plot of *Cinderella* was written by someone who'd had trouble about cab fares,' she said to me once when she was telling me about her embarrassments with these rather insensitive and callow friends. 'People born rich don't know what a nightmare taxis and tips can be, and not having the right pair of shoes, and trying to keep your bag out of sight because it doesn't go with your evening dress.' It was doubtless through the ordeal of pitiful little economies and sartorial makeshifts that she learned what enabled her, ultimately, to appear so exquisite.

Mr. Leverett's enforced retirement made it necessary for Jocasta, while still in her teens, to set about earning her living. She had only the vaguest qualifications and was glad, after an inauspicious attempt as a doctor's receptionist, to get a job in the showroom of a milliner. She now seldom saw Mrs. Bentham-Lyall's grand-daughters, who were busy with all the seasonal activities of the debutantes' world, and if it had not been for a chance meeting with a son of Lord Tandon's who had taken up photography as a hobby, her uncertain links with that family might have been finally broken. This boy of twenty had asked her to pose for some experiments with lighting. The resulting pictures had been shown to a leading fashion photographer, who was impressed with the qualities of the model and asked if he might 'borrow' her for an experiment of his own. The outcome was that Jocasta's portrait appeared on the cover of a magazine, and that she began seizing spare-time opportunities of modelling for the camera, while studies of her by the heir of the Tandons accumulated in numbers sufficient, it may be gathered, to alarm his family.

Suddenly Mrs. Bentham-Lyall resumed her benevolent if intermittent interest in her protégée and advised her sagely to aim at some proper training for a career, promising that, if she would decide what she wanted to do, help would be forthcoming. Jocasta acknowledged a desire she had formed to become a professional model, and mentioned a course of evening classes advertised by a Mayfair agency. Mrs. Bentham-Lyall, slightly disconcerted, asked for a few days to think this over, and came back with a generous counter-proposal. The best training for mannequins was surely in Paris. She had consulted Jasky who made clothes for her and many of her friends, and had shown him Jocasta's photographs, and he had undertaken to place her in the home of one of his colleagues while she was being trained, and even to consider giving her some experience in his own salon later on. Mrs. Bentham-Lyall would take care of the expenses.

Jocasta did not need persuasion to enter into a project so far surpassing her expectations, nor could her grandparents, who had been unhappy about the job at the milliner's, fail to appreciate that this would be a progressive step. The plan, whether devised by Lady Tandon or her astute mother, proved in short entirely efficacious, and Jocasta might never have divined the fear that prompted it but for a resentful hint thrown out by the object of their precautions. She was in Paris ten months, having worked for a season at Jasky's before returning home as accomplished in beauty as so young a girl can be, and soon able to live by her own exertions in the nerve-racking world which exploits women's love of dress.

She was having a redoubtable success, a fact as strange as it was gratifying to her grandparents, who were both in their seventies, and in any case unworldly. In their younger days, girls who dressed up in expensive clothes that other women would possess were only just ceasing to be regarded as pathetic; and though they were pleased that her features should be selected for demonstrations of cosmetics in the glossy magazines, and that her figure and carriage represented perfection to the makers, vendors, and photographers of clothes, they remained bewildered. I doubt if they ever really grasped what it was all about.

This beauty of Jocasta's, whatever it might mean to others, was not regarded by her as primarily an attraction, a means of sex appeal. It was at once her profession and her art, and she devoted herself to perfecting it as fervently as a poet to his poems or a singer to the production of musical and compelling notes. She was as free from vanity about it as any good artist when he contemplates his talent, finding it rather a source of anxiety than of complacence, a sacred dower which it would be base to misuse or squander.

She had taken her training at the school for mannequins very seriously, being resolved to attain the expertitude that would put her in the loftiest hierarchy of those priestesses of fashion; and was as strict in her performance of the essential rituals—the exercises and abstinences—as if she were really dedicated to a religious cult. She would experiment with make-ups as a poet will experiment with metres, joyfully adopting one, gravely admitting another to be a failure, acknowledging with a detachment that sometimes made me laugh this or that limitation of her own endowments. The propriety of a particular style of walking, a way of removing the coat, a method of facing cameras, would be the subject of critical and eager discussion with fellow-devotees. As for clothes, the *raison d'être* of all this elaborate ceremonial to which she so completely gave herself, I'm bound to say that if I hadn't been in love with her, I might have found her minute and constant attention to the subject exhausting.

Jocasta's preoccupation with the gods to which she ministered made her, as far as men were concerned, somewhat remote and inaccessible, which was possibly just as well for me, since, even in an epoch when one's wife may go out to work, it's hardly permissible to marry without the assurance of being able to support at any rate oneself: and as to possession without marriage—I won't say I never thought of it, but only that I never thought in that environment of attempting it. In the full restricted and old-fashioned sense of the word, we were engaged, and I was almost grateful for her coolness of temperament since it spared me from any physical or moral struggle with myself.

Her room, which I now occupied, did not reflect, except in small and touchingly inadequate ways, the nature of her avocations. She longed for money and luxury because they could provide beauty with appropriate settings and make its achievement more durable: but when she had paid her share of the housekeeping—a matter about which she was punctilious—the necessity of keeping up a good professional appearance left her no margin for the enrichment of her background, which was almost unchanged since her schooldays.

It was endeared to me by the reminders it offered of her adolescence and some extremely happy days of my youth. I would lie on her bed, with its fancy brass and ironwork, which she had painted turquoise blue, and recall how at twenty I used to meet the little, round-faced girl of thirteen on the stairs and say a kindly, patronising word to her, not dreaming—though she was always good-looking—how she was destined to eclipse so completely the memory of the woman I had then loved that it was only with an effort I could summon up a faded, wavering image of her.

And yet I *had* loved her, and in the room on the first floor, where I was reading classical languages with Mr. Leverett, I had hugged to myself the delicious knowledge of how I would be spending my night, and the Greek and Latin texts over which we pored were made more vivid to me by my awareness of the contrast between my innocent afternoons and my guilty evenings, and my pity too for poor virtuous old Leverett who had never had a highly illicit affair with a married woman.

Now there were two new contrasts to enjoy, the chastity of my present love and, curiously enough, the ribaldry of my present studies—for I had been busy with Byron's Venetian phase and its great product *Don Juan*. In the bottom of Jocasta's wardrobe of stained oak (which, to Mr. Leverett's pained surprise, she had also insisted on disguising with turquoise paint), I kept my card index, hoping to improve the anything but shining hour of her pursuits elsewhere by some work that would set me a little further on the road towards beginning my book.

But after meeting Earl Darrow I knew I wasn't going to begin it; or at least that the book I was beginning would have to be concealed from her for ever as a creation of mine. There was nobody, absolutely nobody, less capable of appreciating a deception. Truth in her was hardly a virtue for she was quite literal-minded. I am myself a fervent lover of truth, the more so as I have reason to know the consequences of deviating from it, but Jocasta sometimes passed the bounds of how far veracity should go. It seemed as if she simply wouldn't bother to think up a lie even when the social conventions called for a harmless one. Silence or deft evasion was the most she would yield. Such an absence of guile gave a memorable quality to her endearments, but it ruled out the faintest hope of sharing any secret with her if it wasn't, so to speak, of the open and above board variety, which after all very few secrets are, and especially not the one that I was hatching.

The difficulty, of course, was going to be working on a book I couldn't show her, and *not* working on the one for which her expectation had been prepared. If I could manage that, if I were able to produce my batch of Memoirs and a satisfactory story to account for them, I didn't fancy she would suspect what I'd been up to. Why should she? She trusted me, and if it comes to that,

I'd always been worthy so far of her trust. She didn't know, you see, about my having had to leave Queenswick. Mr. Leverett did know once, but I believe he'd more or less forgotten. He mostly did forget anything to the disadvantage of people he liked, and he'd thought at the time that the headmaster had been too drastic. In any case, he never would have told Jocasta.

Both Mr. Leverett and his wife were so full of confidence in me that they naturally got the best I had to give. That slight tendency of mine to create private dramas I was always able to suppress in their house. I realised I was a kind of substitute for their dead son, and it was a sincere grief to me that my brilliant new plan was going to involve deceiving them: but the benefits we should all reap if I could carry it through successfully were an incentive too powerful to withstand.

After I'd slept on my inspiration and woken up to find it still irresistibly attractive, and spent another slack day at Rossiter's elaborating the possibilities, I had an idea for dealing with Jocasta which seemed distinctly superior to several I'd rejected.

I had promised to call for her at the Savoy where they were holding the dress rehearsal for an international fashion show of some kind. Twelve countries were presenting models, and Jocasta was delighted to have come so near the top flight as to be among those selected. According to her calculations, she would be free to leave with me at about six o'clock, but she had reckoned without press photographers and newsreel cameras, and I had a long time to wait. By getting myself mistaken for a textile man, however, I eased my way into the ballroom where the show was being staged, and watched what was going on with considerable interest.

I don't know much about clothes, but I find it enjoyable to see them being shown off by lovely girls who are trained to efface themselves in favour of what they are wearing and never, as far as I'm concerned, succeed. Their special little graces, the various mannerisms of their carriage—sometimes, it's true, amusingly silly ones—their hair and faces so beautifully imperturbable, the way the most gifted of them bloom grandly and consciously like rare exotic flowers that seem to know their own splendour, all this used to entertain me more than the spectacle of the clothes, though I wasn't incapable of admiring those. But what gave such a fine edge to my pleasure on the occasions when I was allowed to penetrate their rites was my being constantly aware that the rarest bloom of the whole lot was practically my own possession.

Quite spontaneously Jocasta had different techniques for different dresses. In a very rich and resplendent garment, she used to walk on to the rostrum like a calm statue into which life has been breathed, her face a little paler than the others and so smooth one would suppose it impossible for any trace of time ever to come near it, her eyes remote, her movements swift (or they seemed so). When she turned, took off a wrap, spread out her draperies, it was with something mysterious of quiet purpose like a somnambulist. If she was showing off a dress that was very new and striking, she appeared with a lively smile which invited the spectators to share her appreciation of the originality. Instead of being fixed on distance, her eyes disarmingly searched round the room as if gathering up the impressions of the audience, and there was so much charm and humour in her look that, before she had left the platform, those whose first reaction to the novelty had been disapproving were already half-way towards conversion. In tailor-mades the poise of her head was a trifle impudent, and her steps, light and firm, suggested energy and adventurousness. When she had to wear, as now and then happened, a *toilette* she deplored, then she was at her most goddess-like, becoming a sort of serene wide-eyed image on which someone had hung a votive offering unworthy but too well-meant to be rejected.

As I fairly frequently managed to see her and other models at work, I was becoming familiar with the requirements and was almost a connoisseur, I imagine, by comparison with most laymen, as to what constitutes good modelling (though I could wish they'd had the sense to invent a new verb instead of misusing an old one for it). I was able, therefore, that evening to observe a little piece of resourcefulness on Jocasta's part which an inexperienced eye wouldn't have seen.

Some film was being taken to go into a news feature in colour, and the officious young man in charge had laid a great deal of emphasis on the expensiveness of the process and the need to get the action carefully rehearsed and timed before shooting. He and the cameraman had rejected all but the showiest confections irrespective of their merits because, as Jocasta explained to me afterwards, film technicians catering for popular taste can't be shaken from a fixed belief that what the public wants is gaudiness pure and simple. In consequence, after she'd been rehearsed in gloves of a neutral shade with a tangerine jacket and dress, somebody wishing to appease the newsreel men hurried up to her with a pair of much brighter gloves in a contrasting green. They approved the change and began to shoot immediately after, with a special admonition that, as they were nearly out of film, they would have to manage with one 'take'.

But the gloves in which Jocasta had rehearsed were kid, tight-fitting at the wrist, and those into which she had changed were of loose suede, so that when she came to remove the jacket and show the daring décolletage underneath, I could see her hands behind her back tugging in vain at the sleeves, which would not slip over her wrists. Most girls would have gone on struggling or said 'I'm sorry, I can't get this jacket off!' and in either event wasted the shot, but before the cameraman, who was in front of her, had even realised the difficulty, Jocasta had raised her hands nearly to her chin, pulled each glove off in a very bold, pictorial gesture, and then, with more effect than in the rehearsal, let the jacket slide deftly over her freed arms.

When she came out to meet me afterwards, carrying her case, that cross between a large handbag and a small valise which is to a mannequin what a brief-case is to a lawyer, she asked me if I'd noticed the tiny contretemps.

'Yes, and I thought you managed it charmingly.'

'I do hope that shot has come off. It matters to Gabrielle much more than to any of the others.'

'And who may he be?' I thought she had said 'Gabriel'. There are quite a number of men in the so-called rag trade who are not queer, and whose attentions to the mannequins kept me on the *qui vive*.

'Darling, Gabrielle's the designer, and she's a woman. There are so few women at the top in England, it's terribly hard for them to compete. Getting into this show was a great break for her and naturally she can do with the publicity more than Hartnell and Amies and Stiebel who can have all they want of it. I think her clothes are nice, don't you?'

'The thing you were filmed in was nice, yes, and you looked sweet in it.'

'It only got into the film because its colour was so vivid. Even then they didn't do it, as you saw, till they only had a few feet left. I was determined not to give them any excuse for leaving Gabrielle out.'

She chattered on with her customary gusto about the clothes and the rehearsal until we reached the Brasileiro, a café espresso off the Marylebone High Street which she patronised a great deal because it had a small roof garden. I was not very fond of it myself. It was generally so crowded that dalliance of an amorous kind, verbal or physical, was out of the question; but the alternative was either going to the flat Jocasta was sharing with her friend, which would be equally un-private, or having dinner in the sort of restaurant we couldn't afford and which was wasted on Jocasta, her diet preferences being for salads and the café espresso type of food.

There were so many people on the roof that fine summer evening, I thought at first I shouldn't be able to mention my literary affairs to her at all, or at least that I should have to take her on to some other place to discuss them, which would make it all very portentous and create the kind of atmosphere I wanted to avoid. But by a stroke of luck, we had hardly given our order than the couple at a reasonably isolated corner table rose and left, and we nipped into their seats before anyone else could get them. We could now converse at least in undertones, and I lost no time.

'Jocasta, I took a pretty big decision last night. You must tell me if you approve of it. I mean, it's a big decision to me. It certainly won't affect anyone else very much. Are you too tired to talk about that book of mine?'

'No. Go ahead, darling.'

'I've decided to write a novel instead of my Byron book.'

'A novel! Can you write novels, Quentin?'

'I think I ought to try. I've got a very good theme for one.'

'Honey, is that sensible when you've spent such ages filling in all those hundreds of cards with things about Byron?'

'I spent ages filling in cards about Washington Irving and William Beckford, and look where it's got me! If I were to write a successful novel, I might be able to sell film rights and television rights and all that, and even an unsuccessful novel probably has sales bigger than an unsuccessful non-fiction book.'

Jocasta didn't know much about either books or the marketing of them. Her affection for me was the sole motive of the interest she so loyally took in my writings, so that if I could only throw up the right kind of smoke-screen, I might work in secret behind it with less danger from her curiosity than if she'd been better informed about literary processes.

The novel I was going to make a feint of being busy with was one I'd begun four years ago and abandoned after a few chapters, losing the impetus because my talents were of an interpretive not an imaginative order. Jocasta had never seen this forlorn attempt, being in Paris when I was occupied with it—and in any case, it was another girl in those days who listened to my confidences.

My scheme was to produce the fragment chapter by chapter at appropriate intervals while actually engaged on my reconstruction of the Memoirs, and, at some stage which circumstances would indicate, to announce that inspiration had failed and I was giving up. That would be, of course, when I'd brought my hoax to its conclusion. It was a measure that would have the character of a convincing alibi if ever any hint of suspicion fell on me, since Jocasta with her transparent honesty would be under the impression that she had followed exactly what I was doing.

'You said Byron would be more popular than those others.' I was a trifle surprised at the earnestness of her tone. When consulted on previous occasions, she had never done more than offer as a duty her acquiescence and encouragement.

'I'm not going to give up the idea of writing about Byron. In fact, I've got something entirely new in mind which I want you to help me with. But all these books about him that keep on coming out—in America as well as England—they must have brought the market to just about saturation point. There's Cline and Willis Pratt at the University of Texas, and Calvert in North Carolina or somewhere, and Leslie Marchand at Rutgers who's been doing a tremendous job for years—and who knows if Iris Origo over in Rome hasn't got something up her sleeve? I feel I could write a novel rather quickly and then get back to Byron when the present spate has simmered down a bit.'

'Isn't it a mistake to change horses in mid-stream?'

'But I'm not in mid-stream, darling, am I? I haven't begun the Byron book yet.'

'You've done masses and masses of research. I was simply amazed, Quentin, today when I saw how much you had done.'

The waitress came up with our coffee and salads and rye-bread sandwiches, and I sat in a faintly apprehensive state until Jocasta was able to resume: 'I rang you up this morning to ask you to bring one or two things I needed, but you'd just left the house, so I went out to Brockford myself and fetched them. I wanted to see Granny and Granpapa anyhow. Quentin, I thought Gran was looking dreadfully tired—'

'Stick to the point, my loved one.'

'Well, to help things on I made your bed and tidied up. You'd left that cabinet of yours on the work-table, the one you keep the cards in. They're not meant to be private, are they?'

I shook my head—wanly, I fear, because I was congratulating myself with a slight shudder on the fact that the unfinished novel was in my locker at Rossiter's and not lying about the bedroom as it might have been. I'd found it only last night in my deed-box and taken it to work with me to refresh my memory of it in case it could be of use.

'I'd never really looked at them before,' she went on. 'I suppose it was disgustingly lazy of me when you'd put so much work into them, but you know what I'm like about poetry. I don't think I've ever read any in my life of my own free will, and especially not Byron's because of the Assyrian coming down like a wolf on the fold.'

'My darling, what are you talking about? The card index contains no poetry to speak of.'

'Only I'd imagined it would, you see—stacks of poetical quotations and criticisms. So I didn't give it a glance almost. But this morning, finding it there, I just picked out a card or two— you needn't worry, I put them back in their right places—and I was fascinated. I sat down on the bed after that and read card after card.'

With my 'alibi' and most of the rest of my plot mapped out, I could see no harm in this. Indeed I felt a good craftsman's satisfaction in hearing praise for my labours, and I asked with some complacency: 'What did you find so fascinating?'

'Byron, of course.'

This wasn't precisely the reply I expected. There was even a kind of silliness in it. 'Which cards in particular,' I inquired, 'did you read?'

'Oh, you can't expect me to remember their names, honey. There were heaps. His appearance, which sounds delicious, his manner, his financial affairs, his relations with friends, his relations with women . . .'

'*That's* not a very edifying series.'

'No. He must have been a terrific Don Juan.'

'Didn't you know that before? His name's a byword for it.'

'In a vague way, but you've got so many enthralling details together.'

'I should have thought you'd say "shocking details".'

It dismayed me to suspect Jocasta of having the common feminine failing, about which Byron himself had made such sardonic gibes, of being attracted by the reputation of rakishness, and I was relieved when she answered: 'Yes, there were things that shocked me—very much. He does seem to have behaved badly to women, but then some of them were simply asking for it, weren't they? What amused me, Quentin, was to see how much you're on his side even when you probably don't realise it yourself.'

'How could you tell?'

She gave the sidelong smile of a child who's showing an adult that it has taken in more than it might be given credit for. 'You had cards headed "Generosity, Examples of" and "Courtesy" and so on, but the cards about avarice and discourtesy were called "Avarice, Alleged" and "Discourtesy, Alleged", and they were full of things that proved he wasn't avaricious or discourteous.'

'Well, he wasn't. I was comparing what was said with what was done. I wish all biographers would do the same.'

'And there was a whole section about unreliable witnesses, and they were nearly all the people who'd written things against him.'

'My dear girl, people who publish books to the detriment of a celebrity whom they profess to have known intimately must have their evidence sifted very carefully. Friends whose word can be trusted don't usually blacken our characters in print—'

'Angel, you don't have to defend yourself against me! If you're on his side, so am I. I can't wait to go back and read some more. Now you understand why I don't want you to write a novel—not just when I've got interested in this.'

The waitress was cornered up against our table while she made out the bill at another, and I took advantage of her presence to snatch a moment or two for self-communion. I could not renounce my lonely but glorious conspiracy, not until at any rate I'd carried it a few moves further. I was newly taken with it, fascinated as Jocasta was with the surprises of my card index. But I couldn't have her going back to read more. Dipping here and there was safe enough, but if she were to apply herself to it, reading solidly, she was sufficiently shrewd, as she had just shown, to make deductions, unpredictable by me, which might turn out dangerous. My version of the Memoirs would necessarily be based upon my studies, which were crystallised in those entries on the cards, and everything I wrote would have, in ways I was quite incapable of recognising myself, a certain slant, the same slant as I'd unwittingly given these matters in my notes and my choice of quotations from other sources. Jocasta was not intellectual, but she was not stupid either, and I mustn't let her become familiar with my approach to this or that aspect of Byron's character or conduct. As it happened, in anticipation of quite another difficulty, I'd prepared a diversion.

If my experiments promised well, and I were to settle down to the forgery (though forgery seemed a hard name for what would be in essence an act of homage and of restitution), the work would have to be done by stealth and I shouldn't be able to spend as much time with Jocasta as I now did. It would be a severe sacrifice but one worth while for the sake of the rich reward success would bring and the certainty that our marriage would follow. I could secure solitude by professing a feverish application to the novel, but I wanted at the same time to ensure that Jocasta should not be without some employment to use up her leisure hours. The risk of leaving so pretty a girl at a loose end when her engagements for the London season were over was one I didn't for a moment underestimate. She was virtuous but she found admiration agreeable, and I'd put some energetic brainwork into the question of an occupation for her, one that for preference would be linked by association with myself. The solution I'd ultimately arrived at seemed likely now to serve the additional purpose of heading her off my index cabinet.

As the waitress moved away, I responded: 'The novel will be done with in a few months. If I go at it positively "all out", it'll be finished in the time it would take me to write a mere fraction of any sort of biography. And meanwhile, I've thought up something that may be rather a neat way of staking a claim in the Byron territory and making a little money at the same time. Which is where you come in, my darling.'

She turned towards me with her fine eyebrows raised. I picked up her hand and kissed it, and held her fingers clasped on the bench beside me while I unfolded a plan which cannot be denied the merit of ingenuity.

'You know, Byron was extremely fond of animals, and that's a popular subject on both sides of the Atlantic. There've been books about his love affairs and about his travels and practically every aspect of his life, but nothing at all on his sayings and doings in regard to the animal kingdom. Now I believe there'd be a definite market for a little anthology containing everything known about his pets and quoting all the observations he ever made on animals; and it would catch the sort of reader who isn't interested in poetry and doesn't normally go for biography. It would be a thing by itself, not competing with any of the others . . .'

'Yes, ducky, but how do I come into it?'

'You could save me an immense amount of time, darling, by simply marking all the bits that refer to animals in the books I'll ask you to read. Unfortunately, the idea only came into my head last night, so I've never collected any material of that kind, but just think how wonderful it would be if you could help me with it while I'm glued to the novel.'

Jocasta had been taught that a too expressive face gathers wrinkles early, and so, apart from her engaging smile, she was usually somewhat impassive, but what I had proposed was so startling a novelty to her that she frowned in a perplexity that very nearly brought a line between her brows.

'Quentin, *dear*! You must have gone dotty! I wouldn't have a notion of setting about a job like that.'

'You don't need a notion, darling. All you have to do is to read, and every time you find a reference to anything like a dog, a horse, a bird—no matter what animal—you mark the margin with a little arrow or something in pencil; and put one of my slips of paper between the leaves. It's as simple as that.'

Still she looked worried. 'Ducky, I don't think it's up my street—honestly.'

I felt a keen disappointment. It had seemed such an excellent device, providing Jocasta with a task that would keep her busy and that she could hardly do without thinking of me. She was an ardent animal-lover too, which is why I'd hit upon that theme: and the prospect of eventually getting a small book out of it, illustrated perhaps and with notes by myself, was a perfectly genuine one. Without even reflecting that it wasn't beyond my power to think up something else, I yielded to my characteristic impulse to break down the opposition.

'Look, my sweet'—I remained entirely suave—'let me give you a clearer idea what I mean. I hand you a book—say Medwin's *Conversations*. You read it—or glance over each page if you prefer. You come upon a statement that Byron bought a monkey in the street because he saw it being ill-treated. You mark it with a pencil, put a slip in, and there you are! Or it might be Lady Blessington reporting that he accused her of bullying her horse—'

'He seems to have been much kinder to animals than he was to women,' she said thoughtfully.

Seeing her interested, I pressed on. 'You come across a letter in which he tells a friend how he shed tears into "a cistern of goldfishes which are not pathetic animals" . . .'

She laughed. 'Why did he do that?'

'Oh, he probably didn't. It was just his jocular way of saying he was sad—his "melancholy playfulness". Or you might find his description of riding with the Countess Guiccioli while her horse tries to bite his horse.'

This time she giggled cosily. I was getting on.

'All you do, my angel, is to put a mark beside it. I suppose the book will end with something rather touching, like Hobhouse bursting into tears when he sees Byron's dogs on the deck of the ship that brought his body home from Greece. I'll do the poetry, since you don't like that, and you do the prose.' Remembering that a beautiful woman likes to be flattered for her intelligence, just as an intellectual one for her looks, I added: 'You're so very observant, darling, I don't believe you'd miss much even if you did a great deal of skipping.'

'I *never* skip,' she broke in resentfully. 'You *know* Granpapa brought me up not to. I'll do it thoroughly or not at all!'

I was aware then that it was just a question of a little extra persuasion to get the thing tied up. And looking back on the whole perilous exploit, nothing seems more ironical than my sense of my own cleverness as I enjoyed my ruse for keeping one of the loveliest girls in London out of mischief.

Chapter Four

Earl Darrow was, of course, entirely unnecessary to a project which, if successful, would be a proposition for publishers rather than collectors of manuscripts; or so I assumed from my very slender knowledge of how in such cases negotiations are carried through. The question of publication would certainly be linked with the question of the genuineness of the manuscript, but the value of that in itself, though by no means negligible, would naturally be much less than in a handwriting accepted as Byron's own. As I should not have dared an attempt to imitate for page after page a writing so familiar to experts, I was glad that I had only to give my script the appearance of furtive, hurried copy by another hand. It was publication that would supply my prize money, and the copyright law in relation to that I must ultimately master, and in secret.

If I could carry the thing through at all, I could do it, as I say, without Darrow, but he was strongly associated with it in my mind, and sometimes during the next few days I felt that if he didn't turn up again, I ought to take it as a warning—I have a Byronic turn for omens—that the enterprise was rash. Besides, there was something about him that had impressed me in spite of myself, something that suggested he was knowledgeable and could be discreet. I had also remembered a point quite obvious and yet the significance of which had escaped me on the day of our encounter. If he had taken the trouble to write to Sir John Murray before coming to England asking permission to visit 50 Albemarle Street, it must be because he was specially interested in this subject—not very well-informed about it, that was clear from his ignorance of facts he would otherwise have known, but possibly having some particular 'angle' which it would be worth while for me to consider.

I was a trifle worried for the first day or two lest he should come before I'd devised a story I could stick to, since, when I was only fooling with him, I'd made some headlong promise to give him one: but this kind of mental exercise I enjoyed and had an aptitude for, and my fear that he'd turn up too soon dissolved by degrees into a fear that he wouldn't turn up at all, so anxious did I become to test his reaction to what I'd worked out. To revert to my former comparison, I was like a novelist who has written a couple of chapters and longs to read them aloud to someone—with this difference, that if the novelist finds he's started in the wrong key, he can, given time and patience, go back and change it, whereas if there was anything unsatisfactory about *my* beginning, I'd have to lay aside the work once and for all.

It was fortunate (taking the short-term view of fortune) that Darrow was ten days in coming, because, had he been earlier, I might have committed an irretrievable blunder in describing the manuscript. I should have said it was in ink—a statement once made not to be unmade. The methods of fading ink to a brownish tint can be ascertained from books exposing fakes and forgeries and are sufficiently simple, though I was troubled about my ability to achieve a uniform effect over several scores of leaves. But what bothered me more was the necessity of writing with a goose quill nib since it was all but impossible that Williams had ever used a steel one. No doubt forgeries of manuscripts purporting to be written with quills had been managed effectually with steel nibs, but modern investigators are so resourceful that I should never feel secure against discovery unless my pen as well as my paper were authentic. On the other hand, to learn to write easily in a disguised hand was going to be effort enough without having to manipulate goose quills, and I thought it risky too to work with any instruments it was not normal to have in my possession.

At first, however, there seemed no alternative, and I went so far as to obtain a few quills and sharpen them with a pen knife, blotting some oddments of paper most discouragingly with them in my attempts to achieve a flowing script. I'm accustomed to use a ball-point pen, which may have increased my difficulty.

One Sunday morning, lying in bed with the Memoirs in my mind as they usually were now, often displacing Jocasta for hours at a time, I happened to think of Hobhouse and the deep-seated jealousy of Moore's place in Byron's affections which unconsciously motivated his zeal to deprive Moore of the gift; and this brought me to meditate on the character of the man as revealed in his pungent marginal notes to Moore's book about their friend—a very mixed character striving to be honest but capable of spite, his loyalty at war with his irrepressible desire to show he was 'in the know'; not the simple manly fellow of the biographical canon, but one with a compulsive need for power over those he loved. . . . Suddenly I had a thought which made me sit bolt upright.

Those notes of Hobhouse's were in pencil! They had become a little blurred here and there, but were still, except for an occasional word or two, legible. The technique of writing with a pencil had not changed at all, neither was there any appreciable change in the chemical composition of pencil lead, otherwise known as graphite.

What more natural than that if Dr. Williams had decided to take a secret copy, it would have been on an impulse born after Moore had asked him to return the unfinished task, and that he would have hurried through it by what was then—before blotting paper, fountain pens, or metal nibs—the fastest means of writing known, a medium soft lead pencil?

The next day, after I'd spent two or three hours experimenting, I knew I had hit upon the right method. My original plan to achieve a handwriting that would have a convincing Georgian look had been to make a selection of typical characteristics and to form a blend of them, but while I was rummaging among our shelves for biographies containing facsimiles of documents, a much less unwieldy method suggested itself. There was in our stock an old writing primer with moral sentiments in specimen calligraphy running across the tops of the pages and rows of blank lines below for the pupil's copy. All the alphabet with its capitals and all the numerals had been introduced. Such books are attractive to certain collectors, and ours, though not in good condition, was priced at ten shillings: I decided to purchase it myself and to do all the exercises just as if I were a child learning its first cursive letters. When I was thoroughly accustomed to the style, I should speed up day by day until I could form the same letters with careless haste. The advantage of this was that the writing that emerged would be essentially an integral one, correct as to period, while the forcing of the pace would ensure that the copybook appearance would give place to the scrawl that adults usually develop; but a scrawl with no peculiarities of my own. I had no sooner conceived this excellent idea than I put the book into my locker and paid its price into our day's takings (I am very scrupulous in money matters).

The following morning when I was occupied with Mrs. Rossiter, who called two or three times a week to be told how things were going, I saw that Darrow had come in without my noticing it and was working his way along a tall shelf examining the contents in his well-remembered knowing-what-he-wanted way. My heart gave a disconcerting plunge. I wasn't afraid that he'd blurt out what had brought him here in front of a third party, but the time he'd chosen was damnably inconvenient.

I went on listening to Mrs. Rossiter as if I hadn't seen him. She was telling me, as she so frequently did, about one of the wonderful deals she and her late husband had done in the early days of their setting up their business. I didn't doubt her stories, but I sometimes got a little tired of the moral I was supposed to draw from them, a moral it was invariably impossible for me to draw seeing that conditions had changed totally since her entry into the book trade by way of a barrow in the Farringdon Market nearly forty years ago. At the same time, I used to be curious about the mysterious instinct by which, without ever reading a book or even opening one, as far as I could see, except to judge its condition and write the price in it, she had acquired a knowledge of how each item was esteemed, not only where books are traffic but where they are literature. It's a knack some dealers have, resembling perhaps the ear for music or languages which may likewise be found as often among the ignorant as the educated.

'It was a real bit of luck,' she was saying, 'us spotting that it might be something special, though we'd never heard of it, and neither me nor Mr. Rossiter could speak Latin; but there it was—we risked a quid on it, which was a lot of money to us in those days.'

With the corner of my eye on Darrow, I asked dutifully what the find had turned out to be.

'Bacon's *Mirifici Logarithmorum Canonis Descripto*.'

Preoccupied as I was, I couldn't help smiling at her reeling that title off perfectly though her diction in English was an incorrigible Cockney.

'We could've sold it the same day for ten times what we gave for it. Old Ditchley, who's now in Cecil Court, offered us a tenner without winking, a thumping big price for him. I'll admit I gave Mr. Rossiter a regular dressing-down afterwards because he didn't jump at it. But he had a motto, Mr. Rossiter did, which many a time I've lived to bless. He used to say'—she paused portentously—'"Buy on spec if you like, but never sell on spec or you'll regret it."'

Mr. Rossiter's numerous mottoes, whatever their wisdom, were seldom very felicitously expressed, but I managed to murmur something appreciative.

'There was a gentleman we called "the Professor"—a genuine professor he was from London University. He collected old books of mathematics, and we kept that one by us in a box out of sight until next time we saw him. And when we brought it out— well, it's worth while being a bookseller to see eyes goggle like that! I wouldn't care to tell you, Mr. Williams, what we made on it.'

'He bought it, did he?' I hoped my brisk tone would speed her up, for Darrow now was edging towards the door.

'No, love, no.' She had an odd way of alternating a strictly formal 'Mr. Williams' with other modes of address, some familiar, some artificially respectful as if I were a customer of considerable importance. I think that for a second or two she sometimes actually forgot who I was. 'He couldn't have afforded what we wanted for it by miles.'

'But you didn't know what you wanted for it!' It cost me an effort to speak with sweet-sounding reasonableness.

'We had a pretty good idea though after we'd seen the Professor's face. It was bought for a museum, that book. Not that I hold any brief for museums, speaking by and large. "Give them a wide berth," that's what Mr. Rossiter used to say. "They expect to get everything for nothing." Now I'm telling you this story, Mr. Williams, because you young people nowadays—'

What moral had been pointed I don't know to this day. Darrow had just slipped out, and the only expedient I could contrive on the spur of the moment for pursuing him was to exclaim: 'I believe that man walked off with a book!'

'Just one moment!' I called, keeping up the pretence, and as he turned, I greeted him with realistic surprise.

'Did you think I'd lifted this?' He held up a leather-bound volume. 'I assure you I brought it with me.'

'What can I do for you?' My voice, amiable but detached, couldn't have given him an inkling of how I had waited for him, the critic-elect of my beautiful fiction.

'Come and have a drink!'

'It's not too easy just now. That's my boss in there.'

'So I gathered.'

'Can you wait a minute? I'll see what I can do.'

I went back into the shop and explained to Mrs. Rossiter that, after mistaking an American customer for a shoplifter, the least I could do was to restore equanimity by having a drink with him—only as she didn't approve of drink, I said a cup of coffee. My junior, a youth-of-all-work, was in the basement making noises from time to time to suggest that he was doing something useful, and he could hold the not-very-heavily besieged fort till my return, so she gave me a permission that might have been either gracious or grudging: I didn't stay to judge.

'Do you know the Three Tuns?' I said. 'It's not much of a pub, but being on the other side of the road, it opens at eleven.'

'Well, I oughtn't to talk. We have States where you can't get a drink on Sunday, States where you have to buy it by the quart, and States where you can't get a drink at all.'

We spoke intently of British and American licensing laws until we were seated on the shabby horsehair upholstery of the private bar at the Three Tuns, just open and as yet nearly empty. I don't care about drinking in the morning, but the barman told me sourly that they didn't serve tomato juice, which I should have liked, and Darrow's request for a well-iced lager being received with equal contempt, we ordered sherry.

'I think that as an institution your English pub is over-rated,' said Darrow. 'Do I hurt you?'

'Not particularly. I've no vested interest in pubs, worse luck.'

'What's supposed to be so hot about them anyway?'

'Red plush, engraved mirrors, jolly barmaids, a cosy atmosphere—that's the tradition.'

'I don't seem to find that kind of pub.' He sounded distinctly out of humour.

'Have you had a successful time?' I asked. 'Did you get those Gissing letters?'

'No, they were too high; but at Sotheby's I spread myself on a nice little item you'll envy, a book by Leigh Hunt with a fulsome inscription to Byron.'

I was just going to exhibit my scorn for Leigh Hunt's fulsome inscription when I remembered that I'd better not be too free with my personal views on Byron and his enemies. 'Interesting,' I said, 'but not quite my thing.'

He stared at me in a cool sort of way that would have been disconcerting if I hadn't felt so sure of my story. 'No? But then why would it be your thing when you've got Byron's Memoirs to play with? That is, if you can bring yourself to bother with them.'

This was just what I wanted. 'Look, I know you think I'm deceiving myself, and perhaps I am.' (It was much subtler not to hint that he might suspect me of deceiving him.) 'But I can't do anything about that business until I get my holiday in September, and even then I shall have to go carefully. I have a very prickly sort of person to handle.' I hesitated effectively, then went on: 'I must rely on you not to repeat what I'm telling you. I didn't intend to go so far when we had our talk the other day, but since you know so much, you may as well hear the rest. The secret's evidently begun to burn a hole in my pocket. And somehow I've got a feeling you might be able to help.'

He said nothing, but settled down in his chair, his elbow on the table, his head leaning on his hand.

'I have a great-aunt,' I began, 'a Miss Williams. She was my grandfather's sister. She still lives in my grandfather's house.'

'Where?' He had a way of being emphatic even when he spoke softly, and he put this question very softly indeed.

'In Wales. She's an old lady who gives her whole life to crusading for various causes which only appeal to her if they appear to be lost causes. She's spent most of her money on them. They always come first. It's important to grasp that.'

'Yes. I've grasped it.'

'She's not an artistic or a well-read woman—unless you count tracts and pamphlets. The house is a jumble of anything that happens to have accumulated there since my great-grandfather built it in 1885, a jumble of furniture and a jumble of books. It's within reach of the sea, so I sometimes go there for a holiday, but only when I'm hard up because it's rather a bore having to listen to the old girl's propaganda about whatever happens to be her latest crusade, and as she's a great believer in plain living and can't afford fancy living anyway, it's a comfortless place. Cold and damp and comfortless. The last time I was there was the summer of 1953.'

By uttering nothing but unvarnished fact up to this point I had, as it were, timed myself in for a true and unwavering performance of my own composition, the cadenza. 'I knew no more about Byron then than any reasonably well-educated Englishman—oh, perhaps a little more because I'm fond of that period. I'd read his works, most of them, and dipped into biographies. If I'd been more familiar with the subject, I might have been quicker in the uptake when I came across the book.'

'Book?'

'Yes, a book for manuscript writing. I was poking around a lumber room where my grandfather or someone put the bindings not good enough for the shelves downstairs, and there, in an old wash-basket, among my grandmother's recipe books covered with spots of grease from the kitchen, and one or two battered albums, I unearthed this thing. I read a few pages and couldn't think what it was, didn't even connect it with Byron at first. I took it for an attempt to write a novel, a pretty good attempt too. Gradually, as I read a bit more, from all the places and people referred to, and especially Lady Byron, it dawned on me that it was Byron himself writing, so I stopped reading.'

'So you stopped reading?' he breathed ironically.

'I imagined, of course, that somebody had been copying large chunks from the published journals and correspondence. I hadn't enough knowledge at the time to realise that these were new revelations. Put yourself in my place!'

'I'm trying to—harder than you know.'

'I was interested, very much so, but if I wanted to go on, which I did, it seemed easier to read from the printed version instead of from a roughly pencilled scrawl that was sometimes quite difficult to make out.'

'Didn't you—? No, I'll keep questions till the end.'

'I can anticipate that one. Didn't I ask my Aunt Beth about it? Well, I began, but luckily I didn't persist. That year, 1953, was the year of the Coronation. The peerage was very strongly in evidence. My great-aunt, who has belonged since 1909 to a society for the abolition of the House of Lords, grows active at the times of Coronations. I'd no sooner let the name Byron fall from my lips than she launched into a tirade about the hopelessness of any peer attempting to write poetry, or to live a moral life, or to be otherwise than a public nuisance. I dropped the subject at once because I was afraid if I drew her attention to the book, it might go into the dustbin.'

'And you minded about that?'

'Certainly. I'm not one for having books thrown into dustbins whatever they may be. I didn't dream at the time about Dr. Williams having done that copying for Tom Moore in Paris, but there's something about a book, even a handwritten one, that seems to merit a little respect. I put it out of sight.'

'You actually did that much for it?' Again his irony was almost impertinently underlined.

I was half-tempted to bring it away because it's generally worth while to collate a copied text with the version in circulation—you can never tell what you'll find—but in the end I didn't bother. I had word while I was there that I'd got a job in Portugal, and I went abroad for more than a year. When I came back and started at Rossiter's, we had in stock the thirteen-volume edition of the Poetry and Letters and Journals, so I started looking more or less casually for the passages I'd thought so striking in that exercise book, and couldn't see a trace of them. I was intrigued. I began to search. I went to the London Library and got out other books on Byron. Not only were the particular pieces I remembered nowhere to be found, but in some cases biographers were completely at sea about matters described fully in the manuscript. I became utterly engrossed. It had grown to be a kind of quest. Yet it wasn't till I'd been at it for weeks that I got hold of Moore's Diary, and worked out what I now believe to be the solution of the mystery.' I made another effective pause.

'I'm all ears,' said Darrow very calmly.

'Moore was in Paris because of his debts. Williams, my ancestor, was probably there for the same reason. He was in extremely low water, so much so that even Moore who was in low water himself lent him money. He undertook to make the copy as an act of friendship but also, we can be sure, because it was a flattering thing to be obliging one of the most famous men of the day by copying the private life of another still greater celebrity. But he was a sociable creature, fond of parties and unable to resist an invitation from practically anyone, so he took his time about it, and after nearly three months Moore decided to put the work in the hands of someone more industrious. That's in his diary.

'Now this is the conclusion I've come to. Williams had been dilatory, but he was piqued nevertheless to have to give up his privilege. I don't think for a moment he had any dishonest intention, though his financial difficulties might lead one to wonder. . . . No, no, my conviction is that to have a secret copy of a document that the most brilliant people in society were delighted to get a glimpse of was simply something that gave him a kick. Before he returned it to Moore, he made a draft of it for himself, and judging by the pages I've read, he wrote hell for leather. How glad Moore would have been to know of its existence when he was working on his biography of Byron and trying all over the place to gather recollections of the script from people who'd seen it! But by that time . . .'

For a most disagreeable instant my tale hung fire. I realised that I hadn't given adequate attention to the date of Dr. Williams's death, but I recovered—and covered—myself dexterously: 'By that time he was beyond reach. He'd never told anyone, never could tell anyone what he'd done. There you have my theory.'

'Do you have a theory to account for the preservation of this precious heirloom without anyone recognising what it was— assuming you haven't been slipping up somewhere.'

Ignoring something unsatisfactory in his manner, I shrugged my shoulders. 'There are so many possibilities. Neglect for example. Neglect can cause treasures to be preserved just as it can cause them to be destroyed. The papers of a man of no property are seldom of much interest to his successors. Perhaps the solid binding was a safeguard. The book may have stood on the shelves with Scott's novels and Moore's poetry for a couple of generations.'

'Very plausible.'

I didn't like either the comment or the way he made it. I hadn't expected that he'd accept my narrative without criticism, but 'plausible'—that word gave me a chill. There's no trap so dangerous to fall into when we fear we are suspected as that of talking too much. I sipped my sherry and left it to him to go on.

'You mentioned you had some papers of Dr. Williams's.'

Fortunately I hadn't forgotten that remark made merely for effect at our first meeting. I'd regretted it since because the Memoirs were going to give me labour enough without expending my skill on what would be no more than hackwork, so I answered with a certain abstractedness: 'Yes. The main item among the papers was naturally this volume, but there were some oddments of one kind and another which I presume were his. I didn't examine them closely, not foreseeing that they might be important. There was a little notebook with some medical stuff in it,' I improvised. 'I think that must have belonged to him. And a few letters. Nothing much else.' These documents could turn out to be lost when I went into action at my great-aunt's in Wales.

'And he was your ancestor? That's kind of vague, isn't it?'

'I fear I am "kind of vague" on the subject. He was either my grandfather's grandfather, or my grandfather's great-grandfather. Or possibly one of my grandfather's great-uncles or great-great-uncles. Let me see! My grandfather was born in 1873. Dr. Williams, who goes back to the eighteenth century, could easily come into the category of "great-great-great".' A little of this could go a long way; at least, I hoped it would. It was evident that I should have to apply myself to the ancestry question later on, but at the present stage, and without having been to Wales, I didn't want to commit myself to anything irrevocable. 'Until recently there were several sons in each generation, which makes it more confusing. And in Wales a name like Williams doesn't help. Williamses married Williamses, just as Evanses married Evanses, and Davises married Davises—'

He interrupted tartly: 'Whoever married whom, they were Welsh?'

'Very much so.'

'Then how comes it that Dr. Williams was an Irishman?'

I have no desire to introduce any elements of drama into this entirely unimaginative record, but I'm bound to write the truth, and the truth is that I felt as if, taking an adventurous but seductive walk, I had suddenly found my feet on the edge of an abyss. I caught my breath and seemed to sway above the gulf.

'An Irishman!' To save my life I couldn't at the moment have concealed my dismay.

'Positively.' He put his book on the table and searched through the pages. I haven't a doubt that if he'd had the right place marked, my fabrication would have collapsed there and then, but it took him a little while to find the page he wanted and during that interim I stepped back from the precipice.

'Listen! Moore's Diary Volume Three, entry for the 12th of December, 1819: "A visitor announced to me, a stranger; said I had done him the honour to leave a card with him last night. Found I had mistaken another doctor for Yonge . . . Proved to be a Mr. Williams, an Irishman, a very gentleman-like sort of person, who offered his services, to take lodgings, or do anything useful for me."'

'It can't be the same man?'

'It's the same man all right. Moore met him, as you've just heard, through the accident of leaving a card on him in mistake for a Dr. Yonge whom he consulted professionally. There's an entry five days later—Here it is: "Called upon Fielding and Lady Elizabeth, who had asked me to dinner; but I had engaged to dine with my new friend Dr. Williams." Moore had a dull evening, but Williams was, as you say, the sociable type, and he's in and out of the diary quite a bit after that. On St. Patrick's day, 1820, they sang duets together, Irish melodies.'

I could faintly remember this, but it hadn't struck me that a singer of Moore's songs would necessarily be an Irishman. My notes had been written at a time when I'd been concerned only with Williams's transactions as copyist of the Memoirs. I'd taken the precaution of going to the London Library to expand them, but the appropriate volume of Moore's Diary was out and, not having had time to visit the British Museum, I'd decided it would be safe enough, temporarily, to rely on the fairly copious data I'd recorded. Inwardly swearing never to commit such a folly again, I concentrated all my faculties now on recapturing the ground I'd lost by it.

'Good God!' I had no difficulty at all in sounding shaken. 'I never heard of any Irishman in our family. I can't believe I've been building all these months on a false premise. No, no! If you could see this book, if you could read it—!'

'I ask nothing better, but as you haven't read it yourself since 1953 . . .'

'I have an excellent memory, and there are parts that are absolutely fixed in it.' I was about to describe an episode or two already sketched out in my mind when to my relief—for I was most reluctant to tie myself down to writing what I might afterwards wish to expunge—he raised a point for which I'd prepared an answer.

'Why can't you, now the Coronation's over, get hold of the book from your aunt?'

'It would have been in my possession months ago if that had been feasible. Suppose I asked her to send it, I'd have to tell where I'd hidden it, and obviously she'd look into it and catch hold of the idea that it was worth money. She's extremely garrulous and gossipy and would consult her friends about it. Moreover, she'd want to sell it so that she could give the proceeds to her latest awful forlorn hope, a thing she calls TAT.'

'TAT?'

'Yes, a league for the total abolition of taxation.'

A frown settled on his face as he signalled to the barman to repeat the drinks, but the alertness of suspicion was giving place to bewilderment. He was finding it hard no doubt to believe a man could invent such a story: and indeed, as to the predilections of my great-aunt, I was inventing nothing.

'But what's stopping you from going to Wales in person to fetch the damn book?'

I smiled that useful ingenuous smile of mine. 'A journey to Wales might seem nothing to you with your transatlantic notions of distance, but it would strike my Aunt Beth as very peculiar. A meaningless visit of a couple of days at a time of the year when I don't normally go—she's no fool though she is eccentric, and she'd be looking for the reason. The problem of ownership is quite a knotty one.'

'There didn't seem to be much problem when you found it. You said you were tempted to bring it away with you.'

'*Half*-tempted: and at that time I took it for a series of copied extracts without value. Oh, you needn't imagine I'm trying to pass myself off as the man Diogenes was looking for, but you see if I just walked off with those Memoirs and they were afterwards brought to light, the source I got them from couldn't be concealed. Inevitably there'd be publicity. My great-aunt in a huff would thereupon lay claim to the property to bestow upon TAT or the Seekers of the Holy Grail or whatever cause she might happen to be enamoured of at the moment. It isn't that I want to do her out of anything, though she *has* squandered what

I ought to inherit, only she gets into the hands of such frightful charlatans.'

'It certainly sounds like it. What are you figuring to do then? I suppose you *are* figuring to do something!'

'I've invited myself to stay with her for a fortnight or so in September. That'll give me some elbow room to carry out manoeuvres. As a matter of fact, I'm pretty sure that manuscript's mine. A lot of stuff knocking about up there belonged to my father.'

There were now two or three other people in the bar and he dropped his voice to remind me wistfully: 'Still, we are up against this trouble about your ancestors being Welsh and not Irish.'

'I haven't digested that yet,' I replied with candour. 'It's incomprehensible.'

My not having attempted any explanation whatever had apparently undermined his original conviction that I'd been hoodwinking him. He may have reflected that so serious a gap in my information about Dr. Williams was evidence in my favour: a man bent on deception would have been better primed.

'You're sure it's Moore's Dr. Williams and no other who's your ancestor? After all, the name's not by any means an uncommon one.' He was actually giving me a get-out.

I took care not to jump at it. 'Yes, I'm sure, or I was sure till you flung this—this hand-grenade at me. Not that it alters my opinion of what the manuscript is—'

'It couldn't by any chance be a *post factum* deduction of yours, this man being your ancestor?'

'You mean I deluded myself that *our* Dr. Williams was Moore's Dr. Williams because of my views about these Memoirs?' I acted the part of a man jibbing strongly at an unpalatable admission.

'I mean you might have read these Memoirs—if they are Memoirs—first and then formed a theory to account for finding them there.'

'I can't agree,' I said stiffly. '*Our* Dr. Williams fits many of the circumstances perfectly.' It would be just too bad, I thought in Darrow's own idiom, if I couldn't, among such medical records as survive from the early nineteenth century, rake up a single

Welsh Williams who could be grafted on to our very adventitious family tree.

'Aren't you afraid you may be building too high on your interpretation of this document? You don't seem to me to have all that much to go on.' The frown he continued to level at his glass was, I presumed, rather one of sympathy for a man probably harbouring an illusion than distaste for the feeble public-house sherry. 'If Moore's Williams turns out to have no connection with your family at all, then where are you?'

'Very puzzled, but still in the position of having access to an enthralling account of the private affairs of Byron written in the first person and as yet unpublished.'

'Frankly, it sounds interesting but doubtful. However, as you're sure to take the first opportunity of showing it to experts—'

'I'll take the first opportunity of showing it to you.'

'Well, I'm—I'm flattered by your offer, but what's behind it?'

'You specialise in manuscripts and you're a neutral observer. I want an outside opinion. It's a necessity. Do you realise that controversies about Byron have been going on with practically unabated fervour for five or six generations? That there are still active Executors to the Byron Estate? That the Byron title is very far from extinct? That there are also direct descendants who're completely alive and kicking? That his various biographers have theories they're wedded to so they can't judge dispassionately? How could they? You write a man's life-story because you have feelings about him, either liking or disliking. Impartiality can't be anything but a façade. I tell you, putting this discovery in circulation will be like springing a whole train of mines.'

'That may well be, and I'd love to be in on it. But I ought to make it clear I couldn't be a neutral observer. I'm a dealer. If that manuscript's genuine, I'll be in the market for it. That's why I took the trouble to do this bit of detective work.' He laid his purposeful hand on the book.

'But you haven't any axe to grind about Byron?'

He shook his head. 'Only as a producer of holograph material that sometimes changes hands. As to that, I've been instrumental in one or two sizeable transactions. It was to check up on one of those that I went to see Sir John Murray. Look, I'll lay my cards on the table since you've done the same. Until last year I was Mr. Nimmo Peascod's librarian. It was he who set me up in this business I have now, in Philadelphia.'

I had, of course, heard about the millionaire paper-manufacturer and his splendid library, and I gave suitable indications to that effect.

'I'm sure, if anything big came my way, I could count on Mr. Peascod for the backing. I mention it because you ought to know that although I'm neutral in regard to who wins and who loses the arguments these Memoirs will settle—always assuming they are Memoirs—I'm not at all neutral as to who buys them.'

'If I sell.'

'If you sell!' He raised his eyes reproachfully to my face. 'So you're back at that—getting coy again!'

His familiarity showed pleasantly that he felt himself on easy terms with me. The watchful wary man who had come to this encounter with a trap laid was subsiding into a friendly inquirer who looked forward to having a stake in the game.

'I'm always a little coy as to that aspect . . . anyhow there's no point in talking about it while everything's in abeyance.' The first time I'd hinted at an unwillingness to sell my fabulous treasure (while it was still no more than a floating bubble of my fancy), I'd been simply taking a little gentle revenge on him and a number of other Americans who weren't present for being arrogant about purchasing power. Now I had a more rational motive.

Realist though I am, I nevertheless hesitate to write the word crime, because crime is something repugnant, something that inflicts pain and misery. To me anything of that nature is odious. My intention was to make my reconstruction of Byron's autobiographical chapters a thing that would give widespread pleasure to readers all over the world and would enrich not only myself and those whom I held dear, but also in a greater or lesser degree everyone who might take part in the publication and distribution of the work. No one would be hurt by it, and no one even annoyed—except a few writers and critics who had persisted in printing opinions I found contemptible and would now compel them to retract. Best of all, my object would be to shed glory on the memory of a great man whom it had always appealed to little men to malign. What I lacked of his wit and variety, I would make up to him by the after-knowledge which would enable me, in seeming unconsciousness of effect, subtly to present his conduct in its most attractive guise.

It will be understood then, if anything about this singular narrative is understood, that I was very far from classing myself as an incipient criminal. Yet I was aware that what I contemplated was illegal, or would be so the moment I had received or required any payment for my creation. The fraud, speaking in this cold-blooded technical sense, would begin only when I sought gain. Until that moment, I should be merely indulging in a hoax. It follows that my policy was never to suggest, or even to admit, my willingness to engage in a monetary transaction until the verdicts on my completed effort removed every trace of anxiety, and I could in perfect confidence yield to pressure.

To avoid any further discussion, I called Darrow's attention with some urgency to the length of time I'd been absent from the shop.

'I'll walk back with you,' he said. 'I have a favour to ask.' We were across the road before he spoke again. 'No, I really can't ask it. It's too much.'

I was in some trepidation as to what it might conceivably be in his mind to put to me when, to my relief, he went on apologetically: 'I'm returning to the States in a fortnight. I got away for just five or six weeks, and I don't see any chance of being here again in September. Does that mean I have to throw in my hand? That's to say, the hand I d like to have?'

He could hardly have given me more welcome news. Though, like most authors, I begin each new composition with a set of reasons for believing I'm going to get through it at a much greater speed than the last, I couldn't pretend to myself, now in mid-July, that I was capable of getting that exercise book worthily filled up before the end of November. Even though I was resolved to renounce all the pleasures of Jocasta's company and to work early and late, I should need four clear months at the job, and I'd been afraid that temporising with Darrow after my visit to Wales in September might prove to be a weak link in the chain I was so artistically forging. Once again, however, I was careful not to meet him too eagerly.

I told him I was disappointed but that he'd hardly expect me to wait an indefinite period before seeking confirmation of hopes I'd been cherishing so long, and that, reluctant as I was to confide in anyone else, having somehow set my mind on having his reaction first, the most I could promise was that I'd write him as to the outcome and wouldn't take any final decision, if ever I became inclined to dispose of the volume, without notifying him.

'Fair enough,' he said, 'and more than I deserve seeing I was about ninety per cent sure until today that you were stringing someone along, though whether it was yourself or me I didn't know. But if the girl I left to take care of affairs back home is managing as well as they tell me she is, it won't be an absolutely "indefinite period" before I turn up again.' He began to enter into the details of his business life in that explanatory American style which reposes so engaging a confidence in the close interest of the listener.

But as we turned the corner that led to Rossiter's, he interrupted himself quietly yet with fervour: 'Say, Williams, you don't know what you've been missing! Look what's come out of your shop!'

He halted and, following the direction of his eyes, I saw Jocasta pause a step or two from our doorway as if undecided whether to wait or to walk away.

'My, that's a stunning girl. If only we hadn't dawdled. . . .'

'That girl's mine,' I said tersely.

'Well, what do you know?' he whispered.

To show him at once where, as he might have put it, he got off, I went forward and caught her by the waist. She was indeed looking particularly 'stunning' that day. I can't attempt to describe her clothes beyond saying that she had on a blue dress, the mauve-blue of certain hyacinths, which suited her eyes and her skin perfectly; and there were some moss roses mixed up with it, and some in her hat too which didn't look nearly so silly on her head as it would in a shop window.

'Jocasta, my dear! I hope you were looking for me!'

'Yes, I came to bring back the book, and to take away the next volume, but there was only the boy in there, and I didn't like to leave it just in case . . .' She smiled. I perceived she meant 'In case I oughtn't to let the boy see that you lent a book out of stock.'

I took from her the only incongruous touch about her immaculate elegance, an old quarto of Moore's Byron—the first edition, in fact, though with various defects. At the same time, I rapidly put to myself the question whether it would matter if Darrow were to hear of the task I'd concocted for her, and decided it was not of any consequence.

He was hovering about not knowing whether or how to go, so I introduced him and mentioned that Jocasta was 'helping me with a bit of Byron research, and seemed to have got off to a wonderfully quick start'. Perhaps my manner may have sounded a shade paternal, as if she were a little girl to be put through her paces and encouraged. If so, it was justified by the extreme childishness of her reply:

'I didn't skip a single page, Quentin, not even the poetry. I think he s such a pet!' She turned to Darrow. 'Don't you?'

'Who? Byron? Depends on what you like to keep for a pet!'

'A pet lion.' She gave her tiny giggle which usually seemed to me so cosy, almost an endearment, but this time it came near to grating on me. 'I can't wait for the second volume, although there isn't much in the book so far about—about what you wanted me to look up.'

Dear Jocasta! She was after all rather sweet, being so discreet about something I mightn't want Darrow to be in on.

'Quentin thought I wasn't going to finish it,' she explained, 'because this is the first biography I've ever read. But now I'm going to read them all.'

'All!' cried Darrow.

'All the ones on Byron, because you can really imagine what he was like.'

'You'll have your work cut out for some years to come, Miss Leverett.' He had performed the customary American feat of catching her name.

'Where are you staying?' I inquired, though it would have been more to my advantage materially to encourage him into the shop in the hope that he would do some more buying. 'I'll ring you up.'

'I'm at Brown's. But why shouldn't I call you? We can have lunch together or something.'

'Anyhow we'll meet before you leave.'

With a small flourish of the hand, which Jocasta returned in kind, he bade us good-bye.

Without even asking who he was, she moved towards the shop door with me, saying: 'I suppose if Byron were alive today he'd be a very important film star—a sort of male Garbo.'

Such a vapid and unworthy comment quite irritated me. I had never regarded my beautiful Jocasta as an intellectual girl, but she had been brought up by highly cultured grandparents, and I saw no reason why she should appear—no, I won't say vulgar, for she had too little pretension ever to be that, but—I can only repeat—childish.

I hung back at the threshold to protest mildly: 'A film star, my darling! Isn't a poet good enough? Just because *you* don't read poetry!'

'I mean a poet couldn't be as famous as that nowadays.' Her diffidence made her falter, picking her words thoughtfully. 'Poets aren't expected to be romantic any more, are they? People don't care whether they're handsome or not. Walter Scott said Byron had a face to dream about.'

I found myself breasting a wave of unaccountable anger. 'That's not in the book you've been reading.'

'No, Granny told me. I can't read Scott, but Gran does. She loves him, and Byron too. She's given me a picture of him that she used to keep in her glove box when she was a girl. Isn't that rather touching, Quentin?'

'A picture of Scott?'

'No, darling—Byron, of course.'

It was the 'of course' that jarred on me.

CHAPTER FIVE

GETTING HOLD of Byron's prose style was about as hard a job as I've ever attempted in my life, but I fancy no one has yet succeeded better than I did. It was plain from his references to the Memoirs in several letters, as well as from Moore's description of them, that the first part had been a consecutive story, sustained and free from vehemence—at least as free from vehemence as anything he could write (had he not been determined that it should be laid before the minutely analytical eyes of his wife?) but before I risked the feat of imitating his narrative manner for more than a few paragraphs, I had to do a little limbering up. I began by seeking to catch the apparently careless tones of the *Detached Thoughts* and certain of the journals, and I wrote a few opinions and anecdotes entirely in that vein. If they were good enough, I could drop them into my MS at suitable junctures, and if they fell short, the waste of work would not be substantial.

My memory and my card index contained most of the material I should want for reconstructing the tale of his courtship and married life; and in fact, since his wife had survived their brief partnership by forty-four revealing years, my knowledge of her character was more complete than any he himself possessed. Using this without appearing to use it, I hoped to give a twist here and there which would win the least-approving reader's sympathy: for even at that stage, monetary gain was not my sole object. Yes, I must do myself the justice to repeat that I set out with the intention of righting many wrongs under which Byron's reputation had suffered.

From the first, I felt time pressing upon me relentlessly. Besides my literary effort, there was the Georgian handwriting to practise until I grew easy with it, and over and above this, the daily reading necessary to help me to project myself into my subject's state of mind and the ambience of another age—not the same thing as factual data but equally essential. I was also obliged to make certain preparations for my impending journey to Wales in September. Moreover in August Jocasta returned home and I had to move.

It took me some hours a day for several days to find new lodgings. The Leveretts were surprised at my persistent refusal of their offer to rig up one of their empty rooms as a temporary habitation for me, but though the prospect had alluring aspects I foresaw difficulties in pursuing a highly secret occupation under the same roof as my betrothed and her family. So pleading the need of being closeted with my novel while the inspiration was hot upon me, I continued searching until I found a room, furnished in a ramshackle but not hideous fashion, in Lowestoft Street, High Holborn. It was dismally far from Jocasta's, but handy for going to my bookshop, and, doubtless on account of its being above a fishmonger's, it had the merit of a privacy beyond the means of most poor men.

Though she was not in the best of humours with me, Jocasta came to give me a hand in getting installed. Hers was an unusually equable temperament, but she was a little hurt at my seemingly unnecessary departure from Brockford Lodge. She tried to suppress her dissatisfaction, to see eye to eye with me when I explained in all sincerity the sacrifice I was making of my own inclinations, yet fundamentally she had not accepted the situation, and when she saw my new apartment, she couldn't refrain from a slight murmur.

'This novel had better be good, Quentin!'

'I'm doing my utmost to make it so. I couldn't do more than give up the chance of being with you.'

'It's quite Byronic, shutting yourself away like this to write at top speed—only I don't think he'd have chosen a fish shop.'

'Neither would I if there'd been any choice about it.' Perhaps I spoke curtly. That word 'Byronic', slipping so glibly off her tongue, as it had done several times lately, gave rise to a faint exasperation. 'He did live over a shop for a time and didn't behave very properly with his landlady.'

'I know—and she didn't behave very properly with him.' There was no comeback to that. 'I dare say you'll get used to the fish. You're two floors above them which is lucky, but they do rather linger on the stairs.'

'Fortunately, I shall not be having many visitors.'

'Poor darling! It must be awful to be in the clutches of a book. Nobody who doesn't write can have any idea what it's like.' She placed on a tray some of the oddments of crockery that went with my furniture. 'If you had some milk, I could make tea for us.'

It was one advantage of having shops underneath that I could slip down for some.

When I came back she was setting out my few provisions in the cupboard that did duty for a larder. I'd never been alone with her before in so domestic a situation. Although her grandparents were not intrusive, I was always aware of the presence of one or other of them in her home, and while I'd actually been living there, she herself was elsewhere. Shabby as the surroundings were, it was charming to see her, wearing a fancy apron she'd brought with her which made her look like a soubrette in a musical comedy, concerning herself so intimately with my housekeeping arrangements. If I hadn't made a pledge to myself before receiving her here that I would defeat temptation in advance by keeping my distance, I should have distracted her with my embraces. Perhaps it would have been better if I had.

'It looks as if you're going to live on tinned soup and sardines,' she said. 'Gran would be worrying about you if I told her, thinking you were going to be under-nourished.'

'And you won't be worrying about me?' It was one of those silly little baits that lovers can't resist throwing out.

'Not about what you eat. Our generation only worries about eating too much.'

'Then what *will* you be worrying about—if anything?'

'Your work, I suppose.'

'You never did before, honey.'

'Because you never tucked yourself away like this before to write a novel.'

'You haven't much faith in my novel, have you?' When the day came for announcing my failure, how convincingly I should be able to praise her for her intuition!

'It's not that, but—well, it seems such a pity, just when you'd got me interested in Byron to go off on to something else. Do you know what I'm doing now, Quentin? I'm reading his poetry!' She turned round from the shelf and looked at me as if she could hardly believe her own words. 'Yes, and I like it! It's different from what I expected. I can understand it.'

'Where did you begin?' Nothing could have been calmer than my inexpressive voice.

'*Childe Harold*.'

'Why, my love?' I felt a curious qualm. So many women had begun with *Childe Harold*.

'Because it was the most famous.'

'*Don Juan* is more famous nowadays. Not that I'm suggesting for a moment you should tackle that.'

'I did. I tried that first as you admire it so much, but it's quite hard for anyone who isn't accustomed to poetry. *Childe Harold* is as easy as anything, only there's not very much about *animals* in it . . . mostly the part about the bull-fight. I'm glad he didn't think much of it as a sport.'

'He went to a bull-fight.' I couldn't help pointing that out.

'But you can see he sympathised with the bull and the horses. By the way, Quentin, do you want me to mark everything about animals, every single thing, even when he only says "To horse! To horse!" or something like that?'

She emerged from the cupboard with the air of a particularly choice advertisement for some product desirable to the elegant young housewife. I wanted her to be *my* housewife—I d come here to work towards the attainment of that end—and I was ashamed of the trick by which I'd set her playing this unapt little literary game in which she was taking such a pride. I longed to have done with it.

'It's a matter for judgment,' I said. 'We can only use quotations that show his opinions or his actions. Anyway, didn't I tell you, sweetheart, that I'd do the poetry?'

'And didn't I tell *you* I like it? Who knows? I may end by liking all kinds of poetry. There's one thing about it—you can read short pieces while you're hanging about waiting for photographers and rehearsals and things.'

I decided to head her off the poetry. 'Darling, have you thought what you're going to want for your birthday?' Living at Brockford Lodge had been an economy, and I'd set aside some money to buy her a present that would normally have been beyond my means. Not that she was selfish, but the childlike vein in her nature made it so joyful an experience for her to receive gifts that one couldn't help wanting to heighten the pleasure by lavish giving. I bore in mind too that, though as a model she was in the habit of seeing all the artefacts most coveted by beautiful women, her home life, with the responsibilities which her affection made her feel so keenly, allowed her few chances of acquiring luxuries for herself. Even the good clothes she regarded as a professional necessity were mostly got at privileged rates after much planning and manoeuvring.

For her last birthday, when I'd begun falling in love with her, I'd bought her a bottle of some alarmingly expensive Dior scent which she said had quite set her up; and at Christmas, just when we were getting engaged, she'd had a pair of Victorian marcasite bracelets I'd heard her admire in a shop window. Lately, being too much tied up to eavesdrop on her wishes, I'd asked her to choose something for herself. It was perhaps too husband-like an offer, implying a matter-of-fact relationship which women never take to very kindly. If so the retribution was fitting.

'Well, I have seen something I'd like very much,' she answered with what I must paradoxically describe as a sort of slow alacrity, 'and I'm sure you'd like it too—tremendously. I feel rather mean about asking for it, you're going to want it for yourself so much. Still, I can wear it, honey, and you can't.'

'It sounds a very mysterious object.'

She stopped in her occupation of warming the teapot to feast for an instant on my bewilderment. 'I give you a hundred guesses what it is.'

'Something we'd both like but that only you can wear? Scent, flowers, make-up—no, I wouldn't want any of those for myself. Was it made for a man to wear in the first place?'

'Oh no! Positively no!'

'Was it made for *anyone* to wear?'

'Yes. It was intended to be worn, this particular one.'

'But not by a man? Then why should I want it for myself?'

'Because it's completely up your street. Oh, darling, you'll never guess. It's a most beautiful miniature of Byron.'

My reactions tend to be slow. I was dead silent.

She hastened to reassure me. 'I know you must be imagining it's too dear even to think of, and so it would be, only it's got some little defects that spoil it for collectors. The enamel's a tiny bit chipped, but you can't see that unless you look into it. And he doesn't think it's an original picture—it may be a copy of one that's well-known.'

'Who "doesn't think"?'

'He's a man who runs an antique shop in the Marylebone High Street. I'll give you the address if you'd really like to get it for me. He swore he'd put it on one side. Of course, we can check up which portrait it's based on.'

I managed to laugh, which was very far from coming naturally. 'Do you mean to say that you seriously want to go round decorated with a picture of Byron?'

'Why not? He's very decorative. And it's mounted like a brooch. It's a lovely setting.'

'Contemporary?' The question was merely to cover my extreme reluctance either to commit myself to this gift or to refuse it.

'The man in the shop says it's antique.'

'That's what I meant. Contemporary with the picture, not with the latest café espresso.'

She appeared mildly puzzled at my ungraciousness. 'I can't help it, ducky, if the world doesn't know whether it's standing on its head or its heels . . . Now don't start wandering round the room the very moment your tea's poured out!'

I was looking for my little index cabinet, and as it was already installed on a handy shelf, it took me only a minute or two to produce the card I wanted.

'"Lady Oxford," I read, "'walks about Naples with Byron's picture in her girdle, in front." That's from Hobhouse's Diary.'

Jocasta giggled. 'Is that meant to be a warning? I promise I shan't wear this picture in my girdle . . . Only, come to think of it, Lady Oxford's waist in one of those Empire dresses must have been under her armpits, so it wasn't as silly as it sounds. She was wearing it on her heart, I dare say.'

Some noise apparently escaped me which caused her to protest, but only half-seriously: 'Sentiment is simply wasted on men.'

'On that man.'

'Oh, would you say so? He spoke of her rather sweetly years after—how her beauty was like a wonderful autumn sunset shedding its last light. Quentin, do you think the miniature I want for my birthday might be the very one she wore? Wouldn't that be nice?'

'Very nice.' I tried not to sound sardonic.

'Was it while she was having her affair with him, or after?'

'A good two years after—1815.'

'How queer, wearing his portrait when everything was ended!' She stared abstractedly across the teacups, and her eyes had in them a hint, no more, of something that deepened my nameless unquiet. 'I suppose it wouldn't have been easy to get over it if one had been in love with him.'

'Women cling to men who treat them heartlessly.' I spoke with a shiver of strange melancholy.

'There was more to it than that, darling, in *his* case. He must have had a lot of glamour—'

'That word has been so much abused, it has no more meaning for me.'

She ignored my priggish and futile interruption, and he was so famous, one would keep on hearing about him, and that would make it harder to get him out of one's system.

She was saying things she had been thinking about beforehand. She had been thinking about what it would be like to have a love affair with Byron. I won't waste words trying to convey the mixture of sensations this perception touched off in me. Who could understand it but one who had spent long months, even years, mastering every known circumstance and detail of another man's life until he has become a completely familiar entity? It was as if I'd rashly introduced a dangerous friend to her—a friend delightful, lovable, yet capable of an unsettling and deleterious influence. I dared not venture a direct warning against him, I who less than a month ago had eagerly brought about this association, but I was prepared now to bear her having almost any other distraction than the one I'd so blindly proposed to her.

I waited to resume till we were clearing the tea-table. 'Look, Jocasta! I've been thinking—it was very stupid and selfish of me to expect you to spend your summer doing dreary literary chores for me. I shouldn't take a bit of umbrage if you gave them up. In fact, I wish you would.'

'It's too late,' she replied, smiling. 'Once I'm interested, I always stick to things. You ought to know that much about me after all these years. And anyhow, I don't find Byron dreary.'

'Wait till you really get going,' I blundered. 'You've only had two or three books so far.'

'No, I've had three you've given me and seven from the London Library. I don't say I've had time to read them all yet, but I will.'

'The London Library, my darling!'

'Yes, you've forgotten Granpapa's parishioners gave him a life membership when he retired. I used to go there quite a lot to fetch books for him, and they remember me there and help me to find things, so I won't have to bother you at all. There's a very nice young man who seems to know exactly what I ought to read. Not that I told him anything about your plan. I simply gave him to understand I'd got a terrific "thing" about Byron.'

She couldn't see my face because she had started to wash the tea things. And now in the quiet and efficient manner which was typical of her in all the practical business of life, she asked me to note some small household requirements I ought to purchase, as, for example, a pan-scrubber, more tea-towels, a packet of detergent.

'I don't want to picture you weltering in a muddle here. I'd bring them myself, but as you've got to be alone, you won't care for me to come tripping in and out.'

I made a little speech about caring for it very much but having to deny myself the pleasure.

'If you had a spare key, I could drop in occasionally during the day, while you're at Rossiter's, and do a bit of tidying up for you.'

'No, no, my angel!' I repressed my tremor of anxiety. 'That would be too tantalising—worse than your not coming at all. Far worse. Let's stick to our resolution to meet whenever I have a chapter of the novel to read to you.'

'*Your* resolution.'

'You'll be glad in the end, darling. If I can pull it off with this book we'll be able to get married. I wouldn't be surprised if I did pull it off. I've got a story that may be good for film rights at any rate.' So I had thought when I'd laboured years ago at that abortive work.

That s all very well, Quentin.' She gently put away the hand that I had laid, contrary to my resolution, on her waist. 'You're lucky I was brought up by Gran and Granpapa, who are educated and able to sympathise with the way authors behave. You might have a girl friend who wouldn't take to this sort of thing. In August too, just when I shall be free!'

'I know, dear. It must seem maddening, but after all, it's not as if I'm going to be chasing about. You'll be free, as you say, whilst I'll be cooped up here in a room over a fish shop, alone with my book.'

The thought of how different it might have been if I hadn't elected to travel so steep and solitary a road couldn't but make me feel some stirring of pity for myself.

She took back my hand. 'Ah, sweetheart, you make it sound so pathetic. The fish shop too! You'll have me in tears. You alone with your book, and I'—a certain elusive and provocative dimple twinkled in her left cheek—'I alone with Byron!'

The small but eloquent pang that shot through me was doubtless neurotic in its origin and owed something to the guilt which must have been subconsciously undermining me. I had a sense of having entangled myself in what might prove to be an utterly baffling kind of competition.

I should have spoken, should have tried with kisses and caresses to explain my apprehension. Jocasta would have humoured me even if she hadn't understood. But I was inhibited by my awareness of the imposition I'd practised on her. I only answered her little jest with a jest.

'Be sure you have your grandmother to chaperone you.'

I didn't see her again until her birthday, for the evening of which I was invited to Brockford Lodge. I took with me the miniature, which she received with raptures, and which thereafter always confronted me from her throat or bosom, but whether because it was the 'face to dream about' or my gift, I never dared to inquire.

'Now I've got a present for you too,' she said. 'At least it's from me and Granpapa. Come and see him!'

We went upstairs to Mr. Leverett's study on the first floor, the room in which I'd once striven to become a classical scholar. I could never cross its threshold without vividly recapturing the sensation of youth, for there hung about it always the most evocative of perfumes—the slightly fusty smell of old books mingled with the clean, austere fragrance of beeswax. The books, most of them with bindings worn and battered, covered two of the walls from floor to ceiling: the beeswax emanated from a mahogany table, where Mr. Leverett had been wont for several decades to write his sermons or work beside his pupils, and a large rolltop desk behind which he entrenched himself when dealing with matters of business.

On the table were placed now, just as they had been when I had first taken my seat there, a pair of brass candlesticks in which candles were burning. There were no plugs for electric reading-lamps in the vicarage, only a single point for light in the ceiling of each room, the installation never having been brought up to date since the dismantling of the original gas jets. Candles provided whatever extra illumination was required, and they had long ceased to be a reminder of the family's slender means and now seemed a kind of pleasing eccentricity.

There was no inducement to the Leveretts to modernise their home even if they had been in a position to do so. The old gentleman was nearly eighty, and the building was ecclesiastical property known to be wanted for a development scheme. Apart from small innovations made here and there by Jocasta or her father, the appearance of the rooms was much as it must have been when Mr. and Mrs. Leverett had arrived here as a young couple.

The furniture, not new when they acquired it, had grown shabby despite the evident care with which it had been handled. The long linen curtains, printed with a design in the William Morris style, were faded to ghostliness. The floor, covered with well-worn linoleum inlaid to represent tiles, was just relieved from chilly bareness by two home-made rugs and a threadbare Oriental runner. There were some very upright chairs of stained oak tightly upholstered in somewhat cracked brown leather and a pair of fancy basketwork armchairs growing a little lopsided with time. In front of the hearth stood a large Indian gong of beaten copper serving as a screen for the empty grate, above which was an *art nouveau* overmantel decorated with heart-shaped perforations and carvings of conventional irises set around a mirror. On the mantelpiece, instead of ornaments, there were pewter tankards containing pens and pencils and in the centre an inkstand.

A stranger would have been puzzled to see Jocasta, dressed like a fashion plate and arrayed in beauty that was a work of art, perfectly at home in that room which could never at any time have had the smallest pretension to social or aesthetic grace; but no one who knew the climate of contentment that prevailed there would have failed to be grateful for its unchangingness.

That climate seemed to be enclosed and held stable by the books, which had nourished generations of learned men and still had treasures to yield up, by the walls where photographs of pupils and parishioners in many bygone styles of dress and portraiture attested a reassuring continuity in the sentiments which had gathered these souvenirs and cherished them, and by the numerous windows whence, in the daytime, poured a light tinted with rose and amber. If Mr. Leverett had been affluent and aware of fashion, he would long ago have removed the rows of stained glass panes above the late Victorian casements, but in his poverty and innocence he had left them untouched, and now they were gradually acquiring the nostalgic charm of a mode that is too obsolete to be stale, yet not old enough to have taken on the stature of the antique.

It was an illusion, I suppose, that Mr. Leverett himself had only grown a little shabbier with time, like his chairs and book-bindings. He was certainly bent and venerable-looking, but then he had been so when I had first been brought to him some fourteen years ago. His hair was perhaps thinner but no whiter than then. His stoop was due, not to age but an arthritic condition. He had a drooping moustache which gave his long face a melancholy air, and in his voice was the quaver of old age, but though his life had been full of difficulty, he was neither sad nor senile.

His personality, serene and trusting, was sustained by a quality I can only call intelligent goodness. I could never decide whether he was good because he was religious, or religious because he was good, or whether he would have behaved with the same altruism and integrity if he had had no religion at all. He was under the impression, at any rate, that he was endeavouring to fulfil the duties laid down for Christians, and his conception of those duties was magnanimous. By a most fortunate dispensation for himself, he had married a woman who completely shared his aspirations, and by what I quaintly regarded as an equally fortunate dispensation for me, their granddaughter, though much less unworldly, was capable of being almost as high-minded. Or perhaps I should say as high-hearted, since with her the generous virtues were not attained by taking thought.

There was a tray of sherry in the study—a regale produced only for celebrations—and Mr. Leverett, welcoming me with a distinguished courtesy from which no one could have inferred that, only a few weeks ago, I'd been a lodger in his house, put a glass in my hand, saying: 'How good of you to come!' It was a feature of his extensive politeness that he regarded even visits from me as a favour.

'There are rewards,' I said.

'Today he deserves rewards, Granpapa. Look at the lovely thing he gave me for my birthday!'

Mr. Leverett put on a pair of spectacles to examine the miniature. 'Oh, this is well-chosen indeed!' She smiled secretly at me. 'In this house it will be a true badge of merit.'

I managed to look gratified.

'You've earned it at least as much as me, Granpapa.'

'As *I*, child, *I*.'

'You shall wear it sometimes round your neck—the Order of—what order shall we call it?'

'Not quite one of the orders of sainthood,' I said.

'Saint Byron!' Jocasta's little squeal of amusement had no appeal for me this evening.

'Saints have been made of still more intractable material,' Mr. Leverett mused. 'He deserves at least an order of chivalry.'

'You judge charitably.'

'Only under the guidance of my wife and granddaughter. Yes, we are all—what does she call us?—all Byron fans here.' I could have groaned but restrained myself.

'Let's show him the surprise, Granpapa!'

'If you don't think it's premature . . . We haven't got very far.'

Her eyes bright with anticipation of my pleasure, she pulled up the roller top of the desk and drew from one of its compartments an oblong box.

'What is it?' I asked feebly. Then with a sinking heart I saw. 'Oh, it's a card index. But what in the world—?'

She turned the box on end so that I might read the label written in Mr. Leverett's exquisite script: LORD BYRON AND THE ANIMAL KINGDOM.

'It's Granpapa's own idea. He's going to save you all that copying.'

'How kind! How very very kind!' I tried to rally the note of enthusiasm called for by her delight. 'I seem to be giving a great deal more trouble than I intended.'

'I'm enjoying it.' His protest was plainly most sincere. 'One needs such occupations, my dear Quentin, with nearly four score years to carry. Pupils are no longer plentiful, one's friends are thinned out. . . . Besides, this is a way of keeping in touch with my grandchild.'

I selected two or three cards and pored over them with as much appreciation as I could muster.

'DOGS. Ah, I see you have a card for each of his dogs. And you've been reading Parry.'

'Jocasta's been reading Parry. She marks, I merely copy.'

She glanced over my shoulder. 'Wouldn't you have given anything to have seen him with Lyon?' Taking the card, she read aloud, simply, a little haltingly, like a child with a lesson (for she had no great dramatic ability):

> 'Riding or walking, sitting or standing, Lyon was his constant attendant. He can scarcely be said to have forsaken him even in his sleep. Every evening did he go to see that his master was safe before he lay down himself, and then he took his station close to the door. . . . With Lyon, Lord Byron was accustomed not only to associate, but to commune very much and very often. His most usual phrase was, "Lyon, you are no rogue, Lyon," or "Lyon" his Lordship would say, "thou art an honest fellow, Lyon." The dog's eyes sparkled, and his tail swept the floor, as he sat with his haunches on the ground. "Thou art more faithful than men, Lyon; I trust thee more." Lyon sprang up, and barked and bounded round his master, as much as to say, "You may trust me, I

will watch actively on every side." "Lyon, I love thee, thou art my faithful dog!" and Lyon jumped up and kissed his master's hand, as an acknowledgment of his homage. In this sort of mingled talk and gambol Lord Byron passed a good deal of his time.... In conversation and in company he was animated and brilliant; but with Lyon and in stillness he was pleased and perfectly happy.'

I smothered an impulse to say that the passage was corny and that Jocasta's sentimentality about dogs was carried too far, and contented myself with a silent malediction on the error of judgment that had led me to enshrine the seductive image here on the very hearth where it could most disturb my peace.

'BEARS,' I read mechanically from another card. '". . . The bear who had taken his degree at Cambridge was also a constant companion at the Abbey. This animal was perfectly tame, and would stand on his hind legs and lick the face of Murray, the old servant, like a dog." Do you think old Murray cared about that much?'

'Oh, but Byron's servants were terrifically attached to him.'

'All the same, Murray grew a little fratchy when he found his master was arranging to have him buried in the same tomb as his dog. He was disposed to be high-handed, you know.'

'That's the way you've got to be with servants—as long as you can combine it with warmth and kindness. Lady Nunheaton's staff stay for years and dote on her though, with all that entertaining, she never stops making demands on them, whereas Lady Tandon has endless trouble, though she practically apologises every time she gives an order. When I have servants, I'm going to be just as high-handed as Byron, and they'll be devoted to me.'

My good humour was somewhat restored by the thought that, sooner than she guessed, I might be able to provide some of the luxuries that, only half-jokingly, she demanded of life; and I was able to make a flattering answer.

I was putting back the cards with renewed expressions of obligation when my eye was caught by some lines:

> ... He had a kind of inclination, or
> Weakness, for what most people deem mere vermin,
> Live animals: an old maid of threescore
> For cats and birds more penchant ne'er displayed
> Although he was not old, nor even a maid.

'That's *Don Juan*,' I said uneasily.

'Yes. Why not?'

'You told me you couldn't get on with it.'

'I couldn't at first, but Gran started me off again by reading some of it aloud. You know how good she is at poetry.'

'And you like it?'

'A lot, now that Gran's got me into the swing of it. It's like— like hearing the voice of a very witty man talking and talking about everything under the sun. So far we've only read Gran's favourite bits, but I'm going to go right through it from beginning to end. There are heaps of things about animals.'

Right through it! Sixteen huge cantos! Hours, days, of hearing that damnably witty and wicked voice discoursing! And there was not a glimmer of hope now that she would tire and abandon the task I'd set her. What with her grandfather's satisfaction in doing work from which he was not debarred by his age and semi-invalid condition and Mrs. Leverett's intense love of literature, which it must be a rare joy to impart to her grandchild, this house was going to be no place to exorcise the all-too-captivating wraith my foolishness had conjured up.

Nevertheless when, later on, I helped Jocasta to get coffee ready, I found myself doggedly trying.

'Darling, I do feel a shade uncomfortable about what your grandfather's doing for me. Suppose I should never get round to compiling that book! After all, it'll be a good while before I can even think of it.'

'Don't tell him that, Quentin! He's been feeling useless and out of things. He never complains, but I can sense it. And he loves working for you.'

'Yes, but Jocasta—'

'Hardly anyone comes for coaching now, though I'm sure he teaches just as well as ever he did. Poor old angel, he can't help growing lonely!'

'Byron will hardly make very edifying company for him.' I was painfully aware of being fatuous.

'He doesn't expect to be edified. He's a classical scholar. In any case, I should have thought if he was bad company for Granpapa, he'd be even worse for me.'

Her manner was gaiety itself, but it was a thrust. I took myself in hand, and with a fairly convincing pretence that I'd been joking, turned off our talk to another subject.

Unluckily, the perilous one was not allowed to rest for long. When we took the coffee-tray up to the study, Mrs. Leverett was waiting for us with a carefully preserved copy of *The Bookman*, dated 1905 and bearing on its cover the ominous words BYRON DOUBLE NUMBER.

'I've been trying to lay hands on this for weeks,' she said, 'ever since you turned Jocasta into a Byronian, and now it's just come to light at the right moment. I thought we might see if we could identify your miniature.'

'Why, you must have kept this fifty years, Gran!' Jocasta opened it with what seemed to me undue alacrity. 'Did you get it when it came out?'

'Yes, I did. Your father used to laugh at me for hoarding so many things but, you see, if you keep them long enough they always come in useful.'

This particular treasure did not, however, live up to that promise, unless its usefulness was to teach me a further lesson in self-restraint. None of the portraits reproduced bore any relation to the one Jocasta was wearing, and I had to endure the vexation of listening to my beloved analysing feature by feature the insolently handsome face that had turned so many heads, and still apparently had power to turn more.

It was perhaps then that I made my first conscious and articulate resolve to do what would normally have been as distasteful to me as the word we use to describe it. I must debunk Byron. Not his genius which I was sure wasn't what primarily appealed to her, but the meretricious charm that had always proved a bane to women, and not merely during the short span of his life. I waited till Mr. Leverett had retired to his early bed and Mrs. Leverett had tactfully left us alone together, and drawing my chair close to Jocasta's, pretended my attention was caught again by her brooch.

'That really was a bargain, darling!' I flicked at it with my finger. 'I wonder how much it idealised him.'

She countered mildly: 'A lot of people said he was better-looking than his portraits. After all, he must have been something pretty good to make such a romantic impression.'

'Romantic men should be thin'—I spoke with a smilingly judicial air—'and Byron narrowly missed being fat.'

'Now that's what was so wonderful about him! He actually dieted—have you ever thought of that, Quentin? He dieted at a time when everyone else was over-eating. It's quite a point for your biography. No one seems to notice what it must have meant in the way of—of strength of mind and all that to be always eating vegetables and vinegar when it was the custom to have endless big dinners. Look at the size of people in some of those caricatures!'

It was evident that I'd chosen the wrong line. Jocasta's training as a model made her sympathetic towards any effort in the cause of physical beauty.

'That is, as you say, a point.' My voice was still cool and judicial. 'I'm afraid, however, that what good he did to his figure by dieting he must have undone by drinking.'

I fancied I had scored because she disliked drink, but her mind was running on one track, and she only answered: 'Yes, they didn't realise that alcohol was full of calories. It would have been much easier for him today.' She swerved away on to a beauty regime she'd seen recommended in a magazine, but suddenly came back to Byron: 'Whatever he drank, it couldn't have made him *fat*, darling! That's an impossibility because some people describe him as thin—very thin. Even Lady Blessington says that.'

'True.' I was cunningly ruminative. 'He was going through one of his thin phases when she came to Genoa. She mentions that his clothes no longer fitted him. They hung on him in the most unfashionable style. He couldn't have had any new ones made for years. Heaven knows why, since he counted as a very rich man in Italy. But then he did have that miserly strain.'

Jocasta's retort though light was surprisingly vigorous. 'Lady Blessington was a silly snob. She'd been hoping he'd make a pass at her and he didn't.'

I ought to have let it go but I persisted. 'Does it affect what she said about the fit of his clothes?'

'Yes it does, because her book's just a gossip column—the kind that's full of nasty little twists to please readers who like to believe they're getting the lowdown on everything. And if he didn't bother to have new clothes made, where's all that personal vanity he's always being panned for?'

Mrs. Leverett, with a discreet rattling of the door-handle—I wish now that it had been needful—came back for her knitting-bag.

'What? Are you two still talking Byron!' She embraced us both with an indulgent and affectionate smile. 'You don't know how fortunate you are to have such an enthusiasm in common. It's a cornerstone of happiness to love the same things.'

She didn't know what it cost me at that moment to give back the smile.

Single-minded as I am in the accomplishment of any purpose I've once resolved upon, I hadn't intended so exceedingly drastic a separation from Jocasta as I forced myself to endure that August. The fact is that I had to grapple just then with an entire revision of my original plan for writing the Memoirs, and it was necessary for me to reconsider all my material in the light of the new approach I was making to my subject; the more so because I would have to depend almost wholly on my index cards while at my great-aunt's house.

Instead of setting myself to invent afresh the manuscript that Byron had handed in a leather bag to Moore at La Mira, the portions of his life story on which he'd laboured systematically and with unaccustomed restraint, I had elected after all to confine myself to the more spontaneous and unguarded second instalment sent to Paris the following year, the section Moore referred to as the 'Continuation'. It was these pages which had contained the reminiscences too bawdy for Regency lords, and evoked the entry in Moore's Journal denying that he had encouraged his noble friend to go into detail about his love affairs.

I had two reasons for making so important a decision—or three perhaps, but if so, since I didn't as yet recognise the third, I shan't mention it till it falls into place.

First, there was good evidence that the later recollections were much more loosely put together than the 1819 batch, and imitation would therefore be less difficult: I could even allow my imagination to move with some freedom. Second, I wanted to get rid of that awkward stumbling-block, Dr. Williams. It was too risky to depend on fictions about a man who might quite easily turn out to have knowledgeable descendants—for, on going with a fine comb through Moore's references to him, I had ascertained that he was married and almost certainly a father, and that he had not been unknown to other celebrated men of his day besides Moore. Earl Darrow had unwittingly revealed a line of retreat from Williams, and in due course I would take it.

I might have laid a clue to Dumoulin, the next copyist (not, it turned out on close investigation, a Frenchman any more than Williams was a Welshman), who had died an obscure bachelor: but as both Moore and Williams himself were looking after him in his last illness, when he was penniless and helpless, the supposition that he had been able to keep a secret transcript hidden from them might well be questioned. I grieved to drop these two young men altogether out of my design, since the fact that each was in desperate straits for money qualified them splendidly to be objects of suspicion, but it was best to play for safety and let the third and last copyist have the honour of having salvaged the precious draft.

The vital entry in Moore's Diary was on the 20th of March, 1821:

Paid one of these days (I forget which) four Napoleons to a man for copying out Lord B.'s 'Memoirs'; he had the conscience to ask eight or nine.

A perfectly anonymous man with the merit, for my purpose, of being rapacious! A man who could ask double the price for the job that Moore, who was generous, had expected to pay! Just the sort of character to be capable of taking, with mercenary motives, an unsanctioned copy. And the papers in his charge had undoubtedly been those Byron had dispatched to Moore in December, 1820, more than a year after parting with his earlier gift.

> Besides this letter [he had written] you will receive three packets, containing in all, eighteen more sheets of Memoranda, which, I fear, will cost you more in postage than they will ever produce by being printed in the next century.

Unhappily prophetic words! The postage had cost Moore forty-six and a half francs, about two pounds, no trifling sum in the year of George IV's accession. The eighteen sheets must have been 'very large, long paper' like those written in the previous year, and each was folded up to make four pages. It had taken Lord John Russell two afternoon visits to Moore to read them through. Allowing that each folio page would contain about as many words as two in my exercise book, I should have to fill a hundred and forty or so, and that was an eminently suitable quantity—sufficient to make a big impact on publication, but not too long a stretch for me to cover without flagging and losing the Byronic *élan* which was already wonderfully invigorating my fancy.

I had thus to achieve one of those reorientations which call for very close application, and as my job at Rossiter's left me with only week-ends and the evenings for writing, I dared not spare much time for Jocasta. We did have a meeting, however, at my room in Lowestoft Street so that I could read her the opening chapters of the novel I was supposed to have in progress.

Despite my own well-established conviction that I was not a novelist, I felt a kind of chagrin as I watched her making a struggle to appreciate what I had written and to conceal her impatient longing for it to be done with, in order that I might go back to the theme she regarded as worth while.

She was reading books on Byron as earnestly as if they were fashion magazines and it gave me what I'm bound to confess was a turn. On both her visits to me, she came carrying volumes she'd brought from the London Library, and that seemed—I agree I was irrational—as inappropriate as she might have thought it if *I'd* become an addict of the literature of women's modes. Whatever effect he'd had on women, the study of Byron was, as I conceived it, a masculine subject.

A few days before I left London for my visit to my Welsh great-aunt, we had what turned out, in its effect upon my future policy, the most momentous of our conversations. Jocasta had arrived with a book under her arm—Mayne's *Life of Lady Byron*.

'You get through them pretty quickly,' I said glancing at the title. 'Isn't it a waste of time to look for what you're after there?'

'You have to look everywhere.' She added, rather ruefully I thought: 'You never know what you're going to find. Anyway, there are a few references to animals in this.'

'You've certainly got a disillusioning one.' I may have said it with some covert satisfaction.

'Did it disillusion *you*?' she asked simply.

I took her youthful and lovely face between my hands. 'I'm seven years more grown-up than you are.'

'You mean that if you've got a grown-up sort of mind, you can understand the—the cruel, unhappy side of people's characters?'

'The seamy side—yes,' I replied magnanimously. 'It's a shock, naturally, to the idealism of youth.'

'I shall never be grown-up enough,' she protested with vehemence, 'to understand Lady Byron! Her cruelty to that poor miserable sister of his and all the while pretending to be so noble! The way she got the credit of that saintly "policy of silence" when she was confiding in practically everybody she knew! Would you believe I've counted dozens of people she confided in? And they all thought they were the only ones. I've made a list of them . . .'

'My dear!' I couldn't quite contrive to repress my exasperation. 'That's not the kind of research you promised to do for me!'

She looked crestfallen.

'I'm a perfect fool,' I went on, 'not to have realised that, if you started on Byron biographies, there'd be all this rancorous matrimonial stuff. I don't know why—I just fancied you skimming about here and there, spotting nice little bits about animals.' (This happened to be true.) 'Somehow I don't like the idea of your delving into hateful scandals.'

'Why? Aren't you going to write about them?'

For a moment I was taken aback. I'd almost lost sight of the legitimate work I'd been planning so long. 'I didn't propose to make much of them,' I said at last. 'There's been quite enough of that.'

'Oh, don't be stuffy, Quentin!'

My face showed her that I was astounded. I had never met anyone with less of a taste for scandal than she had. Indeed, it was her emphatic *distaste* that had almost prevented her from appreciating my book on William Beckford.

'You can't leave them out,' she went on reflectively, 'when they were such a *thing* in his life. And it's fascinating to see how people behave—when they don't behave like us, I mean. Even Granpapa, who practically won't hear an unkind word against any living soul, simply laps up dreadful revelations about historical characters. The longer they've been dead the more he can take. When he gets to the Roman emperors, anything goes. I don't care myself what went on with the Roman emperors. They're not real to me, but Byron *is* real . . .'

'And so you want "dreadful revelations" about him?'

'Not me personally! But since he was considered shocking and still is, and it has to be written about, I'd much rather that was done by his friends than his enemies. It's just prissy of his friends to ignore it. If he were alive, you wouldn't. You'd be defending him.'

If he were alive! I ought not to have suppressed my natural impulse, which was to tell her that if he were alive, I wouldn't let *her* come within twenty miles of him: but it's instinctive with me, as it is with many possessive men, to mask my most vulnerable feelings. Jocasta, secure in her beauty, had no coquetry. She would never have deliberately set out to hurt me, but I'd been hurt by others and my automatic reaction was to keep susceptibilities concealed. Nevertheless they found expression in one way or another.

'If he were alive!' I repeated. 'Yes, I'd be defending him, but I doubt if you would. His conduct to women was not very defensible.'

'You must admit they were a fabulously tiresome lot of women. All that mopping and mowing at him! None of them seemed to have a glimmering of humour.'

'He didn't give them much cause for it.'

She paused at this, intent upon arranging some flowers her grandmother had sent me from the South Brockford garden. Then she said: 'Anyone who could have laughed with him would have been all right. Look at all the fun there is in his letters! Look at *Don Juan*!'

'*Don Juan*—so you're ploughing on with that?'

'I've nearly finished it.'

'I should have expected you to be put off by such an utterly cynical poem.'

'I don't find it altogether cynical.'

'What! With all its flippancies and its mockery and its coarseness?'

'Coarseness! Where? The shipwreck's pretty grim, but I suppose that was part of the attack, wasn't it?—the attack on— on the flowery way of writing about such things. That's what Gran says. I admit it's ribald, but isn't that the way men do go on among themselves? When I'm shocked I tell myself it wasn't written for girls.'

'It certainly wasn't—and I rather wish *my* girl wouldn't read it.'

'Oh, Quentin!' She gazed at me reproachfully over the vase of dahlias. 'Lately I do believe you've been showing signs of a puritanical streak. I hope you're going to take yourself in hand.'

I changed my tack. 'You've been making the most amazing progress, darling. When I remember that only a few weeks ago, we could scarcely have discussed this subject for two minutes, and now here you are with quite strong opinions about it! You must tell me exactly what you've been reading. I'll make you a list of books you may have missed.'

'Yes, do! Isn't it nice that I'm beginning to understand something about your work at last, Quentin? I was hopeless about it before. I did try, but William Beckford never appealed to me much. There was something completely repellent, something that made me shudder, about the letters from that woman—the one who took part in those horrid Oriental fantasies of his. And the affair with that boy—Courtenay or whatever his name was— you can't deny it was wickedness! I dare say he was a clever writer, if you can stand all the chi-chi, but he wasn't in the least a person I could be fond of.'

It was then that the seedling of the idea that was gradually to become an overwhelming compulsion began to germinate. It's ironical to recall that the dear girl herself planted it in my mind, under the impression that she was encouraging me to work on a theme worthier of my talents than the follies of Beckford. (Though I must mention here for the benefit of any reader who hasn't come across that book of mine—which is to say almost any reader *this* book may happen to have—that the scandalous material was merely incidental, for I was concerned more with his extravagances than his perversions.)

I may have critics who'll think I must have been out of my mind to worry about a man who had been dead at that time a hundred and thirty-two years; but let them imagine the situation in other and more familiar terms. Let them imagine *their* beloved engaged in ardent daily contemplation of some celebrated film idol or world-famous pin-up girl! The object might be utterly remote, no physical meeting within the bounds of possibility, and yet, even though the emotion aroused might lack the immediacy of actual jealousy, wouldn't there be an irritating envy? A fear of being measured by unattainable standards? And in my case there was the disturbing complication of a loyalty to both parties. I too was a Byron fan.

It was with a singular feeling of treachery that I got my notebook out. 'I must give you that list while I think of it. Since you've become a Byronian, you ought to pay some attention to Shelley as well. Their lives were linked together in so many ways.' I wrote down the names of two or three works I might rely upon to represent Byron in the meanest light that could be cast upon him. There's no one like a good old-fashioned Shelley biographer for that, preferably one of the Garnett-Forman school.

'Thanks, honey! I'll try to read them all before you come back from Wales. Now you'll get along with that novel as hard as you can go, won't you?' She put her arm round my neck and gave me a placid and good-natured kiss. I didn't return it for the anything-but-simple reason that it came into my head when I felt the cool touch of her lips to wonder how she might have kissed someone else. . . someone who probably received very few placid kisses.

It was a relief to me, in the conflict of my various kinds of guilt, that she presently remembered to tell me of a chance meeting with a former professional colleague who had married a rich Argentino, and had come home for a holiday with a parure of pink topaz set in diamonds and clothes from Buenos Aires which were described in detail with an endearing zest.

When my daring project was accomplished, how much I was going to enjoy unpinning that miniature and putting pink topaz and diamonds in its place!

Chapter Six

THE HOUSE which my great-aunt Beth had inherited from her brother was a grey stone villa standing half a mile out of the town of Penrhyndeudraeth. It was square, symmetrical, and without any touch of fancy excepting two rather snobbish-looking lions, couchant and regardant, who flanked the steps leading to the front door. In my childhood, I had believed them to be observing everyone who came and went with a contemptuous amusement, and though they seemed to have grown smaller through the years, I was unable to shake off that impression.

When I arrived, my great-aunt, undismayed by a light drizzle, was working in her garden at the side of the house, tending certain dim, scentless, obtrusively hardy flowers with which she frequently filled her vases. She greeted me cordially, but as if she had last seen me yesterday instead of three years before.

'Oh, it's Juggins! And needless to say, in good time for a meal.'

That nickname and the pretence that I was still a greedy boy—she never dropped such small threadbare jokes, or perceived that they could become distasteful. I had forgotten—I always did forget—how many little ways of getting on my own and other people's nerves the poor woman was given to. That anyone so benevolent could find it so irresistible to ruffle one's self-esteem remained a source of painful wonder whenever one met her. Yet, she had likeable qualities, and I resolved to fix on those whatever she said or did to me: otherwise I might defeat the ends that had brought me here.

I embraced her and told her she was looking well, which as to health was no falsehood. Like her flowers, she was a most hardy perennial, and though plain of feature, might have passed for at least a dozen years younger than her seventy-three.

She moved before me to the house with quite a nimble step, talking vivaciously about nothing that much concerned either herself or me and, as I say, with no more ceremony than if we'd parted yesterday, leading me in by the back door so that she might deposit her garden tools in the outhouse and her cut flowers in the pantry. There for some minutes she kept me standing beside my suitcase while she filled some jugs of peculiarly coarse and lopsided pottery.

'These were made locally,' she said with pride, 'by members of the Spare Timers' League. I help to run it. I bought them to replace my grandmother's vases. Do you know, several of them turned out to be Old Chelsea, and those dust-traps encrusted with flowers that used to stand on the spare room mantelpiece—they were Coalbrookdale. I got a pretty decent price for them.'

'What have you been up to, Aunt Beth? Selling the family vases! I was quite fond of those flowery ones.'

'My dear boy, they were old-fashioned when I was a girl. I was tempted to turn them out long ago. These are really modern and practical.'

I followed her through the kitchen and down a short dark passage, into what had once been the dining-room. Since she had—very willingly—bowed to the necessity of saving domestic labour, she'd converted it into a general living-room. Now it had undergone another change, and one which struck me somewhat disagreeably. Where once it had been cluttered, now it was stark. The late-Victorian furniture had been denuded of all the bric-à-brac which had accumulated in her childhood and before, and with it had gone everything I had ever either liked or laughed at. Startled, I stood at the threshold trying to grasp what it might mean to me.

'There!' she said. 'Isn't it improved? I wanted to do it for years, and now I've done it!'

'You haven't been making a clean sweep all over the house!'

'That's just what I have done, and oh! the difference! I only wish I'd had the courage years ago. What stopped me? Sloppy sentimentality, I suppose.' She paused, then added with her customary frankness, 'That and not realising what dealers would pay for things.'

The scheme which had brought me to Wales absolutely hinged on the fact that I would find there a fairly large house filled to overflowing with the minor family possessions of three generations and left in the keeping of a decidedly careless housewife who never bothered about them. I'd relied upon being able to persuade her, forgetful and indifferent as she was, that a manuscript book she'd never seen before must have been lying amongst the lumber for years unnoticed. But if there had been this idiotic clean sweep, my task might not be easy or indeed possible. I couldn't invent a new finding-place for my treasure because I'd already informed Earl Darrow that it was here, and wherever I might ultimately negotiate, I should have to stick to that story.

It may be conceded I deserve credit for suppressing any but the mildest sign of my apprehension: 'Don't tell me you've got rid of the books! I was looking forward to them.'

'What was the use of them? They were hopelessly out of date, and who read them? No one except you, and you only come here once in years.'

'But Aunt Beth! I'm in the book trade. You might have offered me the first refusal!'

'No, no, Juggins, never do business with your own kith and kin! It leads to trouble. If you'd asked for them, I should have felt I ought to give them to you. As it was I had quite a nice little cheque for them from a dealer in Caernarvon. Now, my boy, you're in your usual room. Would you like to take your things upstairs while I get the table ready? I don't have any help on Saturday evenings.'

Scarcely believing my ill-fortune, I went up to what had once been known as the junior spare room. I'd slept there so often during my father's lifetime that its discomforts had always been to some extent mellowed for me by an old familiarity. The roses that climbed up the trellises on the china jug and basin set seemed to be striving to atone for the absence of running water: the vivid greens and scarlets of the cross-stitch hearth-rug apologised eloquently for the chilly expanses of brown linoleum around it. If icy and incorrigible draughts crept round my shoulders as I lay reading in bed, if the windows rattled, and the wardrobe door unaccountably swung open just when I was dipping into an odd volume of *The Mysteries of Udolpho*, nevertheless there *were* those captivating odd volumes to dip into; and the photographs in plush frames, the fretwork paper-rack carved by my great-grandfather, the firescreen with unrecognisable flowers stencilled by my great-grandmother, the big kaleidoscope on a stand near the window—these had a sort of cosy and absurd charm for a youth born in 1926.

Since my last visit the room had become merely bleak. The marble-topped washstand, the fretwork, and the photographs, all alike had vanished; and the heterogeneous decorations on the walls, varying from a colour print of 'Love Locked Out' to an embroidered sampler, had been drastically reduced. Little remained except a cabinet portrait of my father as a subaltern of the First World War and water colours by deceased relatives who were not talented.

I can't describe my dismay. A clearance on this scale would have a catastrophic effect on the plan I'd spent the last two months perfecting. Everything must have been rummaged through and by my great-aunt's own hand. Though she was absent-minded and unobservant, the probabilities were not in favour of her believing that, in all this tidying up, a substantial leather-bound book had escaped her attention. Or if she believed it, such evidence of her own abstractedness might make her examine the manuscript with extra care.

Perhaps I ought to explain more precisely what I'd decided to do, because my reader may be puzzled as to how I could plant the Memoirs in this house when they were not yet written. I'd been composing them, whether piecemeal or in consecutive passages, since the end of July, but even allowing for the use of those random anecdotes and 'detached thoughts' I'd worked on to get my hand in, they weren't so much as half-finished. Yet, for the business to appear casual and natural, they must come to light during my September holiday, and I'd devised at quite an early stage a means of coping with that difficulty.

I had, it may be remembered, two antique exercise books, and it was my original intention to fill only one of them, keeping the other against possible contingencies. In the course of learning to disguise my handwriting, however, a more immediate use for it occurred to me. I would copy into it all sorts of passages from Byron's letters and journals, gaining practice as I did so both with my Georgian scrawl and the Byronic idiom. This volume was the one I would 'discover' in the jumble of books I'd hoped to find at Penrhyndeudraeth. Aunt Beth, supposing it to be nothing more than some bygone enthusiast's collection of excerpts, would almost certainly agree to let me keep it. My request would be timed so that this decoy book would be in her hands just long enough for her to make the sort of inspection that would convince her, if later she were asked to identify it, that she could do so without hesitation. By then, of course, I should have substituted the other volume, the one which was actually going to contain my reconstruction of the later Memoirs. To the most searching investigator, the provenance would thus be completely satisfactory, since my great-aunt, though eccentric, was a woman of honourable reputation.

How, after contriving this ingenious scheme and building up all the structure to sustain it, could I bear to see it toppling into nothingness! For a moment my suavity deserted me. I rushed out to the landing and called to her impatiently over the banisters.

'What is it?' She came running into the hall below, and I managed to put a sudden check on myself. It wouldn't do to let her see that I was seriously put out.

'Where does one wash now that the washstand is gone?' It was all I could think of to ask her.

'In the bathroom of course. Oh dear! I've forgotten to put out a towel for you.' She started up the stairs.

'It's all right. I'll find one.'

'You wouldn't know which.' Poor Aunt Beth! She was the worst housekeeper I've ever met, but the fussiest about meaningless little details. While she was letting everything slide that could make for her own or anyone else's comfort, she would be niggling over some triviality. 'Don't touch the linen cupboard!' she pleaded. 'You'll muddle it up.'

I stood by on the landing watching her select, by a process of mind not to be guessed at, a meagre khaki-coloured Turkish towel that felt like a rasp.

'Do you think you'll need two?' she inquired grudgingly.

'Mayn't I have one for shaving? Or did you'—I couldn't resist saying it—'sell those too?'

'Oh no, I only sold what they'd give good money for.' She never minded a little rallying.

'Did they give you good money for the washstand?'

She came to my bedroom door with the second towel, shaking her head ruefully. 'They wouldn't touch it! Mr. Caradoc—the man who bought the china ornaments—told me it wouldn't be worth his while to send a van for such stuff even if I gave it to him for nothing. It's gone down to the cellar. You can't get anyone to carry slop-pails about nowadays, so I just had it put out of the way.'

I saw a tiny sparkle of hope. 'And all the other things that used to be here? The collar boxes with that barbola work or whatever you call it? The raffia pyjama bag? The framed photographs of cathedrals? Did you find a market for those?'

She laughed. 'Now then, Master Juggins! Don't be sarcastic about your father's old home. I made that pyjama bag myself. It was all the rage in the nineteen-twenties, raffia work.'

'I'm not sarcastic. I shall miss some of those things, especially the kaleidoscope.'

'Ah, that's gone. Mr. Caradoc was keen on that. But the rest you'll find in the cellar whenever you want to look for them.'

'The cellar? The dampest cellar in England, Aunt Beth!'

'Well, what was I to do? The attics have been full for years.'

The sparkle warmed into a glow. 'Then they didn't clear the attics for you, these dealers?'

'Not yet. To tell you the truth, that was something I thought you could help with. It's a bit much for me, lugging round those old trunks and mattresses and coal-scuttles, and Mrs. Evans won't do it because the dust brings on her asthma. I know you want to do some writing, but it wouldn't take you more than a couple of afternoons.'

With considerable artistry, I feigned a lack of eagerness. 'What is it you want me to do exactly?'

'Just straighten up the chaos so that I can get at whatever there is to sell. I have to raise quite a lot more money yet.' She went back to her dinner preparations, leaving me hugging myself. Hitherto I'd always been intensely irritated when she produced some disagreeable task to mar one's holiday—some labour her formidable servant, Mrs. Evans, explicitly refused to perform: but her command to turn out the crowded attics gave me a joy proportionate to the shadow of frustration that had loomed upon me when I thought she'd already emptied them. I didn't even react with much annoyance to the knowledge that she'd disposed of the best things in the house, which ought in the natural course to have descended to me, so sure did it seem in the moment of relief that my secret *magnum opus* would place me beyond caring for such trifles. Indeed, as I sat down to table with her after helping her to bring in the meal, I inquired amiably whether the money she was trying to raise was for TAT.

'We call it TACT now,' she said, spooning on to my plate a very small portion of hot-pot. 'At least, some of us do, but others want to call it TROCO, which sounds silly to me. It's a great nuisance because the argument's holding up the printing of our new leaflets.'

I knew she would explain whether I asked her or not, but like Mr. Interlocutor in a minstrel show, I didn't fail to put the question: 'Why has TAT changed to TACT or TROCO, Aunt Beth?'

'It's a matter of strategy. The total abolition of taxation is too progressive an idea, we found, for general consumption. Taxation has gone on for thousands of years, and people can't believe it needn't go on for ever. We did everything we could, held meetings, distributed ninety thousand leaflets in two years—we even had a sandwichman walking about Cardiff with very striking placards—but we were simply called cranks. Then along came John Ockrington, a really live wire who recently took a cottage on the way to Portmeirion, and he suggested that we should re-form and aim at something easier to realise. I backed him from the first, and I believe all our members will gradually come round.'

I swallowed a mouthful of very moist cabbage and delivered myself of the next question: 'Come round to what?'

'A more moderate policy. Taxation According to the Choice of the Taxpayer—that's TACT. TROCO is Taxpayers' Right Of Conscientious Objection. Both mean the same fundamentally, but we must fix on the name that will be best for propaganda.'

'Conscientious objection to taxation!' I murmured it with the air of one who ponders. I confess, however, that what was weighing upon me was the unpleasant stickiness of my knife and fork handles. Cutlery at my great-aunt's was liable to be washed by a mere swishing around in lukewarm water. Her mind was too preoccupied with battles against the accepted usages of the world to place a value on the delicacies of life, either social or domestic. It was a defect I'd been aware of, naturally, before this visit: but so many early reminders of it were none the less disconcerting.

Her sturdy, argumentative voice went on. 'People are so accustomed to various forms of slavery that total freedom is a conception they can't grasp. Our platform now is going to be partial freedom. We shall establish the right to refuse taxes only for expenditure we don't approve of. I've every hope that it will have an immense popular appeal.'

How often had I heard her say those words! She never launched upon a campaign without a quite touchingly vernal belief in imminent victory, and from each experience of defeat she rose undaunted.

'It's so simple and workable. There are figures published every year of how our national income is spent, and all you have to do is to find out what proportion of the money goes to support something you consider wasteful or morally wrong, and register a conscientious objection to paying taxes for that purpose. There'll be tribunals modelled, to some extent, on the tribunals for C.O.'s in wartime. If nuclear weapons cost—say—twenty per cent of everyone's income tax and you object to them, then you withhold twenty per cent and state your case to the tribunal. If you feel that all those offices in Whitehall are costing too much—'

I was impatient. 'But what if they've deducted the tax before you get your income?'

'We shall abolish that form of coercion. Sheer interference with the liberty of the subject! The worst despots of history would be shocked by such extortion!'

'There I'm with you, Aunt Beth! Down with Pay-as-You-Earn!' The thought of that weekly exasperation infused my voice with fervour.

'Aha! You see! We've got the hang of it at last—a cause that will win support from everybody.'

'If only you could make it work!' I subdued any ring of scepticism for I wanted to please her, and, as a matter of fact, the present crusade was so much less crazy than some she had set off upon that it seemed, by comparison, almost to deserve encouragement.

'It will work. Men care more for their money than their lives or their children's lives either. Once the right has been won, there'll be plenty of conscientious objectors to having our substance squandered on things like the H-bomb. Coming face to face with the arithmetic of it will bring block protests. Sixty or seventy thousand at a time will insist on going before the tribunal. Oh, we shall harass them, I can tell you!'

'You've definitely got something. I hope, however, it isn't to promote this scheme that you're selling your goods and chattels.'

'Well, it can't be run without cash. We must have publicity.'

'Couldn't you let someone else stand the racket this time?'

'They'll pay me back. That's agreed. John Ockrington's launching an appeal, and obviously it has to be financed. He's going to write to people with influence—going to see them personally. There'll be printing, travelling, entertaining and quite a lot of expense. It's bound to bring results, because John has a wonderfully persuasive manner.'

I was sure he had, but I doubted, knowing something of the history of Aunt Beth's enthusiasms, whether his persuasiveness would be exerted upon anyone but herself. Through her mixture of benevolence and pugnacity, it was her destiny to be exploited. Benevolence made her willing to devote herself to improving the lot of mankind, but because she was also pugnacious, she adopted only those causes that went against the grain of approved custom, and formed alliances with individuals who were for some reason themselves at odds with society. Her description of John Ockrington's unfortunate circumstances was superfluous. I could have told her before she told me that he was hard up, in flight from some form of vendetta, public or private, merited or unmerited, and a man whom it was her special mission to aid and sustain.

There had been among her protégés—though she never regarded them as that but rather as her teachers and counsellors—a deserter from the navy, a doctor who had been struck off the register, a not-quite-cured dipsomaniac, and a playwright whose sole renown lay in having had a very morbid play banned by the Lord Chamberlain.

John Ockrington, it seemed, was a clergyman who was suffering persecution from a bishop. His name was known to me in connection with a scandalous divorce in which he'd recently figured as co-respondent but my great-aunt was convinced that he had risked his living for the reform of doctrine, and the divorce proceedings were, in her opinion, a frame-up sanctioned if not initiated in the See of Canterbury. It was never of the slightest use to attempt disillusionment, so I didn't try. She was unshakably loyal to each charlatan or near-charlatan who bamboozled her, and none ever slipped from her good graces except by choosing to slip from her hands. Luckily for her, the hospitality she so much enjoyed dispensing was Spartan enough to send even the most determined sponger packing after a few weeks or months, and when that happened she was inclined to take umbrage.

As her next-of-kin, I had a right to begrudge what she'd thrown away on harebrained plans for the regeneration of mankind, but this philanthropy of hers had been going on so long, I recognised it as incurable, as my father had done before me. Her all too frugal personal habits and a certain fundamental sense of day-to-day responsibility prevented her from becoming penniless, and that was a matter for gratitude, though she had steadily diminished the property she'd inherited when my father was still a schoolboy.

Looking round the denuded room while she was out fetching the pudding, I reminded myself that I must on no account be let in for paying her anything more than a token share of my gains when I sold my manuscript. It would be the irony of ironies if the proceeds of my toil and invention went to support some unscrupulous impostor.

'I've made an apple pie,' said Aunt Beth kindly, setting a small dish on the table. 'It's specially for you. I never take more than one course myself nowadays.'

I concealed a tendency to recoil. Aunt Beth's pastry resembled nothing so much as the little cakes of dough that children bake, heavy as clay and with a most disturbing greyness. I would have preferred to remain hungry, as I still was, but it wouldn't have done on my first evening to reject what was meant for a treat. As I dug my spoon and fork into the helping she served, I wondered whether I could possibly afford to take at least a few of my meals at the Portmeirion Hotel, and whether she'd be offended or relieved if I suggested it.

I cast a fly over the stream. 'You don't mind my having invited myself here to work? It'll keep me from getting in the way round here.'

'Work? Oh yes, another of those books of yours. Have you got to be at it morning, noon, and night?'

She always displayed an indifference bordering on contempt towards my writing, and to do us both justice, would have taken the same attitude if I'd been a famous Nobel prizewinner, for she looked on all art and literature as a frivolous waste of time unless the aim was propaganda.

'I'll certainly keep my promise to turn out the attics for you, but I do want to get a chapter finished in the next two weeks.'

'I don't know why you bother. You've never done very well out of it, have you? And frankly, Juggins, your books are about such trumpery people, they don't deserve to have biographies.'

'I did warn you I'd be writing, Aunt Beth! This fortnight away from London means a lot to me.'

'Yes, you did warn me. The only thing is—where are you going to do it? John usually comes here in the evenings to map out the campaign and we use this room which is the only one which has a fire when it's chilly.'

'I'll sit in my bedroom.' I was glad of the prospect of retreating in privacy, though my bedroom's north aspect and the fact that she'd never had it wired for electric heat were depressing.

'Perhaps,' I ventured, 'if it goes on raining and being cold, I could light myself a fire upstairs?'

'Oh no, Mrs. Evans wouldn't hear of that! She'd have to do the grate in the mornings, and besides, coal fires make the rooms dusty.'

It was curious that so much good will towards the human race should be combined in my great-aunt with an inveterate reluctance to allow any member of it whom she saw at close quarters to be comfortable. Once again, I admonished myself to pay cheerfully the price I'd known would be exacted for her unconscious collaboration, and I was assuring her that I would meditate earnestly on the respective merits of TACT or TROCO as a title for the reformed society when, before we had cleared the table, the front door bell announced the arrival of the Rev. John Ockrington. I stayed just long enough to take a strong dislike to him over a cup of Nokaff, a coffee substitute my great-aunt had recently discovered, before retiring to the junior spare room, where I had in my locked portmanteau, both the work I'd really come to do and the typescript of the unfinished novel which I'd silently designated *My Stalking-Horse*.

I didn't, of course, write the Memoirs straight into the exercise book in which I should ultimately present them. They required intense care in composition, and the first draft would be succeeded by a second and probably even a third before being irrevocably committed to the final text. I was still a long way from that stage—not, as I've said, half-way through the writing; and yet it was going faster than I'd dreamed of hoping when I'd laid my first foundation. It was so much easier to devise random reflections and disconnected adventures, many of them imaginary, than an account corresponding to Byron's own description—'long and minute'—of his courtship, marriage, and separation, containing numerous particulars which could be checked by evidence.

Instead of perpetually consulting sources of reference, watching lynx-eyed lest I should slip up on a date or a detail, I found I could give a fairly loose rein to my fancy. Moreover I was no longer under the anticipated necessity of being an advocate in disguise. Provided I never forgot that I was impersonating Byron, I could say more or less what I pleased, since it was safe to assume that the second instalment of the Memoirs was in essence a reaction against the first, and justified a treatment much looser in every sense of the word.

Byron had taken great trouble to prepare a record which his wife would read, and had invited her to express her opinion as to its accuracy. He had promised that 'her mark should not be erased', and given Moore—who was to publish it after his death—explicit injunctions to that effect. Her refusal even to glance at what he had written had the effect her icy negations always did have on him. The more she held herself in check, the more he let himself go.

In applying himself to the production of a document which would stand her closest scrutiny, he had keenly looked forward to getting some response from her. She had withheld from him even a flicker of human curiosity. The frustration must have been acute, and a hinted threat of reprisals in her terse reply was highly provocative to a man who never failed to rise to a challenge.

He would go on recounting his memories as and when he chose, and this time he would dispense at will with circumspection. He was no longer trying to move, to chide, to argue with one hostile reader, to wring from her an admission that he, as well as she, had 'suffered things to be forgiven'. He had nothing now to gain by keeping a curb upon himself, nothing to lose—or so he imagined—by blackening himself with all his usual gusto. In any case, he'd flung the last shreds of his reputation to the winds by continuing to publish, against the advice of almost every friend he had, cantos of the execrated poem *Don Juan*. A fresh storm of obloquy had broken over his head, and though, when he resumed his prose work in Ravenna during 1820, he was actually living in circumstances comparatively decorous, he was in no mood to apologise to posterity for his past conduct.

Picking up the thread as if just after Lady Byron's rebuff had been received, I could be ribald, gross, anything that he in his most reckless mood might have been. And that was proving much simpler than the restrained style of writing. I even entered into it with a certain relish.

I'm afraid the truth is that I'd lost my desire to place Byron in a favourable light. I told myself to begin with that, if I was to forgo using the best-selling ingredients I'd been counting on at the outset—the first-person narrative of his conjugal disaster—I'd have to surrender to the popular taste for the exposure of a famous man's frailties; but I soon acknowledged that this was a secondary motive, and that what I was primarily bent upon was shocking Jocasta out of her exasperating crush on the poet.

I'd done everything I could at those recent brief and unsatisfactory meetings of ours, but since it was I who had unwarily fired her with the enthusiasm, I wasn't in a very good position for any overt attempt at quenching it, especially with both her grandparents throwing their weight into the Byron side of the scale.

No doubt after having resigned so much of her to a career that was alien and mysterious to them, they were delighted to be able to have her with them for a while, sharing an interest they could understand. Mrs. Leverett reading the poetry aloud while Mr. Leverett made his neat and intelligent arrangement of index cards and Jocasta sewed or knitted—I could see the charm of the picture. In a spirit that was none the less eager because it was also playful, the little family seemed to be cultivating a veritable Byromania. True to the tradition that his most ardent defenders have always been found among the respectable, they were for Byron against all comers, and made a kind of game of contriving excuses for his most outrageous behaviour. It was part of the joke to send me postcards, since I now seldom saw them, recommending points I ought to make for the confusion of his enemies when I came to write my biographical work.

As for my artful scheme to set Jocasta reading Shelley biographies, it came to grief ignominiously within a fortnight. I will repeat, absolutely verbatim, the telephone conversation I had with her that brought it to an end.

'Quentin,' she began, having rung me up at Rossiter's one afternoon shortly before I left for Wales, 'I'm sorry to bother you at the shop, but your not having a telephone at that hideout of yours makes things a bit difficult. It's about those Shelley books. Is there any special reason why you want me to read them?'

'None at all.' My words were airy but my voice quavered with surprise. 'It was only that I thought you might like to know something about him. He looms up pretty large in Byron annals.'

'Yes, but do I have to read *three* books on him? Won't one do? Granpapa's got one at home.'

'Which, my love?'

'It's a dreadfully tedious, heavy-handed affair. I can hardly drag myself from one page to another. Anyway, I dislike books that set out to debunk people. . . .'

'Oh, my dear, you can't expect everyone to admire Byron as we do.'

'Honey, your line must be bad! The book's about Shelley.'

'About Shelley. *Debunking* him?'

'Yes. It doesn't leave a rag on him, and it's such a bore. Still, it'll save taking three out of the London Library if it's only the facts of his life you want me to know.'

'What *have* you got hold of, darling?' I asked helplessly.

'It's called *The Real Shelley* by Somebody Jeaffreson.'

'But that was written in the Eighties! It's appallingly out of date.'

'So are the ones on your list, darling. Didn't you know? The young man at the Library says there've been masses of new Shelley books in the last few years with things that were never published before giving quite a different picture of him, and not nearly so unsympathetic to Byron. He's offered to round up a few, but it's no use my bothering to take them out if you've got some special reason for wanting me to read the others. . . . Though honestly, I'd much rather stick to Byron. Shelley's not my dish at all.'

The young man at the Library! I was tired of the young man at the Library—blast his helpfulness!—and more than tired of my far too successful device for keeping Jocasta busy.

'Look here!' I cried. 'You don't have to read about either of them. I shouldn't have wished them on you. Why not jump into a bus and come and talk to me? We're very quiet here today.'

I could all but hear her smiling. 'Aren't you losing your head a little, ducky? You couldn't have another chapter ready!' And as I mumbled some protest, she said heartlessly, 'You made the rules, you must keep them!'

It was true that even the flying visits she occasionally paid me at Rossiter's had been vetoed in advance by me. I did, at this slack season, get some brief opportunities of private work, and being anxious lest she should come upon me without warning, I'd told her I must set my face against distractions.

'Don't you even want to see me?'

'Of course.'

'"Of course" means nothing.'

'I do want to see you, but I'd truly rather not until you're normal again.'

'Normal?'

'Yes, you never have been, darling, since you took up with this—this—what do you call the Muse of fiction?'

'There isn't one,' I said hastily.

'I'm sure there is, and she's a most horrid harpy who's trying to separate us.'

'But, Jocasta, I'm begging you to come right over here!'

'It isn't possible this afternoon. I've got Gran with me. She's waiting in the Library Reading Room. I actually induced her to leave Granpapa at home and go to the National Portrait Gallery with me. She doesn't get out nearly enough.'

'Why the National Portrait Gallery?'

'Sweetheart, I got into the habit of wandering round picture exhibitions when I was living in Paris without enough money to do anything else.' I waited, feeling there was more to come and there was. 'We've been looking out for Byron pictures because we still haven't tracked down the original of my miniature. They've got the one of him wearing Albanian dress. Isn't it luscious?'

'You're becoming quite a connoisseur of Byron ikons.' I said it with a semblance of amusement. 'You'll never be able to get back into the mood of your fashion shows.'

She took me literally. 'It's always hard to go to work again after a holiday. I've got lots of engagements, thank goodness! Still, darling, I'll be able to do a certain amount of reading for you—'

'No, no, Jocasta. I entirely release you—'

'I refuse to be released. At least, I don't mind giving up Shelley, but you're not going to tear me away from Byron.' The turn of speech was one of the jokes—or we pretended it was. To talk of Byron as if he still had a physical existence had become a recognised pleasantry of hers soon after I had, as it were, brought them together. I have a theory that, not only is many a true word spoken in jest, but that almost every jest expresses a truth that might be uttered in earnest if it were not for an inhibition of fear, pity, or good nature; and to me Jocasta's gaiety as she teased me about her romantic attachment altogether failed to mask the sincerity of the sentiment.

Romantic attachment! And who was to blame for that, I asked myself in a rage! Who had gone out of his way to set up this intolerable rival for himself?

A remedy had been open to me from the first moment she'd shown the first symptom. Was it too late even now to use it? To devote myself wholly to reminding her that I was the very much alive young man who was to be her husband? No, I couldn't abandon my great venture. I had put too much into it, and for some months to come it was bound to occupy me exclusively. I could only intensify my efforts to disillusion her. My version of the Memoirs would present the gingerbread ruthlessly denuded of gilt.

That was the third reason I lately alluded to—the reason why I'd decided to apply my skill to a graphic portrayal of all that was most dissolute in the poet's life. If I were not (at bottom) an honest man, I needn't confess to it, but being determined not to mislead either myself or the reader, I acknowledge that it must have been—little as I perceived it at the time—the motive that really weighed with me in making my change of plan.

In the first portion, composed in 1819, he had undeniably been concerned to make out a case for himself, but my reconstruction would demonstrate that by 1820, he'd thrown caution to the winds. He would be writing prose as he was writing poetry at that period, when, to the dismay of nearly all his circle, he'd found his level completely as an artist in *Don Juan* and *The Vision of Judgment*.

'My finest, ferocious Caravaggio style'—that was his own phrase for his later manner; and that was the style I was aiming at, an interplay of light and shadow that would rivet the attention and, ultimately, draw the eye to darkness.

CHAPTER SEVEN

MY FORTNIGHT at Penrhyndeudraeth was trying, to say the least. I hadn't expected to enjoy myself, but the various nuisances I was obliged to put up with went beyond what I'd anticipated.

To please my great-aunt and get her into the mood where she would not deny me the small favour I was to ask of her, I professed a lively interest in her latest crusade, and this had the irritating consequence of my being roped in for a meeting that took place in Caernarvon. There the crucial argument about the title of the organisation was settled, much to her dissatisfaction, by a majority verdict in favour of 'TROCO', and it was perhaps to assert herself after having been worsted on this issue that she suddenly offered *my* services for redrafting the brochures which were to be printed, recommending me to the assembly as a professional writer of high standing—the first time she'd ever given me such a testimonial. It was vain for me to insist that I wasn't even a member of the Society. I was proposed and seconded there and then, and Aunt Beth passed me a note across the table to tell me I should have my subscription paid instead of a Christmas present.

I was thus committed to the most uncongenial little job, and one which required consultation with John Ockrington, of whom I was already compelled to see too much.

Neither my great-aunt nor her house had grown cosier with time. The years seemed merely to make her more wiry and resistant, deepening her conviction that a young man who liked hot bathwater, complained of an insufficiency of blankets, and didn't want to go for walks in the rain, was a sorry example of post-war laxity and self-indulgence.

Her housekeeper, Mrs. Evans, fully shared this view and added unspoken but manifest criticisms of her own. She had never forgiven me for breaking a lamp when I was fourteen years old, and although that accident had been unique, behaved invariably as if I were sure to do some damage to everything I handled. She would rush up to me and snatch things out of my hands with exclamations of relief at having reached me in time—which made me very nervous—and when I offered to wind the grandfather clock, she entreated my great-aunt not to let me go near it, as if my touch were disaster.

A stout, hale woman twenty years younger than her employer, she had resolutely diminished the number of her duties until now almost every task was done 'to oblige'. Aunt Beth was too afraid of not being progressive, of proving out of sympathy with a modern trend, to put up any opposition. Like many another doughty fighter, she quailed before the eye of her servitor, with the result that guests, except the few that Mrs. Evans singled out for favour, were being given shorter and shorter shrift. This was useful to me in one way, as it provided me with an excuse, when the weather was good enough, to walk to the Portmeirion Hotel for my luncheons, and thus I had a little freedom and was spared the penance of my great-aunt's table; but of course it was expensive, and conditions when I was compelled to remain at the villa were acutely uncomfortable.

I can't deny that I felt my lot was hard, and yet some curious inner energy bore down the obstacles, and I found my ideas expressing themselves with uncanny facility. Every artist dreads that perverseness of the spirit which allows imagination to sag just when all the circumstances for long spells of work appear propitious. I was having precisely the opposite experience, rarer but not unknown, a period of intense productiveness while beset with difficulties.

On the long walks to Portmeirion, I used to think out my next move, for that is how I regarded my day's work—as a series of stratagems, each one designed for the disenchantment of Jocasta. I wasn't indifferent either to the fact that I was killing two birds with one stone. The immense sales of Boswell's London Journal had not been attained solely because of its literary merit, and to make up for the materials I was losing by neglecting the first twenty-eight years of the poet's life story, I felt I must get all the benefit I could from supplying new scandals. Still, that was only an incidental motive.

Sometimes I enjoyed my own cleverness, counting each coarseness of phrase, each damaging anecdote, as a score against an enemy, and sometimes I was as bitterly ashamed as if I were discrediting a friend: but always I was borne along by an afflatus (I won't dare to call it divine) which gave the true Byronic speed and vitality to everything I wrote.

It may be supposed then that I was anything but pleased, on a morning two or three days before my return to London, to encounter John Ockrington coming up the road to the villa as I was going down it, and to guess as soon as I saw him that he would offer to turn back with me.

Although his behaviour had been so unclerical that his bishop had virtually excluded him from his own parish church, he affected so much of the clergyman in his bearing that he resembled an actor overplaying the part, a form of defensiveness no doubt and one which had probably grown more marked since he had openly come into conflict with authority. He was a man of about forty, but seemingly much older, grey at the temples, tall, narrow and pinched-looking, and as sage and sanctimonious in a dried-up kind of fashion as if his career had been as wise and well-guided as in fact it had been indiscreet and ill-starred.

'Ah, Williams!' He hailed me in a paternal style that suggested much more than ten years between our ages.

'Lunching at the hotel again? Aren't you setting off rather early?'

'I thought I'd wander round the gardens first and do a bit of writing.'

'Always industrious, Williams. I'll go a little way with you if I may. I was hoping to see you at your aunt's. I'm taking up the press cuttings. We're in the papers this time all right. Miss Williams will be very much gratified. TROCO must have all the publicity it can get.'

Oblivious apparently to the possibility that he might be awakening some recollection in me of the less welcome attentions he himself had had from the press only a few months ago, he brought from his pocket with a smile of satisfaction a notecase in which were folded three or four cuttings.

'Our last meeting only had a few lines in the *Caernarvon Weekly Advertiser*. Now, you see, we've got nearly a column in the *Advertiser* and a jolly good mention in the *North Wales Courier* as well as headlines in the *Aberystwyth Gazette*. Our outlook's beginning to change.'

I opened out a cutting and read:

NEW STYLE OF CONSCIENTIOUS OBJECTOR
WELSH AUTHOR CLAIMS RIGHT TO REFUSE
TAX PAYMENTS

I was wondering what Welsh author had mixed himself up in this absurd business when my eye lighted with incredulity on my own name. Described as a member of a well-known Penrhyndeudraeth family and a specialist in Regency biographies, I was credited with having been an enthusiastic supporter of the meeting and volunteering to write the propaganda for the campaign the Society was launching.

'Your aunt did quite right to bring you forward,' said Ockrington a shade enviously. 'I was the first to warn her that I myself was under a small cloud at the moment . . . The Caernarvon reporter was naturally glad to make the most of a local character, and other Welsh newspapers have done their paragraphs from his.'

'But I'm not a local character. I've never been more than a visitor here.' I seized this point only because I couldn't be frank about the chagrin I felt at seeing myself identified with a group of cranks.

'You come from a local family. I think it was very sensible of your aunt to let you have the—shall we say?—limelight.' His wistful little laugh apprised me clearly where he preferred the limelight to be shed.

I was assuring myself that the likelihood of these minor provincial papers being read by anyone I knew was luckily remote when he went on: 'Personally I'm very much in favour of your putting your signature to the brochure. A real live author, you know!' He gave another little laugh, this time magnanimous. 'That's quite an asset.'

'No, no!' I cried. 'I carry no weight at all. The people who get the brochure will never have heard of me.'

'Nonsense! We must make them hear of you. We'll give them the titles of your books—'*Why Britain Needs TROCO*, by Quentin Williams, author of So-and-So and Such-and-Such. You do write under your own name, don't you?' Relying on my obscurity to get me out of the embarrassment, for once the reminder of it didn't make me wince.

'Your aunt . . . she's your great-aunt really, I know—but so young, so amazingly young for her age! Wonderful woman! She tells me you're working on a novel. What is it about?'

'It's a difficult thing to say in a few words.'

He didn't press for an answer but hurried on: 'A marvellous gift if one has time to exercise it. Now if only *I* were to write my life story. I've often thought of doing it, and one day—who knows? It would have an immense interest for people, though I dare say there are a few who would shake in their shoes . . .'

This man seemed to have learned all the most tiresome ways of conversing with an author. In a moment or two he would be hinting that he could make my fortune by letting me write his biography. I excused myself for interrupting and pretended to discover that I'd forgotten to post my letters, which might miss the midday collection if I put them in the letter-box at the hotel.

The diversion was successful. He offered to take the letters back to Penrhyndeudraeth for me and was even obliged by the *empressement* of my tone to face about and get on his way.

One of my letters was to Mrs. Rossiter and the other to Mr. Leverett. I'd written to him instead of to Jocasta the previous evening because I couldn't trust myself yet to reply to one I'd had from her without showing the vexation it had caused me.

Dearest Duck (she had begun, striking at once the note of misplaced levity),

Why didn't you tell me that Newstead Abbey was only ten miles from Nottingham? Or did you forget I had an engagement to go up for that great Nottingham lace jamboree? I might never have got to Newstead if it hadn't been that one of the models, Lorelei Hannen, was brought up in the district. How cross I should have been if I'd got back to London only to find I could have visited Byron's old home and didn't!

I stayed with the other girls at the Black Boy Hotel, and as we had an evening show as well as an afternoon show and a rehearsal, we were there two nights. The others went back to London next morning, but Lorelei's parents, when they heard how keen I was to see the Abbey, suggested that we should stay till the afternoon and they ran us there in their car. I wouldn't have missed it for the world. Everything seemed right, even the grey weather. It's just exactly what I'd pictured—only perhaps a little grander and less ruinous. They tidied it up a good deal in Victorian times. But as you've been there yourself I shan't waste words describing it all.

We had a special piece of luck which saved us from having to go all round in a large party with a guide. At this lace manufacturers' 'do' the night before, we had the Mayor and a lot of Civic people in the audience, and one of them was the City Archivist. She's a woman and her name's Miss Walker. Well, she happened to be at Newstead today arranging some letters in a glass case, and when I asked her a question about them, she recognised me. So then I told her I had a very particular reason for being interested in Byron, and she seemed surprised and pleased—but not nearly so surprised as Lorelei. After we'd talked a bit, she could see I was serious, and she was fascinated with my miniature, so then she took us and showed us all kinds of things and it was thrilling.

Darling, that marvellous draped bed of his! It's the grandest Regency bed I've ever seen. All that furniture must have been the last word when he bought it, and I suppose it was one of the reasons why he got so much into debt at Cambridge. Long ago one of the owners of Newstead let some visitor sleep in Byron's room, just to feel what it was like. I could never be brave enough to do that. I *know* I should meet a ghost.

There are some pictures of B. at the Abbey that I've never seen before, and a marble copy of the bust by that Danish sculptor—I can't spell him. I looked at it a long time because Hobhouse and others said it was a very close likeness. It's different from the paintings, a harder stronger man. You can see the stubborn side that went on writing what he believed in no matter how much he was attacked, and made him stay in Greece when everyone else was getting out.

Somehow or other we got to talking about whether his hair was naturally curly or not. There's a lock of it in the collection there, and Miss Walker, who's a Byron addict herself, opened the cabinet to let us see it closer. I admit I oughtn't to have done it, but I had a sort of irresistible temptation to touch it, and while she was showing the others something else I did, and darling, it coiled round my finger like a live thing. I can't explain what a curious sensation it was, that contact with something that really was *him*.

I was sorry we didn't have time to go to the church where he's buried a few miles away, but Lorelei wanted to get back to London to keep a date. I thought I couldn't go to bed without telling you what an exciting afternoon it was. I do wish you'd been there.

The affectionate admonitions and endearments with which she ended hardly registered in my brain, I was so tingling with anger. In spite of my precautionary silence Jocasta had been at Newstead. At Newstead behind my back! Steeping herself in his atmosphere! Impressed by his ancestral grandeurs! Gazing at the face chiselled by Thorwaldsen! Artlessly displaying her enthusiasm to strangers! *His hair curling round her finger!*

That—that alone was enough to drive me to distraction. She must, she should be cured of what was, I perceived, rapidly becoming an infatuation. Last night I'd lain awake thinking what disgraceful episode, what impudicity of language, I could concoct for the Memoirs that might be counted upon for turning her admiration into repugnance. I realised that up to now I hadn't gone far enough. My inventions might shake her, but without effecting total disillusionment. To do that wasn't going to be child's play, because both she and her grandparents had that large-scale tolerance which is often, in charitable minds, the accompaniment of innocence. Some individuals had been singled out for incomprehensible temptations which grew at times beyond their strength: they deserved Christian compassion when they fell and unstinted applause when they resisted. How often Byron had fallen and how much he'd resisted were matters about which their notions were hazy, but they were persuaded that there had been a rousing high-spirited struggle in which the Pilgrim of Eternity had proved himself a hero in the Pilgrim's Progress fashion.

Jocasta was a trifle more sophisticated than the old people, nevertheless she had the habit of a remarkably uncritical acceptance of those who won her affections. (After all, hadn't she accepted me?) I was sure, however, that if once she drew the line it would be firmly and without compromise. Where would she draw it? That was what I now strove daily to decide.

To think out ways of shocking and distressing her was not always an occupation I could regard with self-approval. As a rule, I was conscious of a certain unmanliness in it. But when my mind's eye saw her at Newstead, talking as one 'Byron addict' to another, gazing round the rooms haunted for her by his presence, feeling his hair encircling her finger—ah, how bitterly I dwelt on that!—I no longer had a scruple.

I was possessed by a will to victory. Victory over *him*—his insolence, his greed for conquest. In my desire to dash her idol from his pedestal, I almost forgot the other end for which I was toiling, the well-earned recompense.

At the moment of meeting Ockrington I was working out a caddish anecdote about Lady Oxford—partly because the *amour* with her was one which hadn't been exhausted by biographers, little being known of it in detail, and partly because Jocasta had observed that he'd spoken 'rather sweetly' of her afterwards and I wanted to dispel the good effect of that. If there was one thing which did seem to trouble her it was his want of respect for the women he had possessed. She made excuses for him, but they lacked the ring of conviction. Ungentlemanly recollections of half a dozen mistresses might undermine him substantially.

I had no sooner heard the last of Ockrington's footsteps than I recaptured the thread of the sentences I'd been constructing. Propping myself against a tree, I jotted a few lines on a page of the loose-leaf book I used for my first drafts:

> The Earl of O— was reputed to be the best-natured cuckold in London—and such I found him when I held on a short lease both his house and his spouse. Lady O— had always been lavish with her beauty—yet an abundant stock of it remained at her disposal. Though forty winters had besieged her brow, she was still capable of adorning her husband's with as fine a set of antlers as even an English nobleman could bear to carry.

No! No good! I wasn't tuned in yet. There was more of the Count de Gramont's Memoirs than Byron's in those conceits. And it was risky to let Byron quote from a Shakespeare sonnet when only the text of the plays was generally available. I walked on, and half a mile further took a fresh page:

> Fame is a greater lodestar to women than fortune. When I was at the meridian of mine—it was in 1813— the Countess of O— had a little passed the midsummer of her beauty—and yet she was a very fine woman still with a most graceful *embonpoint*. I have never liked thin females and was being plagued at that time by her whom I have alluded to as the Mad Skeleton—I think the desig-

nation was of Mr. Hobhouse's contriving. Lord O— was reputed to be the best natured cuckold in England—and to be sure I found him so. . . .

That was the key. I went on from there referring to the short lease of the house and the spouse but leaving out the phrases which immediately followed, and explaining in a parenthesis that the house was a dower house and not his Lordship's great house, because Byron was extremely literal-minded: and on the wasted page I noted, as a reminder to myself, that Lady Oxford, who was forty, was the only middle-aged woman who had ever attracted him. I might bring that in at some point, and since middle age in his day was estimated to begin at thirty, I could put it strongly and in terms distinctly unchivalrous.

Or wouldn't the case of a much older *grande dame* give a better opportunity? A mystery for which it would be amusing to provide a solution. I jotted down while I thought of it: 'Lady Melbourne—did she go to bed with him?'

He had told his wife that she did, but that might have been one of those statements meant to shock, to scarify, but not to be seriously believed, with which it was his habit to tease her. Yet there was always a possibility that, even with a woman of sixty, his capacity to evoke and to respond to an amorous excitement had proved irrepressible. It was worth exploring.

I took a long time to reach the grounds of the hotel, having strayed into the woods and lingered wherever there was something to sit on or to lean against, concentrating now on my literary, now on my emotional, problems. In consequence I was late for my lunch and almost the last in the dining-room. This had the advantage, however, of giving me a window table usually reserved for hotel residents, and I looked out with keen enjoyment on the expanse of glistening sand left by the outgoing tide, feeling limbered up for a beautiful afternoon's work. My ill-humour had gone because I had set the scene for two or three particularly unseemly revelations; and at my present rate of going, I should have the manuscript ready much sooner than I'd calculated when I had planned to write an elaborately disguised defence.

Out of the corner of my eye I saw a dark form approaching and prepared to conciliate the waiter who doubtless hoped, in presenting my bill, to clear the room. My exasperation when I found no waiter leaning over me but John Ockrington must have shown itself on my face. He made haste at any rate to apologise for this second appearance.

'I came down on my bicycle to bring you a message from your aunt. She thinks this would be a good afternoon for some work in the attics.'

'What! Today—with the sun shining?'

'She reminds you that you're going back to London on Sunday, and today's Thursday. I told her I'd met you and that you were absolutely absorbed—the poet's eye in a fine frenzy rolling and so forth—but she was very insistent. She's a lady of indomitable will-power. A wonderful woman!' he added hurriedly to acquit himself of mockery. 'I suggested you might prefer to do it this evening, but it appears the attics have no electric light.'

'Damn the blasted attics!' I checked myself at the sight of his piously lowered eyes and pursed lips.

'If there's any help I can give—'

'No, thanks all the same. I did promise to do them and I will. I'd better catch the next bus.'

It was a nuisance when I wanted to think out how I ought to proceed to have Ockrington at my side on the walk to the bus stop. Intoning about the tax objection business too, which was rapidly becoming the most boring subject on earth to me! I switched off my attention from him and, with non-committal mutterings of response, meditated on my next move, which would be crucial.

I'd used various excuses to put off turning out Aunt Beth's lumber because the sooner it was done, the longer the decoy manuscript would be exposed to the risk of some caprice on her part. From the first I'd been taking it for granted that she would willingly offer it to me when I expressed the wish, but as the hour drew near, I suddenly perceived that this was merely theory, and between theory and practice there might be an unpleasant divergence. When I'd gone over it in my imagination, the little scene had always been played according to my requirements—the casual request casually granted: but now that it was to be performed in real life by flesh-and-blood characters, one of whom had never learned the lines, I saw the ending might not be as I'd envisaged it.

Suppose I brought the book to light this afternoon, could I defer asking for it till I was on the very verge of departure? No, that was hazardous. She might take a freak that she wanted to keep it, and to leave it with her would be fatal. She must have time to look at it so that *I* would have time to cope with any difficulties she might make. How much safer I should have felt if it hadn't been for the daily visits of Ockrington!

All the same, I must account it a piece of luck to have had the opportunity of exploring the attics forced on me. That circumstance would be to the advantage of my story when the provenance of the document came to be explained. . . .

It filtered down to the level of my mind where these reflections were forming that names of significance had been uttered. Leverett—South Brockford—In one of those instantaneous backward jumps the startled brain is sometimes able to perform, I not only switched my attention on again, but was able to take in almost the whole statement that at first only my ear had registered.

'. . . I couldn't help seeing your letter was addressed to my dear old tutor, Mr. Leverett. I was delighted to learn he's still in the land of the living. At the same old house in South Brockford too!'

'Oh, did you know him?' I was a trifle disconcerted.

'Yes, indeed. I read Divinity with him during several vacations. A charming old man and a most able tutor. But he must be immensely ancient—ninety or more.'

'Seventy-nine,' I said tersely.

'Is that so? Why, he looked as if he was not long for this world when I knew him twenty years ago. Of course, anyone over fifty seems antiquated to a youngster, and he was very bent with arthritis or some such complaint. Are you one of his old boys too?'

'Yes.'

'It was sad about that son of his committing suicide, wasn't it? It happened quite shortly after I was ordained. What was the reason of it, do you think?'

'That was before my time.' I was resolved to be as uncommunicative as possible.

'A brilliant young fellow, amusing, good-looking, full of fun, but alas! not well balanced. A certain *excess* in everything he did. I caught glimpses of his wife. The marriage was an unfortunate one.'

I would have liked to know more of Jocasta's mother, a topic Mr. and Mrs. Leverett avoided since they could not speak well of her, but there was something about Ockrington which inhibited me from showing my curiosity.

He mistook my unresponsiveness. 'You mustn't think I read your envelope deliberately. The name caught my eye just as I was dropping it into the pillar box. I glanced at the address almost automatically.'

I said I quite understood, and we walked a few more paces in silence. Then he began again:

'Does dear old Leverett still strive to practise the Christian virtues?'

'Certainly.'

'One never knows. Sometimes advancing years bring intolerance. My bishop, for example! Not that he has the excuse of really great age; he's only in his sixties. If Mr. Leverett is still the man I knew, he would be shocked by the unchristian hardness of heart I am now experiencing at the hands of the Church. Would you believe the machinery is already in motion to eject me altogether, to expel me from Holy Orders?'

Having some recollection of the divorce reports in which he had cut so startling a figure, I could believe it very easily, but I managed a polite feint of surprise.

'Yes, the day is appointed. The judgment is pre-ordained. But I shall not submit. I shall put up a fight, be sure of that! The Church still has some faithful servants who are not possessed by envy and all uncharitableness. There are a few quite ready—

clergymen but never likely to wear lawn sleeves—ready to sign a protest. . . . I shall seek advice as to how it can be done. Legal advice. "You take away my life when you do take away the means whereby I live." No one has the right to take away my life except the Supreme Arbiter. It may well be that I can appeal from sacred to profane authority. Many of my congregation would support me . . .'

Heartily embarrassed, I quickened my step. If I missed the bus, I might be accompanied all the way back to Penrhyndeudraeth by this troublesome man.

He kept pace with me. 'Mr. Leverett was always the soul of charity. I can't doubt he would be a signatory to a petition against the persecution of an old pupil. Don't you think I ought to try him?'

Pretending not to hear, I hurried on.

'Perhaps I shall call on him when I return to London. After all, there was nearly a divorce in his own family.'

I was obliged to speak. 'I shouldn't recommend involving him in any dispute with the Church. He's dependent on it for his house, among other things.'

'And would they penalise that good old man for expressing an honest opinion? Could they stoop to such hypocrisy, preaching the gospel of truth?'

My conviction that Ockrington was the most accomplished charlatan, as well as my determination to prevent him from gaining the smallest foothold in Jocasta's home, roused me to reply: 'It mightn't be his honest opinion.'

'What? Has he forgotten his son—?'

'That's the bus!' To my relief I had a genuine excuse for breaking into a run. The bus really was coming up the hill, and as I leapt on to it, I pushed Ockrington as far out of my consciousness as I could. I had reached that stage in the execution of my plan when a mistake would be irretrievable.

I shouldn't be able to go back now on anything said or done in connection with the document on which fortune and future hung suspended, and I felt like a circus performer as the moment approaches when the orchestra is silenced, the long roll of a drum announces the danger of the feat to be performed, and poised in fearful isolation, he advances by precarious steps along his tight-rope.

Chapter Eight

IT WAS AN irksome restraint upon me that I perpetually had to remember what I'd said to Earl Darrow, so that nothing that happened in the sequel to my story would be at odds with the first part of it. I had told him I'd come across the book of Memoirs in an old laundry-basket and hidden it somewhere else for safety afterwards. The place where I now professed to discover it must be one in which I might conceivably put something I wanted to be sure of finding again. It wasn't until I'd practically emptied the first of the two attics that I lighted on what appeared to me the perfect repository.

By removing an old cot, a perambulator, a combined hat-rack and umbrella-stand, a feather mattress, two tea-chests of crockery oddments, a dress basket containing shabby curtains, and a wicker deck-chair with no seat, I reached at last a folding screen so covered with dust that it had evidently not been touched for years. On pulling this away from the wall so that I might judge whether Aunt Beth had any hope of selling it, I saw on the floor a late-Victorian portable desk. It was made of heavy stained oak with brass mountings, and contained a multiplicity of neat compartments for such requisites as envelopes, inkwells, pens, stamps, and rulers; a sloping hinged flap with a section for correspondence underneath it, and underneath that again a small drawer.

I couldn't recollect having set eyes on it before and the initials engraved on the tarnished mounting didn't correspond to any name known to me, but it was completely in keeping with many late-Victorian objects that had been scattered over the house before the recent clearance and appeared to be essentially the sort of thing my great-aunt would desire to get rid of. Wouldn't it be diplomatic therefore to ask first and foremost for the writing-case, and then to affect to find the exercise book inside it—admitting to Darrow afterwards that in the interests of literature I'd been obliged to practise a slight deception on my great-aunt? No sooner did this thought occur to me than I hastened down to my room to fetch the counterfeit volume from my locked suitcase.

There was no one about. I slipped it into the drawer, which had a lock but no key, and having let a little time elapse, during which I did some impressive work in sorting and stacking, I strolled down carrying my prize.

'Worn out already?' Aunt Beth glanced up ironically from some silver she was cleaning.

'Not at all. Wait till you see how much I've done! I can't go on till you've made up your mind about what you want to part with. Besides, it must be nearly tea-time.'

'Is it? Oh dear, yes! So it is—and I've still got these things to polish. Mrs. Evans will be cross.'

'Why doesn't she do them herself?'

'She won't clean silver.' Aunt Beth dropped her voice to announce the stern decree, but made no attempt to explain it. 'Personally, I'd be glad to sell some of these pieces, but you know what *they're* like!' She jerked her hand furtively in the direction of the kitchen. 'You lose caste unless you've got the right sort of paraphernalia—toast-racks and sauce-boats and all that. Still, I think I'll try to off-load these big meat-dish covers. They're only plate but they're old. They belonged to my grandmother.'

I decided to take this as an opening. 'You won't get anything for them, Aunt Beth. Better hang on to them, and if you live long enough—as I hope you will—late Victorian stuff will come back into fashion.' I lifted the unwieldy writing-case on to the table. 'Take this, for example! It must have cost quite a bit of money in its day, but I doubt if you could get ten shillings for it now.'

'What is it?' She looked at it with an unenthusiastic, indeed an unrecognizing eye. I was much encouraged.

'It's a folding desk—evidently meant to be portable but much too heavy to carry about.' I began to open it. 'I was wondering whether you'd let me take it back to London. It's rather nicely designed, and I could do with something to keep all my writing things together.'

'Did you find it in the attics? I don't know who put it there. Those aren't the initials of anyone in my family.' She raised the lid but without any real curiosity. 'It must be something my father or one of my uncles bought second-hand.'

'Or perhaps *my* father,' I said, insinuating a claim.

'Oh no! Your father had no time at all for Victorian things. In his day they were considered horrors. Well, if you want a cumbersome, old-fashioned piece of junk like that, you can have it.'

'Here! Who's giving away property as doesn't belong to them?' To my unspeakable vexation, Mrs. Evans, portly but brisk and baleful, swept into the room and laid on the desk a hand quivering with resentment.

'Oh, is it yours?' No apology could have been more abject than my great-aunt's agonised laugh. 'Mr. Quentin thought it was mine.'

'I don't see as that gave you the right to make him a present of it, Miss Williams. Old-fashioned it may be, but it's not junk, I tell you. It was bequeathed to me by the Honourable Honoria Eastree!'

Though she hadn't a trace of snobbery in her composition, the name of that former employer, richer, grander, more worthy of consideration in every way than my great-aunt, had so often been used to put her in her place that by mere reflex action she looked humbled. She who had defied policemen as a young suffragette in 1910, had made pacifist speeches in 1915, joined a hunger march in 1926, and driven a van with anti-capital punishment posters in 1937—the brave advocate of unpopular causes through a long lifetime—had been bullied mercilessly for sixteen years by her employer.

It took all the courage she could rally to protest mildly: 'It was a natural mistake, Mrs. Evans. My nephew found it in the attic.'

'I dare say he did, seeing as it's been lying there ever since I moved my bedroom downstairs during the war. However, now I know it isn't considered good enough to mix with your things,

Miss Williams, I'll take it where you won't be troubled with it no more.'

I had the presence of mind to circumvent her with a swift step as she made for the door bearing the wretched desk before her.

'I'm so sorry,' I said. 'I think it's a very nice desk and that's why I asked for it.' My conciliatory smile wasn't a success.

'You asked the wrong person,' she retorted crushingly.

I saw there was not going to be the slightest possibility of retrieving the manuscript in secret, so I put the boldest face I could on it. 'There's a book in the drawer. Do you mind if I take it out?'

'Depends whose property it is.'

'Well, not yours, Mrs. Evans.'

My tone, half angry, half hurt, had no more effect than my smile. She clasped the desk defiantly in her arms. I was compelled to reason with her. 'Why don't you look at it and see for yourself?'

With an unerring instinct for my discomfiture she demanded: 'Whose is it then?'

If I replied that it was my aunt's, there was a considerable risk that she (Aunt Beth) would at once, on seeing it, disclaim possession, and then Mrs. Evans, simply to score over me, might carry it off. If, on the other hand, I announced that it was mine, my tale of having found it in the attics went overboard, or at any rate would be lacking confirmation from this house. I hedged.

'You seem to think I'm trying to make off with something of yours.'

'And so you did! You tried to make off with my legacy from Miss Eastree! What right have you got anyhow to put things in a desk as isn't your property?'

Luckily for me, she was being so stupidly recalcitrant that even Aunt Beth was stung to a quite brisk reproof. 'Oh, do stop squabbling, Mrs. Evans, and give Mr. Quentin his book!' She explained slowly as to a child: 'He thought the writing-case was mine and that he was going to take it to London and that's why he put his book in it. It isn't a crime! I'm sorry if I called it junk,' she added with unwonted tactfulness. 'As Mr. Quentin says, if one lives long enough, things always come back into fashion. I'm a bit behind the times, that's all. Now, get the tea, there's a dear woman, and let's have peace.'

Thus both admonished and coaxed, Mrs. Evans grudgingly opened the drawer and handed me a volume. As she went off hugging the unresponsive oak to her bosom, Aunt Beth and I exchanged glances of mutual commiseration.

'I'm afraid I let you in for that,' I whispered.

'Poor creature! There's something pathetic about her making such a treasure of that miserable little legacy.'

'She only does it to annoy, my dear. The treasure has been thick with dust lying behind a screen since the war.'

In the relief of breathing freely again, I was tempted not to disturb my great-aunt's timely assumption as to my ownership of the book, but to have come all the way here and spent two such comfortless weeks and then to go back with my purpose unfulfilled would be a serious failure. I couldn't convincingly produce a copy of a document which had been burned in the presence of seven persons without a very circumstantial tale of how I'd acquired it; and that would need the support I'd been building up for it. My witness-elect couldn't be left out. I took the plunge.

'I'm not sure whether this really *is* mine, Aunt Beth. I let you say so because I didn't want to go on arguing . . . I found it among the loose books lying about up there. They mostly belonged to my father, didn't they?'

'I can't say, Juggins, not having had a real turn-out there for years. I'd forgotten there were any books left. Is there anything good—anything that would fetch money?'

'No, a dingy lot, I'm afraid. A dealer might give you a pound or two for them, not more. I brought down this one to see if you could remember whether it was my father's.'

An actor would have commended the ease and naturalness of my performance, but as I laid the counterfeit book before her on the table, my heart, in Byron's phrase, was beating at my fingers' ends.

She looked attentively at the shabby leather binding, then opened the leaves. 'Oh, it's written by hand!' she remarked with surprise, and after skimming over a page or two: 'It's not a handwriting I can recall. It goes back long before your father's time, I should say.'

'Yes, but it might have belonged to him all the same. It seems to be somebody's copy of bits out of Regency biographies—which, according to the local paper, are right up my street.'

'But not up your father's street.'

'No—though he may have picked it up somewhere or other because it amused him. There are some pretty racy bits in it.'

'Is that why you want it?'

'How do you know I want it?' My great-aunt's point-blank style for once wasn't distasteful to me.

'Because you're trying to persuade me it was your father's. It may just as well have belonged to anyone else in the family.'

My real reason for seeking to establish a right to the book was in case, when it later turned out to be valuable, she became inclined to demand a share of the proceeds. Not that she was covetous but one of her crusades was sure to be wanting money. I wasn't averse to her mistaking my motive, since it simplified my approach, and I pressed on ingenuously:

'Well, give it me whoever it was, there's a dear!'

'Wait a minute! I want to look at it first. Where did I put my other spectacles—the reading glasses? Are they on the mantelpiece?' She moved to her chair by the fireplace and I handed her the glasses with the most nonchalant air in the world, though my hand was still unsteady.

'It's very bad writing,' she said. 'I can only just make it out.'

With much stumbling she read, having turned a leaf or two at random:

> 'In going to a rendezvous with a Venetian girl (unmarried and the daughter of one of their nobles), I tumbled into the Grand Canal, and not choosing to miss my appointment by the delays of changing, I perched on a balcony in my wet clothes. My foot had slipped in getting into my

gondola to set out (owing to the cursed slippery steps of their palaces) and I flounced like a Carp, and went dripping like a Triton into the sea and had to scramble up to a grated window:

"Fenced with iron within and without,

Lest the lover get in or the Lady get out."

The father was laid up, and the brother was at Milan, and the mother fell asleep, and the Servants were naturally on the wrong side of the question—'

She looked up with a pained smile. 'What is it? Casanova?'

'No, it's a letter or a journal entry of Byron's. I've seen it before somewhere.'

Mentally I made a note that a passage about this escapade, which I'd copied in a slightly garbled form from published correspondence, must figure in my invented recollections. Aunt Beth's memory was unreliable, but might attach itself like a limpet to any particulars which struck her. It wouldn't be amiss to use much the same words again, Byron being lazy at times about varying the phrases in which he recorded incidents that caught his fancy. Provided I didn't overdo it, there would be no loss of plausibility if here and there in his Memoirs a paragraph or so followed fairly closely the wording of a letter; and it would save labour in composition.

My great-aunt had found another piece to read, a garbled copy like the first:

> 'Of late I have had a notion that I might take my natural daughter with me to Venezuela and pitch my tent there for good and all. I am not tired of Italy, but a man must be a—

'A *what*?'

I leaned over her shoulder and read, as if I were deciphering with difficulty, 'A Cicisbeo.'

'What's that?'

'I can't imagine. Something to do with music perhaps. Look, it goes on, "A singer in duets and a connoisseur of opera here".'

'Ah yes, I see.' She groped her way a little further:

'Better be an unskilful planter, an awkward settler, better be a hunter or anything than a fan carrier to a woman. I like women—God he knows—but here the polygamy is all on the female side. I have been an intriguer, a husband, a—a—'

She couldn't quite bring herself to say 'whoremonger'. Her eager progressiveness was social and political and stopped at the changes in manners which permit a woman to quote such a word.

'Let *me* try and make it out, Aunt Beth!'

'No, thank you, I can read it. More Byron no doubt! I haven't a word to say in favour of that man. I can't believe it was your father's doing to get hold of this. It just isn't his style.'

She ran her eyes over a few more lines here and there, but with such supercilious and superficial attention that I felt it unnecessary to go on checking closely what she was reading. I was tremblingly anxious to make sure of getting back the book because she was taking its existence less casually than I'd anticipated. My policy of copying somewhat 'shocking' passages so that the text I was planting would correspond in spirit to that which I was writing had its tricky elements.

'Personally, I should be inclined to throw this on the fire. It would keep it out of the hands of anyone impressionable.'

'My dear aunt, it's 1956—a little too late to start protecting people from Byron!'

'Well, I dare say that's true.' I thought she was going to hand me the volume, but she closed it and laid it down on the further side of her armchair. 'Let's put it on one side till we hear what John Ockrington has to say.'

'Ockrington! Now, honestly, Aunt Beth!' How I contrived to speak playfully I don't know. The thought of being obliged to confide my decoy to that nest-feathering busybody filled me with dismay. 'I should hope you can make up your mind about letting me have an old writing-book without having to consult a clergyman. What does he know about it that I wouldn't know?'

Her mouth extended in a wavering apologetic smile. 'That's just it! You're a bookseller. You might have an ulterior motive.'

'As what, for example?' She spoke lightly and so, with an effort, did I.

'Oh, you're quite capable of it. I know you of old, Master Juggins. If the book is worth anything, it should be sold for the benefit of TACT—I mean TROCO. Why *did* they fix on that name?'

'Do you suppose I'm going to take it to the shop? It never entered my head. I simply want to read it and see if there's anything in it that I haven't come across before. It's the sort of thing that interests me.'

In spite of myself I must have conveyed the idea of eagerness, automatically setting up an impulse of opposition in her. 'All the same, we might as well show it to John. He'll be looking in this evening. Here's the tea.'

Mrs. Evans was still surly and my great-aunt's attempts to placate her allowed me a brief space for weighing the consequences of one move or another. Everything depended on the inspection of the MS being rapid and lacking in any real curiosity about the contents. From what I'd seen of Ockrington, I felt sure he had an eye to the main chance and was uncommonly inquisitive. Moreover, my having kept him at arm's length in our conversation about the Leveretts doubtless hadn't endeared me to him. At all costs he must be left out of this.

When Mrs. Evans had retreated, I turned the conversation to other topics as if the matter of the book was too trivial to dwell on, and, although I was on tenterhooks, it wasn't till tea was well over and I'd agreed to resume my work upstairs that I went back to it. I made a dive and picked it up from where she'd rested it on the floor, and staged a little scene which, considering I played it impromptu, came over pretty well.

'Now look here, Aunt Beth!'—I was huffy but not without an air of amusement—'I'm going to take this back to the attic and restore it to all the junk I found it with. You're not going to get me to ask favours of John Ockrington. If it belonged to my father, it's mine. If it belongs to you, I would have liked you to give it to me. But John Ockrington isn't a member of the family, and I don't see why you should bring a stranger into this at all.'

The implied accusation of unfairness was one I'd guessed she would be susceptible to. 'My dear boy, he's not quite a stranger.' She was flustered. 'You know all I'm concerned with is raising money for TROCO.'

'If you think Ockrington is a better judge than I am of what's worth anything in the book trade—'

'No, no, Juggins . . . only perhaps more disinterested. I mean more devoted to TROCO,' she corrected herself good-humouredly as I gave her a mock-baleful glance.

'You're becoming quite grasping on behalf of TROCO, Aunt Beth. I do believe you're trying to sell me the book.'

To chaff her into giving it to me was of course my object, and I was disconcerted when she came back at me with a laugh: 'Certainly. I'll sell you anything in the house if you'll pay the price. We positively must start a TROCO campaign somehow in London. Without that we shall never get going. One just can't operate a big national thing like this from a backwater in Wales.'

I asked as sympathetically as I could: 'Won't Ockrington take it on?'

'He can do a great deal privately—seeing important people, getting subscriptions and all that, but this infamous hypocritical bishop dragging his name in the mud . . . it means we daren't give him an official position in the society. He was the first to point out that the publicity wouldn't do us any good.'

I tried to look as if I were weighing her problem while in reality I struggled with my own, which seemed to have reached a desperate pass. But suddenly, rubbing her fingers over her short untidy hair in one of her youthful but ungainly gestures, she exclaimed: 'I'll make a bargain with you. Take the book if you've got such a fancy for it, and let me put your name forward as Appeals Organizer for the London section of the TROCO Committee!'

'London section? There isn't one.'

'There will be as soon as we can work up the enthusiasm to form one.'

My thoughts seemed to rush about helter-skelter in my brain, tumbling over one another; and all that was sanguine in them hurried to seize on the improbability of survival for a venture so plainly at odds with modern trends of opinion. Taxpayers' Right of Conscientious Objection forsooth! What chance was there that even the maddest orator at Hyde Park corner would espouse such a hopeless cause? Surely I could safely make that pact! It occurred to me too that, since I hadn't been able to persuade her the manuscript was my father's property, here might be a means of limiting her claims upon me when it turned out that she'd parted with a treasure.

'It's rather a tall order,' I said, 'seeing you've got rid of so many of the things I liked. I wouldn't do it for just this one book—that's absurd! The binding isn't even in good condition. Throw in something to make it worth while—you who went and sold the kaleidoscope!'

The red herring was beautifully effective, leading into an exchange of jocular recriminations on my part and somewhat sheepish protests on hers, and enabling me to say facetiously at last: 'Well, if I consent to do anything for TROCO after all the sacrifices I and my heirs have already made for it, it'll be the noblest deed of my life.'

'You will, though, won't you, Juggins? We could even pay you when the campaign's a success.'

'No. I can't do more than a spare-time job, and it's no use offering money you haven't got yet. To have my choice of the few decent books you've left in the house will be my only recompense—that and the pride I take in being a dutiful great nephew.'

'I'll hold you to that promise,' she said triumphantly.

I was too discreet to reply that I'd hold her to the gift. One word too much might undo all that my artistry had so perilously accomplished.

With a sense of having just managed to clear an exceedingly stiff hurdle, I went back to the attics, stopping on the way to lay the decoy on my dressing-table. After the incident with the writing-case, there was every chance that Mrs. Evans's curiosity would tempt her to a little prying; and I deemed it an advantage, in view of the inquiries which were inevitable when I brought my remarkable wares to market, that my great-aunt's testimony might have support, however ungracious, from a third party who was, to some extent, a witness. The more evidence the better. I wouldn't even have minded John Ockrington if I hadn't suspected that somewhat shady character of being likely to suspect me.

Chapter Nine

I RETURNED to London in a very good mood. To escape from the rigours of Aunt Beth's housekeeping was in itself a pleasure; to have brought off my little ruse was an important victory; but what was best of all was that, thanks to my decision to deal only with the later and less cautiously written Memoirs, and the spur of what I admit to have been a sort of jealousy, I'd been able to proceed with a celerity unprecedented in my private history as a writer, and for once I could hope to finish my task in advance of what Earl Darrow would have called (if he'd known about it) my 'skedule'. This was a great comfort to me because I didn't want to temporise too long with him. Jocasta too would think it odd, when she heard about my splendid find, if I'd allowed months to pass before I mentioned it. As it was, provided I could keep up the pace, there would be no greater lapse of time than I could account for with very reasonable excuses.

The pace—it was wonderful! Even on the train journey to London I managed to rough out my Lady Melbourne story and get it to a state where it only lacked that air of spontaneity which gives Byron's prose its indolent forcefulness. I led up to it by some typical reflections on platonic friendship:

There is no such thing as genuine platonism between the sexes because the feminine will not endure it—and they are right, their power being all in the senses and the sentiments—The virtuous Miss Milbanke excelled in platonic performances, but the end of our chaste friendship was that for her sins or my sins (*she* made a point of never committing any) she bestowed her immaculate hand on me. It was an honour I never did anything to deserve before or after.

Friendship with a woman must have its admixture of sentiment, and sentiment will sooner or later awaken the senses, and the senses will claim their hour of dominance—and then—and then one party will grow tired and the other affronted, and there's an end of your friendship.

I never knew it otherwise but in a single instance and this so strange I scarce hope to be believed. Lady M— was above sixty when I met her and I four and twenty, she a great lady and I in Tom Moore's phrase 'gentle and juvenile, curly and gay' and the favourite for a season or two of the cheating goddess Fame. Besides grace and grandeur Lady M— had so much wisdom that I consulted her about all my loves and though some of them shocked her, I never found an instance of her betraying me. I could not venture such a boast of any other daughter of Albion. They are for the most part as perfidious as its rulers. (I except my sister and would my mother too, but she was a daughter of Caledonia.)

Lady M— was born many years before my mother and it will be allowed that, though I owed her gratitude and affection, it was beyond reason to expect more of my one score years and six—the precise time of life I had reached when the lady suddenly gave such signs as no man may politely ignore of wishing to confer on me a very particular favour generally called the last. So sweetly unreasonable is the sex.

What attraction she had seen or suspected the reader must guess if he can—perhaps none but the fancy to test her once invincible powers of fascination. I must own I was fain to have misunderstood the invitation. It was on a winter night and we were in her dressing-room—for she followed our grandmothers' custom of receiving her select circle there, which was quite comfortable and all that because she was a grandmother.

I had paid a few innocent compliments to her person which remained handsome and was well preserved, when she let fall her cachemire and treated me to an untrammelled view of a bosom ripe but not to any grave extent overblown, with the whitest skin I ever saw except that of a German woman, Constance, of whom more in good time. Besides this display there were sundry further manifestations more seemly to be imagined by the reader than described by me—yet not so very seemly either. In short she made it pretty plain one way and another that I should oblige her.

Never was an oblation to Venus offered more reluctantly. It was less the disparity in our years that incommoded me than the value I placed on our friendship which seemed imperilled whether I indulged or rebuffed her caprice. However, being as ill-fitted for the role of Joseph as Lord M— was for Potiphar, I made a valiant stand and contrived to go about the business energetically enough, and it was better than I hoped, for she had the good sense to snuff out the candles.

We are bred to believe that none but the young are fit to minister to our carnal appetites, yet let us but consider that the progress of human decay, more especially in the female, commences at the top with grey hairs and descends by stages down the frame, and in the dark we shall not be much worse off with sixty years than sixteen—ay, better if experience in gallantry be taken into the account. (Nevertheless I acknowledge this is mere philosophising on my part and, although sage, no more likely to affect my conduct than my reader's, who will continue foolishly to go staring into women's faces.)

The day after my soberest relationship with a woman had taken this inebriated turn, I was in the greatest perplexity. I neither wished to pursue an intrigue which would have rendered us both ridiculous nor to offend Lady M by shunning her society—which had formerly been so agreeable to me. My relief then was measureless when her page brought me a few lines couched with equal vivacity and delicacy begging me to *excuse* the previous evening's incident and to ascribe it to feminine curiosity. Her explanation—perhaps more tactful than truthful—was that she had desired to investigate at first hand the grounds for the persistent (and very troublesome) attachment that a member of her family professed to feel for me.

'I hasten to give you my assurance,' she wrote, 'that I am *fully satisfied* and need make no further trial. Let our friendship continue without even an allusion to my inquisitiveness, which your generosity and my discretion will consign to oblivion.'

She was as good as her word, and we resumed our platonic intercourse upon the easiest footing. In a few weeks—or days even—it was with difficulty I could recollect the adventure, and she never seemed to remember it at all—the only woman I ever knew who forbore to make a scene or at the least to hold the threat of one over my long-suffering head.

I have never yet re-read my first batch of Memoranda, not having had it in my hands since Tom Moore was in Venice—so I cannot recollect whether I described the long exchange of effusions decorous enough for a young lady's letter-writing manual which passed between myself and Lady Byron before she did herself—and by Heaven me—the injury of taking that name. The very postmen must have been the purer for carrying them—

That was as far as I had got when we steamed into Paddington, and though it would need further touches to polish it into the impromptu style and give it the requisite strain of a caddishness beyond hope, I tucked the pages into my valise with self-respecting contentment.

Jocasta actually came to meet my train, and in the delight of seeing her fresh beauty and serene elegance repelling with their own magic the grime of the station, I didn't resent the sight of the miniature on the lapel of her coat. Such was the mellowness of my humour that I could believe she wore it as a compliment to the giver.

I d asked her to come to my Lowestoft Street room to hear the latest chapter of my novel, having maintained the pretence that I was working devotedly at that; but she told me her grandfather was not well, and that she would prefer me to go home with her so that she might give some assistance to her grandmother. It was a disappointment but I quickly reconciled myself to it. I always admired the spontaneous sweetness of her attentions to the aged couple, whom so many girls would have regarded as a burdensome tie.

We went together to South Brockford and spent a thoroughly domestic evening there, and, as I'd had little enough of anything that resembled a settled family life, I was grateful for it and looked forward keenly to the day when—thanks to the secret draft now nearing completion—I would no longer spend my nights alone in lodgings. Mrs. Leverett being worried about her husband who was in bed with a bronchial attack, the little jokes in the Byromania vein which had been current last time I was in the house were in abeyance. I didn't breathe the disturbing name, and Jocasta's talk, when she wasn't busy with the dinner and the clearing-up afterwards, was chiefly about her engagements and the joyful possibility that she might fly to Rome to take part in a show and be photographed in British clothes against famous Italian backgrounds.

'The gimmick,' she explained, 'is "classic". Classic clothes against classic architecture.'

'What? Classical draperies! Are they going to be the fashion?'

'Silly! I'm talking about suits and coats.'

'What is a classic suit?' I liked to see her pleasantly absorbed in her own innocuous subject.

'It's—I've never really asked myself! I suppose it's a suit that doesn't go out of fashion. . . . Not that there is such a thing if you come to think of it. A suit ten years old would look nearly as dowdy as an old dress.'

'Then it's just one of your errands of deception. You're always using your beauty to persuade people of something that isn't true about clothes. You turn what you wear into fictions.'

'Fashion is all fictions. All illusions anyhow. I don't mind being photographed in illusions, as long as they're beautiful enough and as long as it's in Rome. I've always wanted to go there.'

'It's very heartless of you, darling, looking forward so much to going away when I've only just come back.'

My regret was sincere, yet I couldn't help thinking how immensely helpful it would be for her to be absent while I was in the final feverish throes of composition.

'I don't see much of you nowadays even when you're in London. How much longer are you going to be working on the novel, Quentin?'

'I wish I knew. I'm getting a bit worried about it. The chapter I've just done seems unsatisfactory somehow.'

It would be better 'alibi', I'd decided, to share with her my supposed doubts and strivings than to abandon the novel suddenly. She would have the impression that she'd watched me at work on it. I might even let the suggestion of giving it up originate with her. The conflict between her truthfulness and her unwillingness to hurt my feelings had been clear from the first, and I could see that she was not sorry to find me beginning to lose confidence.

It was a relief to me tonight to be able to abstain from dwelling on matters which belonged to my private conspiracy, and I was glad I'd left the typescript at the tube station Luggage Office in my portmanteau.

I didn't see Jocasta again for several days because her grandfather took a turn for the worse, and she spent all her free time helping to look after him. It was distressing and I should have liked to make myself useful at Brockford Lodge, but I was obliged to snatch every available moment for my writing.

Mellowness still prevailed. Indeed it grieved me that so much of the work I'd done was calculated to prove painful to Byron's admirers, and I wondered if, perhaps, before I finally copied out my recent inventions, I might tone down their grosser improprieties. I'd always had spasms of remorse for having twisted my intended tribute into an attack on the memory of a man whom I still fundamentally envied and admired, and the absence of any new provocation so revived my loyalty that, to make amends for its failures, I attempted two or three anecdotes reflecting most creditably on him; but they cost me great labour for very little effect. My picture in the Caravaggio manner wouldn't take that kind of light.

I did what I could to redeem a particularly scurrilous part of the text by dropping in a handsome eulogy of the genius of Shelley, but placed where it was, it had the tone of sarcasm.

Still, its composition served the purpose of making me feel more respectable than when I was devising episodes to 'bring a blush to the cheek of the young person'—*my* young person too, whom I ought to have protected from such unseemliness.

The trouble was that I had developed a Byronic style which was part of the very matter I wrote, and which was at its best when I was being outrageous. So I put most of the virtuous passages on one side for reconsideration.

The style assuredly was everything. As long as that would hold, I had no fear of being betrayed by any mechanical slip. Every pitfall of that kind had been taken fully into account. The paper was contemporary, the handwriting I had absolutely mastered; the pages of the used exercise-book had been destroyed in my own fire, the stiff leather binding torn up and consumed in small fragments. My great-aunt was already convinced that I'd found the manuscript in her attic and would become more than ever so when she learned that it was worth money. Her housekeeper would by no means weaken my story if she averred that I'd attempted at first to conceal and make off with it. Thanks to my long preparation for a biographical work, dates and verifiable details in the text would stand the most vigilant scrutiny.

If the reminiscences themselves rang true, I didn't see what could go wrong ... unless it was some copyright complication.

My ownership of the script would place me in an extremely strong position, but was there anyone who could interfere with my disposal of it? I hadn't dared to make any overt inquiry about copyright before my journey to Wales. Preceding the discovery of the document that would have been a rather suspicious circumstance. Darrow, who alone was in the secret, or believed he was, couldn't advise because in this field American legislation differs widely from ours. I'd contented myself with trying to learn the law from books, which isn't an easy thing to do unless, so to speak, you already know it.

It was safe now to venture some inquiries, though I couldn't even yet announce quite candidly what I was trying to find out, being determined not to make any stir about so very stirring a subject as Byron's Memoirs until I was perfectly ready to produce the MS. In consequence of my guardedness, the talks I had with knowledgeable people, including my publisher and a customer who held a post in the Society of Authors, were anything but conclusive. I was told what I already knew—that the copyright of literary works which had never been published would belong to the heirs of whomever had written them. As long as there *were* heirs, it didn't matter what time had passed since the date of the writings. I asked—what if the licence to publish had been sold before the death of the writer? Then the copyright would be vested in the heirs of the purchaser. Suppose the purchase had been made a hundred and thirty-odd years ago? One of my informants believed the contract would have lapsed, nullifying itself by non-fulfilment. Another said he thought it would still be enforceable.

I was impatient for the day when I could state the case plainly, for there was no doubt at all that John Murray II had paid two thousand guineas for the document entire, but equally there was no doubt that he had consented to its destruction and had afterwards accepted repayment of the sum. Assuming one could prove the act of destruction had in part failed, who would have the right to control my use of the property? Commonsense seemed to answer that, notwithstanding the absence of contract, the heirs of the man who had repaid the money would have a claim. If Thomas Moore had no heirs—and I was gratefully certain he hadn't—wasn't I at liberty to do what I liked with the exhumed treasure? It would be as well nevertheless to put myself in the clear first with the reigning John Murray.

Preoccupied as I was with these matters and with holding down my job at Rossiter's, I couldn't at first repress a feeling, despite the painful twinges of conscience it cost me, that Mr. Leverett's illness was providential. Yet soon I realised I wasn't getting on as fast or as satisfactorily as when I'd had the impetus of anger. My energies were flagging and the moment I had a hopeful bulletin, I seized the opportunity for a respite, and begged Jocasta to come and hear my chapter. She was appearing in a tea-time fashion show at the Dorchester that day, and although she was at first insistent that she ought to go home directly after it, her grandmother, who was in the room when I telephoned, prevailed upon her to come to me in Lowestoft Street.

She had led me to expect her arrival at about half past six, but it was half past seven when she turned up. 'They gave us champagne after it was over,' she said, 'and I stayed to drink some. It's bad for the figure, but this has been such a worrying time. Did you think I was never coming?'

I kissed the cheek she turned to me.

'I believe you're just snobbish about visiting me over a fish shop.'

'And well I might be! I'll be glad when you leave this place.'

'So shall I because when that happens we'll be getting married.'

Chilling my heart with silence, she sat down and began pensively to draw her gloves off finger by finger as if the operation required the most meticulous attention.

'We're engaged, aren't we?' I tried to ask it flippantly.

'Yes, we're engaged . . . but getting married somehow doesn't seem real any more.'

'Doesn't seem real? What do you mean, Jocasta?'

'I don't know exactly. Once it did seem real and now it doesn't, that's all.' She sighed. 'Perhaps it's a sort of reaction after a hateful week. I've had to fulfil my engagements because of the money and everything, and it's been miserable leaving Gran alone to cope with things.'

I grasped eagerly at that bearable explanation. 'You must have blamed me for not coming out to you, but what with being at the shop all day and going through a sort of crisis with this novel . . .'

'It's all right. You explained that.' She stared remotely at her outstretched hands.

'I only work at it intensively like this because we can't marry until I make some money.'

'No, we can't.' There was not the slightest expression in her voice.

I had never thought her selfish for not wanting to take a husband who was so far from being able to support a wife. It was quixotic generosity in her, whose circumstances oscillated almost daily between harassing economy and extravagant luxury, to have promised herself to a man who could give her so much less than she longed for and could easily have had from others. In the fear she had inflicted on me, I had an impulse to make myself less ineligible by telling her how I'd brought from Wales a neglected heirloom that couldn't fail to enrich me: but I checked myself. The tale of my Byron find would be bound to arouse her excited curiosity, and fobbing her off when she asked to see it would be hazardous. The kind of lie that might do very well on a minor occasion, such as that I'd left it in my bank or with a friend, was to be resolutely avoided when it was vital to keep my statements verifiable at every point.

I contented myself with a cheerful hint. 'All the same, it may not be as long as you imagine, darling, before I'm in a position to lead you to the altar.'

She thought I was still dwelling on my novel, and offering me a rather effortful smile of conciliation, said: 'Well, here I am, waiting to be read to.'

The sequel to the reading wasn't quite what I'd looked for. Instead of the concern she'd so palpably tried to conceal on previous occasions, the longing to deflect me from a mistaken course that I seemed set upon, she spoke almost with indifference; at any rate with the air of one not personally involved in the problem.

'Perhaps it *is* the kind of book that makes money, Quentin. That's a thing I wouldn't know about.'

'But do you think it's any good? Do you like it?'

'What does it matter whether I like it? You wanted to write a book that lots of people would buy, and for all I can tell, they might.'

I was cut to the quick, not by her distaste for the novel—that had always involuntarily shown itself—but by a detachment which in her seemed like harshness.

'I don't want to make money by producing bad work. If you didn't respect it, I'd hardly be able to go on with it.'

'How can I judge? You know I don't read many novels. Not many books at all if it comes to that.'

I found myself saying acridly: 'What about your passion for biography? And poetry?'

'Don't be sarcastic, Quentin! It was you who started all that anyhow.' She leaned back resting her head on the faded velvet of my one armchair. 'I'm not at all sure now it was a good thing.'

'Why?' I held my breath to ask it.

'One tries to live outside one's own life. That's not good.'

'No, it isn't.' I didn't know whether to be glad or sorry that she recognised her danger. 'If I wasn't obliged to earn my living and struggle to write a book at the same time, we could enjoy a little more reality together.' I drew my chair as near as I could to hers and put my arm round her neck. 'I'm quite aware that being plighted to me hasn't been a very vivid experience lately.'

I bent over to kiss her. For the second time, she turned her cheek to me. I tried to reach her mouth, but she drew further away. Then abstractedly, as if she hadn't noticed my attempted embrace—and I hardly think she did—she said: 'I believe I'm going to give up Byron.'

It was the first time his name had been mentioned between us since my return from Wales, and in such a context I ought to have rejoiced to hear it: but that her thoughts should be on him as she rejected my kiss was wounding.

Our established bantering style tided me over. 'You fickle creature! Why, it's only about a fortnight since you were at Newstead Abbey behaving like a pilgrim at a shrine.'

'That's what I felt like then.'

'What did he do to turn you against him?'

Such is human instability that, as I waited for what should have been welcome enlightenment, I was for a moment disconcerted. Perhaps since I'd laid such a train for disillusioning her, I didn't want to find that I'd been toiling needlessly. Perhaps on the other hand, it was a sort of reflex movement of my old affection for the man I'd always, till these last few months, hoped to defend.

'I shouldn't be surprised if I hadn't turned against *men*.' She was much more than half serious.

'Men? Why?'

'It's a thing you could never understand, being a man. Whatever you may say, you're in a kind of freemasonry. There's something in your nature that's hostile to women.'

'Hostile to women, darling! Men!' I repeated stupidly.

'Yes, you don't mind if women are deceived and belittled. You joke about it. It's one of the great masculine traditions.'

'My love, how can you be so absurd? When have *you* met with hostility from men?'

'All the time, I dare say, if I'd only had the sense to see it.'

'Darling!' I was really exasperated. 'Is this because Byron was unchivalrous?'

'He wasn't worse than his friends—all those men he wrote his witty letters to. They encouraged him. He was like a child that does what someone dares it to do. They were daring him to have fun at the expense of women. Their sentimentality and their silliness and their—their—'

Her command of words, which was never more than moderate, broke down under the strain of trying to express such unwonted ideas. I was about to take advantage of what seemed a superb chance of darkening the shadows that had evidently begun to gather about the image of the hero when I recollected in time that it would be a considerable indiscretion to put it into her head that I was no longer 'on his side'. So far I'd managed to give my criticisms an indulgent or at least a dispassionate tone. If I began to send openly the same barbs as I was preparing to dispatch from my ambush, she might later on make deductions perilous for myself. After all, she and her grandparents weren't ignorant of my being uncommonly well-versed in Byron history.

I took her hands in mine and pulled her out of the chair. 'Let's fry ourselves some bacon and eggs!'

She shook her head. 'I had a lot of canapés and things at the Dorchester. Besides, you're only trying to change the subject.'

'Of course I am. I must, if you will talk about the shocking way men treat women. How can you in the presence of a Galahad like me? I can't look at you without thinking how virtuous I am.'

'Only because your mind's on something else.'

I couldn't be sure whether she spoke ruefully or mockingly; but the effect was to make me want to prove to her that my mind and body too were capable of a most tenacious attachment to herself, and I clasped her in my arms with a fervency I hadn't dared to yield to for a long while. She struggled against me, not with violence, as if she were repelled, but stolidly as if fending off an inconvenience.

'Don't do that, Quentin! You know I can only come here if you behave sensibly!'

The bloom of her skin, its scent, its delicacy, the movement of her shoulders under my hands, nearly deprived me of self-possession. I drew her to me, pressing my face against her neck, while she as firmly drew away from me.

'Quentin, *please*! I'm not in the mood.'

I let her go. I almost pushed her from me. 'It seems I *am* in the mood. Perhaps you'd prefer me to take you home.'

'You may as well.' If I were her brother, she couldn't have been more casual. 'Granpapa might be able to see you if we don't arrive too late.'

'Fond as I am of your grandfather, it wasn't him I was longing for this evening.'

'But, honey, you can't switch on and switch off like that. You wanted to be Galahad while you were shut up with this blessed novel of yours, and you mustn't grumble if you get your way.'

I couldn't help seeing the justice of this, and in a spasm of the pitiable optimism that overcomes uncertain lovers, I was inclined to lay her fit of pique at my own door. It was more endurable than laying it at the door of a rival, dead or alive.

I began reassuring her. 'It isn't my usual method of work. You won't always have me doing this ivory tower business. . . .'

'I'm sure the fish shop has never been called an ivory tower before!' She said it with the particular teasing laugh that brought the dimple to her cheek, so I shouldn't have been offended, but I was. I didn't even kiss her before we set out. The fishy vapour that always clung about the staircase was more humiliating than ever.

On the way to the tube station, she described the fashion show. I tried to listen, but now I was regretting that I hadn't let her say her say about the grievances of women. I wanted to know precisely—quite precisely—what she had come up against in *him*, the tireless trouble-maker I'd let loose upon myself, and whether it was really bad enough to turn her from him.

It was about quarter to nine, an hour of slackness on the Central Line. We were the only people on the escalator at Chancery Lane and the platform below had an air of such total desertion that one could hardly imagine there had ever been a rush hour there. With its dim, unbeautiful light and the all-encircling arch of its colourless tiles, it seemed a sort of Limbo between the upper and the under world, where one might stand forgotten waiting for trains that would never come, with nothing to remind one of the vanished life above ground but the strange fictions of posters.

Jocasta's cautionary tale of a mannequin who had fallen from grace and allowed herself to gain weight between the fitting of a skin-tight dress and the wearing of it in public, straggled to a wavering end, incongruous, incredible even, in these surroundings. Preoccupied with my own dejection, I was as unresponsive as a husband of ten years' standing.

The train, of course, did come, announcing itself from the distance with a gentle but menacing thunder, as from some milder circle of inferno. Dead souls appeared behind the windows of the coaches, and we joined them. A few heads turned, as heads always did turn automatically upon Jocasta's entrances, but the faces remained blank. The noise as we were rattled into the tunnel was heightened by the comparative emptiness of the carriage, so that we couldn't speak without straining our voices.

Again I was humiliated. It occurred to me that never in his life had *he* been obliged to take a girl home in a public conveyance. For him fine saddle-horses, or a carriage with lackeys saying 'Yes, my lord' and 'No, my lord,' or a gondola gliding among the palaces of Venice. His rendezvous would be in a private casino, a mansion in Piccadilly, a villa looking over a Swiss lake. He would not have wanted for the means to buy Jocasta pink topaz . . .

My umbrage mounted as I measured the contrast between our situations, and with it mounted my anxiety to know at any cost how he stood with her now. Yes, I was under a compulsion to know it. The noise diminished with our slowing up at Holborn, and I struggled for my suavity again to ask: 'What is it you've been reading about the Noble Bard?'

She tilted open the lid of her professional handbag and revealed among the lipsticks and eyebrow pencils a copy of *The Last Attachment*.

'Oh, the book about the Countess Guiccioli.'

'Yes, poor creature!'

'You call her that? His one thoroughly satisfactory love affair!'

'That's what I thought. I was *happy* about her. She was such a nice person, and she must have been very attractive even if she didn't have a mannequin's figure. Anyhow, if you come to think of it, a figure that was wrong for those high-waisted dresses, might be an asset nowadays. Look at all these film stars—and even television stars!'

'My angel, there's nothing about *them* in *The Last Attachment*!' Her habit of translating the characters on the Byron scene into the setting of modern life irritated me because it so evidently gave them a dangerous reality for her. The train had started, and she made a little gesture signifying that the effort of contending with its noise was beyond her.

The glazed eyes of our travelling companions were fixed upon us. There we sat side by side, Jocasta beautiful, myself not unpresentable, a couple whom everyone must take for sweethearts, and instead of the conversation the onlookers would suppose we were having, about ourselves, our emotions, our future together, we were absorbed in a love affair of phantoms. I was on tenterhooks for the halt at Tottenham Court Road to see whether she would resume without my prompting, and she did.

'The great point is that she was nice, and that she loved him and he seemed to love her. He *was* in love with her—Oh, he was!

Those first letters were ardent . . . ardent!' The need of subduing her voice and crowding in all she wanted to say before the train went on lent a kind of force to her ineloquent speech. What he wrote in her book was romantic and touching somehow. And she did make an end of all that debauchery in Venice. We've got to admit it was debauchery however fond we may be of him.' Even in the Underground Railway, she was giving me an uneasy feeling of his imminence. I admit she stopped him from writing *Don Juan*, but only for a time, and if she'd never met him, he mightn't have lived to write it at all, racketing round in such bad company. He owed her everything. Yet he wasn't loyal to her. I can't tell you how it affected me.'

We were in the tunnel again. It was a good moment to use the actor's technique of throwing away a few lines. 'No, no, you re wrong. No matter how flippant he may have been about it to his worldly friends, he behaved very well to her.' She leaned closer and I shouted, 'He followed her about Italy even though he hated uprooting himself. He was good to her family.'

The reverberations rose to a crescendo, and I flung out several more points in his favour which I could count on her only hearing confusedly. I got what I wanted—the effect of being his advocate, for at Oxford Circus she said with a reproachful smile:

'There you are! Men always hang together against women. No, Quentin, I just can't take those letters. They were a betrayal.'

'Don't forget he'd been led to believe she was going to betray *him*—to parade her conquest and then jilt *him*.'

'How stupid of him to swallow that!'

I brightened. There really did seem to be a hope that he'd gone too far, and it cost me no effort worth speaking of to say magnanimously: 'After all, he'd had some rather unnerving experiences with women.'

'But Teresa wasn't a woman, only a girl in her teens—that's what makes it so cruel. She was four years younger than I am. Imagine being married at eighteen to a sinister old man! I can't think of anything nastier!'

We were *en route* again, and I waited for the lull at Bond Street before remarking as if I were amused: 'You're identifying yourself with Teresa.'

'You have to identify yourself with characters you read about to bring it all to life.'

'Do you also see yourself as Caroline Lamb and Claire Clairmont and the Draper's Wife and the Baker's Wife?'

'None of those, thank you. It has to be someone sympathetic to me, naturally. I mean, I've got to picture myself reacting more or less like that person in the same circumstances.'

I hadn't felt such a pang since the day I'd had her letter from Newstead Abbey.

'Not that I'm the same kind of girl as Teresa. I'm probably more straightforward, and I wouldn't be so long-suffering—no, not even for Byron. I simply can't understand how, when he was at the very beginning of his affair with her, he was making passes at other women. I was so depressed, I wanted to fling the book across the room.'

The anger that embittered me suddenly had the flavour of grief. She had begun by finding him 'fascinating', had gone on to play a little game—which wasn't quite a game—of flirting with his shadow, and now, in her fancy, she was his mistress. At Marble Arch I sat in silence, sustained only by the knowledge that, in my locked deed box there was my draft of the Memoirs with some two dozen pages still blank—pages over which I might spill out words of vitriol, words that would strip the last shred of glory from the idol, and leave it pitilessly exposed, defaced, defiled, an object of revulsion.

She turned towards me with a challenging smile: 'Well, defend him! You will, I'm sure.'

As a matter of policy that was what I ought to do—to maintain the long-familiar partiality that would be utterly irreconcilable with the authorship of the document I was about to bring to light. And as I wondered what I could write worse than I had already written, I did frame a defence; and not a bad one either.

'It was *because* he was so much in love with Teresa that he made those passes. She was a new kind of experience for *him*, and he wanted reassurance. Whenever he was off his guard, he showed that she was desperately important to him: when he was put on the defensive, then he bolstered himself up with ogling another woman or writing something cynical.'

'Is that how men behave?'

'It isn't the way *I* behave but then I'm not the conquering type.'

All the way to Lancaster Gate she was apparently turning over my theory in her mind. With a gesture I recognised as ill-timed even as I made it, I caught and tried to hold her hand. She gently pulled it away, and in a crisis of wrong-headedness, I made a snatch at it. She let me keep it then—the alternative would have been to give our neighbours the undignified spectacle of our mute wrangling—but her fingers lay in mine; limp and unloving. I couldn't repress my uneasiness, and like a fool I whispered while the train stood in the station:

'You didn't mean it, did you, when you said that about our marriage?'

'When I said what?'

'That getting married to me didn't seem real any more.'

'I'm not certain whether I meant it or not. Perhaps it was the champagne. That makes everything seem a little unreal.'

'Hasn't it worn off yet?'

'Yes, but you can't expect me to explain a mood. Anyhow it may have passed by the time we're able to get married.'

I might have replied—I wish I had!—that it was a mood that would only pass when she ceased to live vicariously in the orbit of a seducer. A moment of genuine candour would no doubt have brought this story to a different end. But it's automatic with me to avoid expressing my deepest sensibilities, and I did so now.

She didn't even wait till we slowed up for Queensway before going back to our other discussion, as if there'd been no hiatus: 'Quentin, I do believe you've got something!'

I pretended not to understand her. 'Got something! What?'

'About the affair with Teresa. It was in the first few months, when there was all that insecurity, that he had a sort of "thing" about being unfaithful. Once they settled down, he never seemed to look at anybody else. You ought to be a psychologist.'

'I ought,' I rejoined sardonically. If only I could be psychologist enough to strike the perfect note for disenchanting her! It was no simple task. Women have a natural tolerance of libertines, and in Jocasta there was beyond that the unusual measure of Christian charity engendered by her upbringing. I would have to be very artful indeed to contrive anything that would defeat the spirit of forgiveness in her; and as long as she could forgive, she could, I imagined, be attracted. Vices were not enough unless they were unpardonable.

Unpardonable . . . or else perhaps—I'd thought of this before—offensive in a ludicrous way! Something to evoke not indignation but ridicule. I determined to cast my line over a pool I'd hitherto left undisturbed.

'There's another theory,' I said as softly as I could while we gathered momentum on the way to Notting Hill Gate. 'Some people think all that pass-making, those spectacular conquests of women, were a cover for the fact that his real tendencies were quite otherwise.'

'Do you mean he was *queer*?'

'I don't say I believe it myself—'

'I should jolly well think not. I'd suspect you were queer if you did.'

I was stung into retorting as by an afterthought: 'Not that it's entirely without foundation, of course.'

She hesitated slightly. 'As to that, most men are liable to go in for some pretty odd behaviour when there aren't any women about. He must have had more temptation than most. . . .'

In the ordinary way I was always charmed to see her reasoning, as it were, with her good nature, and so I should have been now if she hadn't continued, undaunted by the increasing volume of noise: 'But as for being *really* queer, like some of the men *I* meet—anybody who could imagine that must be dotty.'

'What makes you so sure?'

'Oh my dear! Honestly! You can't fool a woman about a thing like that.'

'Darling, I doubt whether you're a connoisseur of the finer shades of queerness,'—I attempted to speak *sotto voce*, but my words were drowned in the din, and I ended in a louder tone—'especially in the case of a man you've never met.'

'Quentin, I do wish you could get rid of your hangover from doing that book on Beckford!' She brought her face close to mine, not in coquetry as our attentive fellow passengers must have fancied, but to hiss in my ear: 'Now he *was* queer. The difference between his style of writing and Byron's—you can feel it through and through. If Beckford were alive today, he'd be a very very chi-chi interior decorator.'

I was taking a risk to press the subject, but it was too telling to be relinquished and I rejoined dispassionately: 'I'm not classing Byron with Beckford but he did have a good many emotional relationships with his own sex.'

I glanced at her out of the corner of my eye, and she was frowning, but whether it was because of my persistence or her difficulty in holding her ground, I couldn't tell.

'He said his heart always alighted on the nearest perch. At Harrow and Cambridge and in the East, the nearest perches couldn't very well be women. When there were women about, it was *us* he always went for.'

Us! *Us!* I couldn't repress the cry that was wrung from me: 'Isn't that wishful thinking? Heaven knows why women always have this mania for men on the borderline of homosexuality!'

It was a cry indeed. I was blaring the protest across a perfect *fortissimo* of clatter in the tunnel when suddenly we emerged into the station and my last words rang out like a clarion.

Jocasta sprang to her feet saying distantly: 'This is where I change,' and the moment the doors opened, hurried down the platform as if she were running away from me.

'I'm sorry about that!' I laughed, catching up with her. 'Did it embarrass you dreadfully.'

She answered as if she hadn't heard me: 'I should get the next train back if I were you. I'll go on alone.'

'But, honey, I'm seeing you home.'

'There's no need. It's early still and you might get some more writing done.'

'You invited me. You said I could look in on your grandfather.'

'I know but I'd forgotten that you hadn't eaten yet, and they'll have finished dinner at home.'

'Are you cross with me?'

'No, I'm rather tired. That's why I'm not offering to cook something for you.'

I was about to assure her that I could postpone my dinner when the mild but unmistakable determination of her whole aspect convinced me that I should be wasting breath.

'Well, when shall I see you again?'

'I'm not sure yet what day I'm going to Rome. I'll telephone you.'

'Then you *are* going?'

'Yes, I meant to tell you but we've never stopped talking about your novel and then Byron.'

I didn't detain her long with questions, being at this moment as eager to speed her departure as she was to go. What had been lacking since my return from Wales was all too poignantly restored to me, the inspiration of a hot resentment. I could indeed get some more writing done tonight.

Chapter Ten

Jocasta's preparations for going abroad and her fortnight's absence neutralised what might have been an estrangement. She sent me postcards from Italy indicating that she was working and sight-seeing at top pressure. The curious terms on which we had parted were not the subject of any discussion between us, for our only meeting before her journey took place in front of three press photographers and a number of other people.

In the last days of October I finished the Memoirs, half of which, wrought to the highest level of verisimilitude within my power, were already transcribed into the antique book—a job I reserved for hours when I could no longer apply myself to the more exhausting toil of creation.

Calculating on the basis that each of the original large folio pages—seventy-two of them in all—would have contained about three hundred words, I had given my composition a total length of some twenty-two thousand. That was going to make a very short book—a fraction of what had been burned in John Murray's grate in 1824; but copious notes and an explanatory preface would give it substance, and the sensational nature of its revelations would compensate for what it lacked in bulk.

Not that it was sensational throughout. I'd been too subtle for that. In making my selection from all the material I'd prepared, I had weighed the probabilities again and again, and studied every available comment by those who'd read the genuine manuscript, comparing the reactions of Lord John Russell, in whose opinion the grossness and indelicacy were confined to a few pages, with those of Gifford who had said without qualification that it was fit only for a brothel; measuring the extreme disapprobation of Lord Rancliffe against the amiable tolerance of Kinnaird in a letter to Byron himself:

> I read with the greatest interest and pleasure your Memoir, at Paris. It is excellent. You curse and swear occasionally in the second part.

The upshot of all my siftings was that I decided to go cautiously with the bawdy element. Much of it must have been such as would seem no worse in our sight today than the improprieties of *Don Juan* which was then deemed a production of odious degradation. Greatly as it would have suited my humour to vilify my subject's character utterly, I kept firmly before me that to disgust Jocasta was only my secondary purpose. I must not fail to win the monetary reward of all my ingenuity and self-sacrifice. An obvious pandering to the taste for ribaldry and scandal might arouse suspicion. The true Byronic style is a perpetual shifting of lights and shadows. He would never have been able to keep up even the amusement of being shocking without relapses into gravity and sometimes morality, but when he *was* shocking, he went much further than any imitator would have dared.

Any imitator except myself. The restraint I exercised by observing, in my completed version, a certain patient decorum in passages where licence might have been expected, gave extraordinary vividness to those other passages where, sometimes wickedly, sometimes with an air of carelessness, I indulged in blasphemy or in recollections of depravity. Generally these recollections were comic and the more scurrilous for that, but occasionally I threw out hints, broad enough to be easily construed, of evils too fearful for light-heartedness.

It was among these darker glades of vice that I staged my final *pièce de resistance*. I have the saddest right to say it was a brilliant set piece. I devised it so that on the one hand it would give Jocasta's infatuation a blow it *could* not survive unless all her natural goodness had been tarnished, and on the other, must promote the widest possible circulation. Reviewers of the least literary papers would seize with avidity on so irresistible a morsel. Readers who never in the normal course opened a biographical work would be besieging their libraries for a story of sex and sin exalted by the name of a genius.

I hadn't after all made him specifically 'queer'. It was necessary to do more than reduce his heterosexual attractiveness. I must present him as morally repulsive. Besides, my disclosures had to be written in the first person, and it was more likely that Byron would have confessed to crimes than invited derision.

By a stroke of cleverness I still take a melancholy pride in, I used the episode, which has never found an adequate explanation, of the body in the sack at Athens. Byron's mysteriousness about this dramatic affair was consistent and sustained. It was the one secret he seems not to have divulged to anyone, and bearing in mind, as I was always obliged to do, that he allowed his reminiscences to be passed from hand to hand while he still lived, I was careful not to make, on his behalf, any explicit confession. But I invented diabolical variations on two themes that appear cryptically in the 1813 Journal:

I awoke from such a dream!—well! and have not others dreamed?—Such a dream!—but she did not overtake me. I wish the dead would rest, however. Ugh! how my blood chilled,—and I could not wake ... Am I to be shaken by shadows? Ay, when they remind us of—no matter—but, if I dream thus again, I will try whether *all* sleep has the like visions.

That was the first, wholly enigmatical. The second, referring openly to 'the Turkish girl's *aventure* at Athens', I linked up with the subject of the nightmare.

L. wondered I did not introduce the situation into *The Giaour*. He *may* wonder;—he might wonder more at that production's being written at all. But to describe the *feelings* of that situation were impossible—it is *icy* to recollect them.

The rumour Eastern travellers brought home was that he had rescued a Mahommedan slave girl from a seraglio who, sewn up in a sack, was about to be flung into the sea for having committed an act of infidelity—some said with him, some said with one of his servants. Lady Hester Stanhope had differed from others in describing the intended victim as a woman of the town. Whoever she was and whatever had happened, the emotions of horror and revulsion left in Byron were sufficient to keep him from disclosing a single factual detail, sufficient indeed to give his wife a lifelong suspicion that he had been implicated not in a rescue, but a murder.

In the nineteenth century, killing was regarded as less reprehensible on the whole than sexual deviation, and many who were deliciously thrilled by the belief that the attractive poet had committed dark deeds in the East, shunned him with genuine terror when told that he had made love to his half-sister. Jocasta wasn't in the least likely to share that outlook. Murder I thought rather far-fetched, however, and I decided that a cowardly connivance would be more despicable. Clothing my allusions in phrases which would have been obscure then but were easy of interpretation now, I suggested a corroding remorse—Byron being given to remorse—for what he had come to regard as the one entirely heinous deed of his life.

To make certain she would find it unforgivable, I carried my treason to its furthest limit, and, in another passage, disconnected from the first but providing in itself a transparent clue, I let fall that the Turkish girl—not saved but abandoned to a most miserable death—had been a child of thirteen.

The effect was altogether dreadful, yet so managed that, in an age which had accepted Trelawny, it might not have seemed as repellent as everyone would now find it. It is ironical to have to assess those devastating pages as the finest literary work I ever did or am ever likely to do as long as I live.

Not until I was revising the second half of the draft did I write to Earl Darrow, using very guarded language, and tell him that my journey to Wales had been fruitful. I had several excuses prepared as to why I'd let a month elapse before sending him the news, but I didn't make them in my letter because I judged that any tendency to offer explanations before I was asked for them might seem defensive, and my strong suit with him so far had been an absolute assumption that I was trusted. I was most careful, of course, not to touch even remotely on the negotiable value of my discovery, but I said that it comprised material that was new and important and capable of electrifying Byron scholars.

That Darrow would contrive to be in on this business somewhere seemed almost certain, and I hoped that by the time I'd had his answer, I should have nearly done the copying. Once having stated that the book was in my possession, I had a sense of emergency, and though I told myself again and again that I was irrational, the knowledge that I couldn't yet produce it for inspection woke me up two or three nights running with feelings not far removed from panic.

As it turned out there was some justification for my tremors. A few days after my air letter to Philadelphia had been posted, an envelope arrived from Italy containing a postcard of the Spanish Steps. Across the back of it Jocasta had written:

While I was being photographed here (cross marks the spot) an American came up and spoke to me, and said you'd introduced us. I didn't remember him. Name—Darrow. He's here to buy some books on Christopher Columbus. He asked me to tell you he's more or less on his way to England. I return Friday. I'll telephone you if possible. Love.

More or less on his way to England! For a moment I thought this was his reply to my letter. Then I realised he couldn't yet have received it. I asked myself in consternation what the 'more or less' stood for. I still had ten thousand words to copy into the book, and although that might be done in a few evenings writing at normal speed, this was work I had to take care about. Any unnoticed slip might be a give-away. The degree of legibility had to be nicely calculated, and what was even more essential, every paragraph finally passed as sound before being transmitted to the page. If I was not to hold Darrow off once he arrived, which was sure to be undesirable, there was nothing for it but to do a whole-time job. I rang up Rossiter's and said I had a touch of food poisoning.

I worked all day in my room on Wednesday and Thursday, on edge in case the door bell should ring, since it was just conceivable that he might have asked Jocasta for my private address. On Friday, though my task was still not quite done, I felt obliged to return to the shop, because I wanted to be near the telephone. She could only ring me up there, for I had no line in Lowestoft Street, and if she were told I was ill she might come calling on me.

Mrs. Rossiter hadn't been getting very good value for money lately, and she was out of temper. My junior being unreliable, she'd had to come and attend to the shop herself, and when I gave a moving circumstantial account of my illness, she merely advised me coldly to be more careful what I ate in future.

'I hope you've got it out of your system, Mr. Williams, so that I can be off. I've other things to do today.'

'Oh yes, I think I shall be all right now.' I spoke as if rallying my feeble strength, but she was not appeased.

'It wouldn't have done for us to give way when we were your age! I've seen Mr. Rossiter wheel out that barrow when he could scarcely trudge—that bad with sciatica he was.'

'I'm afraid he would have had to give way to food poisoning, Mrs. Rossiter.' I felt as if I'd really been suffering from it. 'Struggling with the symptoms in public might be rather indelicate.'

'Well, it's cost you something, I can tell you that,' she retorted so callously that I gathered she suspected me. 'I sold that run of *Ackmermann's Repository* for fifty pounds, and those *Monthly Museums* for twelve pounds. So there's your commission gone bang!'

Under my hand on the desk I saw that the purchases were invoiced to a woman who was essentially my own customer. 'That sale was really mine,' I said. 'I showed Miss Adamson those books weeks ago, and she's been in twice about them since.'

'It couldn't have been your sale, dear, when you weren't here. Fair's fair.'

I needed the money, and though my position was tricky, I was driven to protest: 'But she was on the verge of buying the Repositories last Monday!'

'Well, it was me that made up her mind for her. It's a pity for your sake you were ill, but there you are—that's fate!'

It wouldn't be edifying to the reader to expound in detail how this petty injustice led to my giving Mrs. Rossiter a broad hint that my days in her establishment were numbered. I shouldn't have done it, I suppose, if I hadn't had a pretty good certainty of fortune and independence in the offing. Even so, it was premature since several months would probably elapse before I could begin to cash in: but I was run down and touchy after my long spell of application to an exacting task, and the anecdotes of Mr. Rossiter and his barrow of books had been an accumulating irritation to me for a couple of years. Besides, I was hurt with her for seeing through my malingering the first time I'd ever resorted to it.

We were taking in the bargain trays before Jocasta rang up, and I wasn't too well pleased to learn that she'd come over in the same plane as Darrow. He had given her and another model, whom she'd been travelling with, a lift from the airport in a car he'd hired, and they were all at his hotel, Brown's, and he wanted me to go and have a drink with them.

I didn't doubt Jocasta when she said they'd met on the plane by coincidence, yet the way he'd been affected by his first sight of her, coming out of the shop with her moss rosebud hat, and his snatching at the thinnest thread of acquaintanceship in Rome, hadn't slipped my recollection. A more pressing annoyance, however, was my fear lest he should let fall something about the story of my manuscript—which he might, after all, expect my girl friend to have heard of.

Naturally, I'd been preparing a tale for Jocasta to explain my secretiveness, but, as I'd never envisaged any prospect of their paths converging, it was to be slightly different from the one I'd told Darrow. Not as to facts—I wasn't such a fool as that—but in the emphasis given to them. The version for Jocasta would be more casual, less dramatic, than the one that had begun as a hoax on an over-jaunty American. I would represent myself as having long been too incredulous about the identity of my find to take it very seriously. But if she and Darrow were going to be able to compare notes, something might emerge to shake her faith in me.

I may not have framed my apprehensions in terms so concrete as this: they were vague and unformulated, I dare say, at that instant, but I can remember well that I was quivering as I asked myself how to respond to their most unwelcome invitation. There was the other worry too—that all day I'd been determined, in what I now perceive to have been an almost insensate way, to get the last of my copying over tonight. Partly no doubt as the result of my exhaustion, I'd developed a neurotic anxiety to destroy my tell-tale draft and enfranchise myself, no matter how laboriously, from the solitary part of my conspiracy. If I went off to have drinks with this untimely party, I should have to take Jocasta home afterwards, and the evening—the evening that might set me free to enjoy her affection and companionship again—would be lost. No wonder I sounded confused and uneasy as I asked, having got the barest politenesses spoken, if I could have a word with Darrow.

She called him to the telephone and we exchanged greetings suggesting that we knew each other rather better than we did. There is a kind of cordiality that ripens faster between people who are apart than those who see each other often.

'You haven't had my letter? I wrote to you in Philadelphia.'

'No, I missed it. I had an unexpected assignment to Europe to attend the Spada sale for one of our collectors.'

'Nice work if you can get it!'

'The best! What's the news on your side?'

'I'll tell you when we meet.'

'Good enough! You can be round in ten or fifteen minutes.'

'I don't know,' I said unhappily. 'It's pretty awkward. I'm very much tied up.'

'You can't be too tied up to welcome these two gorgeous women home.'

'The other one's also gorgeous, is she?'

All the well-remembered percussive quality of his utterance was in his reply. 'She's right out of a Seedsman's Catalogue! Say, Williams, do you think you have the monopoly of beautiful girls?'

I was reassured. Jocasta in any case would be bound to go home to dinner on her first evening after being away. I could see her tomorrow with my burden lifted and a mind comparatively at rest.

'Are they with you now?'

'Certainly they're with me.'

'I mean—at the telephone?'

'What do you think this phone booth is? The ship's cabin in *A Night at the Opera*?'

'It's just that I want to say a word alone to you. That manuscript—it's still a total secret.'

'A secret from Jocasta? Pardon me, but after a flight over the Alps in bumpy weather, you get to call people by their first names.'

'A secret from everyone. There's a reason.'

'Still the same old mystery-monger. Well, I haven't spilt a single bean so far. Answer me one question! Did it turn out to be what you thought?'

'Not precisely, but still a terrific discovery. I'll get in touch with you.'

'You can't be induced to come over then?'

'I mustn't—positively. You'll hear from me tomorrow or the day after.'

'Don't linger over it! I ought by rights to be on my way home. Couldn't we make a date now? I'll buy you lunch tomorrow.'

I braced myself and took the plunge, arranging to meet him at Brown's. I should be able afterwards, it being a Saturday, to go out to Jocasta's.

But when she returned to the telephone and heard that I wouldn't be joining them at the hotel, she became—it was as understandable as it was unusual—grudging and evasive. I dared not use the novel as an excuse again, not if it had been a glorious masterpiece instead of the failure I was about to acknowledge; and I said that, having been away for two days through illness, there were things I was absolutely obliged to do for Mrs. Rossiter, and added in my most cajoling tone that she ought to sympathise with me, longing as I was to be with her.

Her soft heart relented when she heard of the illness, and she promised to see me after my appointment with Darrow.

'He seems like a nice person,' she said. 'What brings you together exactly? Is he a customer?'

'A kind of counsellor, darling. I'll tell you all about it when we meet.'

I had now committed myself to both of them, and although I was afflicted with spasms of fear that I would break a limb on the way home or suffer some other accident which would prevent my covering the vital last lap, I felt on the whole relieved. It was a close finish, but better perhaps than fumbling on pretending to devote myself to an insipid novel. I don't think I could have kept it up much longer.

* * * * *

'It's a pity it didn't turn out to be what I used to think it was,' I said to Darrow with my hand on the shabby leather cover of the book. 'There are some very amusing remarks about Lady Byron, but it's not the record of his married life by a long way. Anything but! Still, what it lacks in domestic detail it makes up in some quite enthralling disclosures about other matters.'

He'd evidently been reading up on the Memoirs since I'd last seen him, and had no difficulty in grasping my explanation as to the portion I was about to lay before him. When I admitted that Moore's Dr. Williams couldn't have been my ancestor and didn't in any case copy this later part of the text, he readily conceded that my mistake had been a natural one. It left me without a plausible conjecture as to how the volume had found its way to Penrhyndeudraeth, but he agreed—indeed himself pointed out—that it was impossible to trace the history of every object that turned up in a family lumber room. The one thing he seemed to boggle at was that I hadn't as yet consulted any expert as to the genuineness of the manuscript.

'If you mean the paper and all that,' I said firmly, 'I don't need to consult an expert. I handle books and paper every day of my life.'

'No, not only that. Not only the paper but what's written on it. I should have thought you'd ask the opinion of some Byron scholar.'

'I suppose I'll have to, sooner or later.' I was unfeignedly reluctant. Confident as I was of the flawlessness of my text, I felt I could afford to be. 'For the moment I'd rather not get involved with Byron scholars.'

You told me that before. It's got a kind of unrealistic flavour.'

'You think it's because I'm afraid of their verdict. You're as wrong as you can be, Darrow! I don't need Byron scholars to prove to me that this is the genuine thing. I've been doing quite a lot of research myself.' This was something he was going to find out sooner or later, and it was best to get in first and give my own angle to it. 'And with all due respect to anyone you may have in mind, as long as the copyright position's insecure, it would be distinctly risky to put it into circulation.'

'I should have thought you could safely consult the Murrays, or Peter Quennell for instance. He must have handled a lot of Byron documents.'

'You're not very grateful,' I said with my frankest laugh, 'for the privilege of being my chosen neutral observer.'

'On the contrary, I'm thrilled. All the same I don't somehow get it. You didn't even expect me to be here.'

'I shouldn't have waited indefinitely for you—I told you so in my letter. But since you're the first person I discussed it with and you *are* here, and you've worked in a very fine collection of manuscripts. . . . When you read it, you'll know why I'm shrinking from the Byron scholars. They're going to find this book a thunderbolt. Having to make up my mind what to do with it is a big responsibility.'

'In other words,' he said sceptically, 'it's just what people would expect Byron's Memoirs to be?'

'Not quite. The writing is brilliant—astoundingly witty and compressed and varied'—I was delighted to be able to represent the merits of my creation without false modesty—'but the whole effect is disillusioning in the worst, the very worst, way.'

'You gave me to understand before that it was *not* scandalous.'

'I know I did.' How thankful I was that I'd tenaciously retained so much of our earliest conversation. 'At least I said scandal wasn't the principal motive for the burning—and it wasn't. But unfortunately, it's there. Much more than I realised before I'd read it right through. You'll remember I told you I'd put it away without finishing it?'

'I certainly remember that!'

'It's funny about Byron. He has this tremendous personal effect on people. You get involved with him.' God knows I could say that much with the ring of truth. 'You either love or loathe him.' I made a telling pause, my eyes set frowningly on the book. 'If this were published, it would deal the last blow to his romantic reputation.'

'Byron's reputation has taken an awful lot of pastings. I wouldn't worry too darned much about it if I were you. It seems to pull through all right. Besides, no one can compel you to publish against your will.'

'Nevertheless, some pretty keen pressure might be brought to bear.'

'Assuming—always assuming—you haven't got hold of a forgery, that's not unlikely . . . if you can be tempted by money.'

'Who isn't? I have less of it than most people and I need it more. I'm engaged to Jocasta, you see, and I'd like to marry her.'

'Who wouldn't?' He parodied my tone. 'Not many men would let a little thing like a dead poet's romantic reputation stand in their way.'

I appeared to muse. 'She herself isn't going to like it much if I publish. I've never dared to let her see this book, never even told her about it yet. She'd insist on reading it.'

'Is it so deadly?'

'Read it yourself and judge.'

'I can't wait.'

I handed him my masterpiece. It should have been a portentous moment, but I was too much in the skin of my part to feel nervous any longer, and he was still being cagey.

'Take care of it! There's no copy.'

'No copy?'

I naturally couldn't explain that there hadn't been time to take one because I'd only put the finishing touches to the MS at one a.m. last night, so I answered, being prepared: 'There ought to be one, or more than one, but I didn't care to send it out to a typing-bureau, and I'm only a two-finger typist myself. I can get Photostats made under proper safeguards when it's been confirmed that it's not what you're afraid of, a Victorian forgery.'

He had pushed the coffee cups out of the way and, after most thoroughly rubbing his hands with his table napkin, was leafing through the pages.

'Why do you say *Victorian* forgery?'

'Because the manuscript must have come into my family's possession before the twentieth century. My great-aunt's sure of that too and her memory goes back a long way. It's been lying there among the junk for at least a couple of generations.'

'Were there no forgeries of Byron's Memoirs before Victoria?' he asked, holding up the paper to the light.

'Nothing that would convince anyone nowadays, because there wasn't any full-scale biography to draw the facts from until Moore's *Life* came out in 1829 and 1830, and not enough of his intimate prose writing known to base the style on. Early forgeries are extremely naïve.'

'You've got it all tied up.' He glanced at me rather sharply.

'I've gone into it thoroughly.' I was eager and innocent. 'I delayed writing to you till I'd checked over all sorts of things.'

'Kind of self-controlled, aren't you?' He wasn't yielding to me yet, though he remarked presently: 'The paper's all right. The handwriting looks authentic. Very odd, though, that it's in pencil throughout.'

'Isn't it?' I would let him work out the why-and-wherefore of that himself.

He read a page or two, bringing a magnifying glass from his pocket for the words I'd so carefully left in a semi-legible state. His eyebrows went up. I could guess that he had come upon one of my more nefarious *scherzi*, and I didn't interrupt his perusal though it was leisurely.

'There'll have to be an expurgated edition for young ladies,' he said with a slight shake of the head. He was caught by something on another page. 'Possibly for young gentlemen too.'

'You see! You can't help thinking of it as a publication.'

He read on for several minutes, amused, absorbed, before responding: 'You've fixed yourself a hell of a problem, Williams, if you plan to keep this out of print.'

That was perhaps the highest moment of elation my beautiful piece of workmanship yielded me. Darrow's face expressed sheer unguarded enjoyment. Already he had surrendered. He believed.

'I'll leave you to it,' I said.

'You'll trust me with it?'

'You're the first person I have trusted. I may seem over-cautious, but you must admit photography has made it hazardous to pass round documents.'

I promise I've no microfilm up my sleeve. How long can I have with this?'

'I could pick it up tomorrow some time as long as you don't let it out of your sight.'

'You can have it back tonight if you're nervous.'

'I shan't want it. I'm going to spend the day at Jocasta's.' I recalled afresh that my four months exile from her was ended and was filled with a happy impatience. 'I'd better be on my way. She lives on the outskirts of London.'

'I know. I was there yesterday evening. I ought to have told you.'

He had a knack of springing these disconcerting pieces of information upon one in the most casual fashion. I was reduced to a silence that must have been vibrant with my resentment, for he hurried on apologetically: 'She had two or three pieces of baggage, and since you couldn't take her home, I tendered my services instead.'

If he'd been about to buy my manuscript outright for the highest price I'd ever placed on it, I couldn't have refrained from showing my displeasure. 'I thought it was the other girl you found so gorgeous!'

'Now, now, Williams!' Boldly he smiled his disarming, youthful smile. 'They're both gorgeous, and I saw them both home. I naturally dropped your girl last as she lives much further out than her friend. She invited me in—I'd every intention of telling you but we've been up to the neck in these Memoirs—she invited me in to meet the old people. What a lovely couple they are!'

I waited balefully for him to say they'd pressed him to stay for dinner, and he did. Even his insouciance couldn't withstand my annoyance, and he tried to placate me. 'They were very much disappointed not to have you there. Jocasta was busy unpacking and helping the old lady and so forth, and I spent an hour or so in Mr. Leverett's study. It's quite a privilege to meet such a fine old scholar. I hope you won't think I was homing in on your territory, but I wanted to persuade him to sell me some of his classical texts. I have a customer for them.'

I pulled myself together, suddenly feeling rather foolish. 'It's no use pretending he doesn't need the money, but I don't think he'll part with them. If you can induce him to, you're welcome as far as I'm concerned. I've practically no market for any Greek or Latin book short of a Baskerville.'

'Well, to come clean, he does have Baskervilles—a few.'

'Really? That room is so infinitely familiar to me, I suppose I've never noticed anything in it.'

'That's the way it is, sometimes, with a place one takes for granted. The Reverend told me you'd been a pupil of his. My, aren't they crazy on Byron, that family! As to that they seem to be pupils of yours.'

'Ah, now you can see why I'm a trifle sensitive about letting loose these Memoirs on the world.' I rose from the table feeling subtle, I acknowledge, and dexterous. 'I dare say I did set them going, Jocasta especially. I wish I hadn't now.'

'You surely are the worrying type,' he declared genially. 'I have a hunch his Lordship will survive anything you do to him.'

For the fraction of a second my self-possession was shaken and I faltered: 'How do you mean?'

'Publish or not, it won't make a cent's worth of difference after the first delicious shudders in the press. He's the established *enfant terrible* of English literature, with the right by now to confess to any moral lapses he pleases. Others abide our question, he is free to do as he likes.'

'Better read right through, Darrow, before you put money on that!'

I took my leave with a sense of well-being. The precious manuscript had clearly made a most satisfactory first impression, and I had little fear that the outcome of further inspection would prove unfavourable. I hadn't said a single word that could be quoted as evidence of an attempt to get money. Neither, on the other hand, had I overplayed my reluctance to publish and be paid. I'd been easy, natural, and completely inside the character I was assuming—that of a slightly quixotic but by no means unpractical enthusiast.

It was going to be somewhat more difficult no doubt to achieve the right key for Jocasta who was so much better acquainted with me, but I'd worked out a tale that was credible, and as to bare facts not inconsistent with the one I'd told Darrow. I didn't intend, however, to do more this afternoon than convey the news of my decision to scrap the novel, and bask in the admiration she would accord to one who could make so immense a sacrifice to literary integrity.

But I wasn't destined to play that scene today. I was taking my overcoat when it came into my head that the Mr. Williams whose name I'd heard called several times by a pageboy might conceivably be me. Jocasta, who'd been aware, of course, that I was lunching with Darrow, had rung up his hotel in the hope of catching me before I left. A celebrated model who was to have appeared tonight in a television programme had succumbed to influenza, and Jocasta had been implored to take her place. It would mean going at once to the studio, and the rest of the day would be spent in rehearsals and the various preparations.

I was so intensely disappointed at having to agree to cancel our appointment that I hadn't even the presence of mind to ask her to meet me after the performance.

Chapter Eleven

Mr. MURRAY
No. 50

STANDING before the big brass door plate worn by innumerable polishings, I asked myself, as visitors to that house must have been doing every day for generations past, whether it was the same doorplate that Byron had gazed at while he waited for admission on that threshold. Over it he had crossed for the last time a hundred and forty years ago, a ruined man, his enemies in triumph, his friends in despair, himself suffering everything a proud man can suffer, yet aware as neither friends nor enemies could be that he had a power to extract from his misery a rarer essence than he had yet been able to distil.

Now that I was avenged I could think of him without animosity. Jocasta had the Memoirs, and I couldn't doubt from her reaction to three or four pages she'd read in my presence that they would have all the effect that I'd patiently wrought for. I had watched her very body recoil, and though she had cried: 'I don't want to go on!' I knew she would force herself to read every syllable.

'Mr. Murray.' So here I was at last on the verge of tasting the fruits of all my self-discipline, my daring, and my skill. The appointment had been arranged by Darrow who was, in his own phrase, completely sold on the document, which he acknowledged over and over again to be sensational.

He had begged me to let him telephone across the Atlantic to Mr. Nimmo Peascod, so that he might be sure of resources to make his bid if I were prevailed upon to part with my treasure and after a show of reluctance I'd lifted the embargo of confidence so far as that millionaire was concerned. Within twenty-four hours a sanction on what I could guess was the handsomest scale had been cabled; but with a reminder that the guarantee of authenticity must be beyond dispute.

Still maintaining that I didn't want to be stampeded into any decision, I'd given Darrow permission to take the book to John Murray's. The inspection had been brief because by this time I'd told Jocasta my story, and I had to have the MS back so that she might read it before it left my hands (as I secretly anticipated) for the last time. I didn't suppose any expert would pronounce judgment without intensive scrutiny and the invitation conveyed by Darrow to bring the script in person for further appraisal the very day after it had first been examined went every inch as far as I'd dared to count on.

When I was asked in a letter brought by a messenger, whether I would object to the presence of Sir Harold Nicolson and Mr. Peter Quennell, I became nervous, of course, but no more than was rather stimulating—no more indeed than I might have felt if my beautiful creation had been the real thing. There might also, if I was willing, be a Mrs. Langley Moore, whom I'd heard of vaguely in connection with some interminable piece of research ('It would be a pity to leave her out,' said the note, 'since she has nearly finished two extensive papers on the Memoirs'), and Professor E.M. Butler, whose book on *Byron and Goethe* was hot from the press.

The hour fixed was 'about closing time'. Members of the staff were still coming out, buttoning their coats as they glanced up at the dark sky. One of them, a tallish brunette whom I could remember meeting on a previous visit, when I'd come to see some letters, noticed me and spoke:

'You're Mr. Williams, aren't you?'

'Yes, I've got an appointment with Sir John Murray.'

'I'm not sure if Sir John's about, but I know *Mr.* Murray's expecting you.' She turned back to escort me into the hall, and gave my name to another girl who was just emerging from a kind of glass cage with a switchboard.

Though I'd only been there once or twice before, my eye had registered things which instantly presented themselves for what seemed familiar recognition: the life-size profile in deep relief protected by glass in a Victorian style—the profile of Byron, gilded, gleaming, smugly noble, portrayed by an artist who perhaps had never seen him: and on a pedestal in an angle of the staircase the Thorwaldsen bust, the work of an artist who had seen him and seen him keenly . . . the vein of hardness in him, the painful turbulence, and, very much in evidence, the capacity, noted by Hobhouse, to put people who took liberties in their place. As I passed it on my way up, the fading daylight from the window behind gave the image a baleful expression. Over my shoulder I cast a look that was at once victorious and apologetic. I didn't tempt providence by whispering 'Quits!' That was a pleasure I could safely postpone till I came down.

On the stairs, on the landing, and in the room between the sanctuaries of Sir John and his nephew, there were memorials of bygone Murray authors; and, scattered on a table below the prints and paintings, books newly published, in bright smart jackets. I wondered with a tremor of excitement whether mine was destined to be among them. As to that, although I wasn't prepared to forgo the advantage of a competitive market, I felt it would set the hallmark on my gift of literary disguise if my book were to be issued with this house's imprimatur.

They might very well fight shy of it. The grosser and more sinister passages wouldn't be acceptable in this quarter, but on the whole I fancied that joy at retrieving even a portion of the lost prize would outweigh the distress of learning that it fulfilled the worst forebodings of those who had sponsored the famous act of destruction.

The publishing rights would inevitably be part of the property, and whoever was to bring the book out, I resolved afresh not to be tempted by any sum Darrow might offer to renounce my claim to some form of royalty. It might be linked up with my having the editorship of the work . . . though possibly the knowledge needed for that was more than I ought to admit to. There were certainly going to be problems, but none of them such as I believed myself unequal to coping with, having already coped with so many.

I could hear voices in the room on my left, and John Grey Murray came out accompanied by Peter Quennell. I'd met them both before, but so distantly that neither of them referred to the fact. I deemed it politic to do so myself lest it should be remembered later; and as we shook hands, I spoke of the occasions in my easiest manner. 'I was trying to find out things about Byron,' I added without enlargement, and I saw no sign that the disarming admission had awakened any misgiving.

'Well, I must say all this is very exhilarating!' Quennell's smile was both congratulatory and expectant. His eyes dropped to my empty hands and then to the table by which I was standing. 'I trust we're going to see the manuscript.'

'It'll be here at any minute. My fiancée was longing to have a glimpse of this house, so I had to agree to let her bring it. I hope that's all right with you and Sir John?'

'I must make Sir John's excuses,' said the younger Murray urbanely. 'He has decided'—he paused and I felt my first qualm, which he didn't allay by going on with a certain soft emphasis—'decided not to be present. Judging by what we saw yesterday, there may be elements of—of embarrassment for us.'

For an instant my heart contracted, then I understood he was alluding not to the possibility of spuriousness, but to the Murray tradition of defending Byron's reputation.

'Of course, we merely dipped into it. The whole may redeem the parts, but Sir John considered that at this stage'—he paused again blandly weighing his words—'he wouldn't take part in our conference. Where's Darrow? Didn't he come with you?'

'No, he's to meet me here. I'm rather early, aren't I?'

'Who's Darrow?' asked Peter Quennell.

'A young man who used to look after the Peascod Library in Philadelphia and now runs a bookshop there, and has dealings in manuscripts. He makes it clear that if Mr. Williams's find is genuine he wants to acquire it.'

I wasn't troubled by the 'if' because I regarded it as a formality. In fact, I was confident enough to exclaim ingenuously: 'What a sell for me if it shouldn't be genuine!'

'It's a pity,' said Quennell, 'it isn't in Byron's handwriting. Is it amusing, Jock?'

'Amusing—yes, very much so, as far as we've seen . . . Oh, here's Mrs. Moore!'

As Mrs. Moore's entrance was almost immediately followed by that of Darrow with Jocasta, I didn't notice her much. I only recall that she was elderly but animated, and eager but harassed-looking. At first I supposed that she was harassed-looking because her 'two extensive papers on the Memoirs' would now be obsolete before they were published, but as she remarked vigorously that she was in the highest hope since, if the script was not a forgery, it was certain to afford triumphant proof of her own theories, I came to the conclusion that the air of anxiety was probably habitual.

The slight irritation I couldn't but feel on observing that Jocasta and Darrow had come in together was cancelled out, more or less, by my consciousness of the prestige it must give me to have so lovely a creature for my girl friend, and I made the introduction with a nonchalance that was ineffectual, I imagine, in concealing my pride. Jocasta, however, was not at her best. She hardly smiled, and when I jocularly taxed her with having left the Memoirs at home, indicated her mannequin's handbag in a dejected silence. I took it as symbolic that the miniature was not in its customary place on the lapel of her jacket.

The reading had inevitably been a profoundly disturbing experience, but though the fulfilment of my intention was gratifying, I didn't want her to cast her gloom over the rest of the party, and as it seemed to be accepted that my volume was not to be examined until everyone had arrived, I asked our host by way of diversion if she might be allowed to go into the Byron room.

'By all means, but how about a drink first? What will everybody have? You, Mrs. Moore?'

'Thank you, I think I ought to keep my head in a state of clarity. It'll be all the more enjoyable to celebrate afterwards.'

Jocasta, who seldom indulged in anything stronger than tomato juice, also refused, and while I was hesitating between gin and Dubonnet and a Tio Pepe, she sidled away and appeared to become diligently engrossed in the numerous paintings on the walls, but I divined by the very fixity of her gaze that her attention was not upon them. I wanted to speak to her, but Mrs. Langley Moore was questioning me.

'Tell me, Mr. Williams—I only had a snippet of information on the telephone from Mr. Murray—how did you come by this miraculous acquisition? You aren't by any chance descended from the Williams who copied the Memoirs for Moore in Paris?'

'Not by *any chance*!' It was one of Darrow's miniature explosions breaking into my ear. 'He once fancied he was, but only because he had no other way of accounting for his family having this thing in their possession.'

'It was confusing, you must admit. There *is* a Dr. Williams among my ancestors.'

'But nary an Irish one!' Darrow was bouncier and jauntier than I'd ever seen him, which is saying a good deal. He was also disposed to assume a proprietory style with me, but I didn't mind that because it was a symptom of his avidity to gain possession of what I possessed. 'Irish or Welsh or Chinese, it wasn't of the slightest consequence, because Dr. Williams had finished his bit of copying before the very enthralling portion we're going to show you was written.'

'So it's the second part. Well, that's twenty times better than nothing, but I could wish it had been the first. One would like to hear Byron's side of the matrimonial story. Not that I have the least inclination to look your gift-horse in the mouth, Mr. Williams . . .'

'His gift horse!' Darrow volleyed the phrase back at her as if he'd been waiting for it. 'I doubt very much, Mrs. Moore, if this is going to be a gift-horse. Williams has quite a keen idea of its value and some very good uses for dollars.'

'Dollars?' She slightly frowned.

'You must pardon my American forthrightness about money. It's the result of having to work fast. I must get back to the States any day now, and if Williams has any last scruples, it's my business to beat them down.'

To my relief she turned aside to greet Sir Harold Nicolson. Darrow was really overplaying the role of alert irrepressible young dealer, and his importunity had a touch of brashness about it which, to do him justice, was out of character.

'*Have* you any last scruples?' He sprang the words straight at me in his jack-in-the-box manner.

'A few, but none that you or some other bidder won't overcome, I dare say. I have, as you've mentioned, very good uses for money.'

'How much?'

The resuscitation of a large and immensely quotable fragment of Byron's autobiography would be front-page news in every literary paper in the world—that was a fact that had never escaped me—and I could guess what it might be worth in publicity to a newly-established firm like Darrow's to have staked a claim to it; but his urgency seemed to have a strain almost of hysteria. He was simply asking me to take advantage of him. I resolved not to go beyond the terms I'd already settled upon in my mind, for whatever temptation he offered, I meant to deal very fairly by him.

'I should want a sum for the manuscript and an agreement to share the proceeds of the copyright.'

'You would?' He became absolutely gleeful. 'A share in the copyright! Now that's an idea we must discuss with Murray. Wait till he's stopped handing out these drinks and we'll put it up to him.'

'No, no! This is a literary party, not a business conference.' My protest was sincere, for agreeable as it was going to be to get down to business, I desired first to savour my literary triumph in all its purity. It was as an artist that I responded to the thrill of this occasion, an actor about to play to the perfect audience. Here in the house of Murray, surrounded by Byron scholars, my little masterpiece was to be submitted to the supreme test. It was nerve-racking but it was glorious too, and I longed for the last guest, Professor Butler, to arrive so that the chatter over drinks might be suspended while I, under the mask of Byron, took the stage.

How much Leslie Marchand, C. L. Cline, Willis Pratt, were going to regret their absence in America at such an hour! Iris Origo and Vera Cacciatore in Italy, Andre Maurois in France—I was genuinely regretful for them, missing what would go down to posterity as a brilliantly memorable event.

Darrow wasn't able to persist in his exhibition of transatlantic hustle because everyone had questions to ask, particularly Sir Harold Nicolson who combined a great deal of charm with a great deal of curiosity, and might have undermined me if I hadn't lived my story detail by detail a hundred times over during the months that had passed since I'd committed myself to it. I was now quite unshakable as to how I'd come upon the book in my great-aunt's attic, how I'd read some of it under the impression that it was fiction, and then knowing little of Byron, concluded that it was an early copy of published writings; how later on, becoming interested, I'd searched in vain in printed texts for passages I vividly remembered and had begun to sift the evidence about the burned Memoirs; how I'd followed the trail of Dr. Williams which had proved false but hadn't misled me in essentials, and what various circumstances had delayed my producing the copy till now. Among these—it was a little extra twist I'd contrived, imposed on me by Jocasta's familiarity with my card index and the knowledge a few other people must have of my preparations for a work on Byron—I instanced in a deprecating way a notion I'd harboured for a while of launching the new material in some sort of biographical piece of my own; thus putting up my not very glittering stock.

I must say I'd been apprehensive about pulling this particular line in front of Jocasta, whom I preferred to be alone with when it was necessary to talk her into believing something doubtful, and if she'd been present my style would have been cramped. But fortunately, during the catechism I had to answer as we stood around with our glasses, Peter Quennell took her into the drawing-room, now called the Byron room; and though in the ordinary way, I shouldn't have been much pleased about that, it gave me the opportunity of playing down the full extent of my Byron studies and dismissing my unwritten book with the very lightest touch.

I was glad I'd acknowledged myself to be an author before Darrow, who was at my elbow prompting me and drawing me out as if he were my impresario, could get in first with it.

'How come you hid your light under a bushel, Williams? It took me a long time to find out you'd written books, and in your case it's certainly nothing to be ashamed of.'

'I'm afraid my publisher's accountant wouldn't agree with you,' I said modestly. 'Naturally I've had a hankering to be concerned somehow or other in the publication of these Memoirs. . . .'

At last, with an apology for not having secured a taxi in time, Professor Butler appeared. From reading this author's works, I had conceived the mental picture of a tall, robust, middle-aged man with—I can't recall what chance phrase, what glancing allusion, had conjured it up—a big black moustache; and when a small lady with white hair put her head diffidently round the door, it took me a few seconds to adjust myself to the demolition at one stroke of the figure I'd been waiting for. There were more introductions, then Miss Butler eagerly demanded, as everyone else had done, where the manuscript was.

I proposed to fetch it immediately (it would give me an excuse for breaking up the *tête-à-tête* in the next room) but Sir Harold intervened: 'Oh, surely the phoenix should arise from the nest where it was consumed? Don't you think so, Jock?'

'That's what I'd planned. Just let me give Miss Butler her sherry! I've even had a fire lighted. We usually have an electric one.'

He vanished briefly into his own room where the tray was prepared, and Mrs. Moore called after him: 'Is it guaranteed to be the same grate where the original was burned?'

'Positively. The same grate but we still have to establish that it's the same phoenix.'

'Oh!' said Miss Butler, taking the glass of sherry from him. 'Do you mean it may be a forgery?'

'Forgery!' cried Darrow. 'Ah, you haven't heard Williams's story or you'd know it couldn't be.'

'Yet one is half inclined to hope it is.' Murray's slow and quiet stress was as effective in its way as Darrow's percussiveness. 'It explains my ancestor's gesture, which we've always until now regretted.'

'Will it turn us against Byron?' Miss Butler's smile wavered between anxiety and incredulity.

'Williams has been worrying about that,' said Darrow. 'He had a certain squeamishness on the subject, but I guess he's conquered it.'

'Is it so discreditable?' Quennell, who had apparently been keeping an ear open for our conversation, spoke from the doorway of the drawing-room. Beyond him I had a glimpse of Jocasta standing in front of the hearth, gazing at the portrait of the tutelary deity of the house, and I could divine from her whole attitude that her expression was one of poignant disillusionment.

His beauty would no longer have any power to move her. The face to dream about would never again grace any dream of hers. She seemed to be searching it for some explanation of the air of nobility which had so obviously impressed the painter and which would henceforth be known for a contemptible sham.

I had an impulse to go to her, to soothe in some fashion the wound I had inflicted, but I couldn't risk missing anything that was being said at a moment when the stage was set for the crucial scene. Until now I'd been glad of the speed with which this little ceremony had been arranged, because I wanted to be committed to my bargain, even on terms that couldn't yet be settled with precision, before she began trying to dissuade me from letting the abominable pages see the light. Though she might cease to feel anything resembling attraction towards their supposed creator, she would assuredly want to protect him from these disclosures. Thanks to Darrow's eagerness to learn the verdict of experts before his return to Philadelphia, there had been no time for me to meet her alone after she'd finished reading the work, which I'd handed her only the previous evening; and I'd regarded that as something to be grateful for. There would be discordant music to face afterwards, but this nevertheless was an occasion for *the fait accompli*. Even Jocasta, with all her high Christian ethic, might be appeased by my emergence from poverty to prosperity: she wasn't in the least indifferent to the things money could buy.

I had welcomed the suggestion that she should bring the script to Albemarle Street, partly because her manifest probity would be a support for me, and partly because the eminent respectability of Sir John Murray and his nephew, and their house with all its associations, couldn't fail to banish any doubt that might arise in her as to my own *bona fides*. Not that she'd so far shown a sign of one, for I'd put my narrative over most convincingly—I was nerved up to it—but should some faint mistrust be latent, it would be dispelled by her being 'in on it' with me here, where she might fancy I'd never dare venture unless my credentials were flawless.

At any rate, these were the motives I consciously offered myself. Much more, I dare say, I was influenced by my simple desire to be with Jocasta again, not to hold her at arm's length, not to shuffle her off with excuses any more, but to bask in her radiance, to share my most vital experiences with her.

It was yesterday that she'd hesitantly advanced her plea to see the house so often visited by Byron, yesterday just before she'd opened the book that was to be her pretext. With my victory in sight, I'd been prompt to yield. Perhaps there was even a touch of bravado in my readiness: and bent on my own objects, I was callous to what she would be undergoing. I should have spared her the ordeal of coming into the midst of strangers while she was still shaken by the evil aspect of my Caravaggio portrait. Yet to be fair to myself, I hadn't expected, when we made the appointment, that the strangers would be so numerous nor that the gathering would so much resemble a party. I was glad she had an evening engagement which must prevent her from staying to see how my composition would be received.

'It's no worse than Boswell's London Journal,' Darrow was saying, and I was obliged to switch my attention away from her to keep the thread of the conversation.

'That doesn't exactly raise Boswell in our esteem.' I don't remember who made that protest, nor who answered swiftly:

'He didn't write it to raise himself in our esteem. Isn't that the whole beauty of it?'

'But we have quite different standards of values for Byron and Boswell. What seems laughable in one would be shocking in the other.'

'Does it matter? After all, he wrote for publication,' said someone else, 'and presumably he didn't mind if posterity saw him as a disreputable figure.'

'But he wasn't a disreputable figure. If that's how he appears the picture must be false.'

'I quite agree. We all know his habit of blackening himself.'

'That could be dealt with in the introduction,' said Peter Quennell who had rejoined the group. 'If it's handled sympathetically—'

Darrow interrupted: 'You Byron enthusiasts always go on as if the man had died last week. He's been in his grave since eighteen-twenty-four, hasn't he? Who can be hurt if the censorship's lifted at last? Here's Williams who told me he was holding back this thing because he didn't want to damage Byron's "romantic reputation". What's it all about? Why? What does he owe to Byron?'

I can't attempt to explain why these words should have affected me as they did. After all, what *did* I owe to Byron? But suddenly all my elation ebbed out of me, sucked down, it seemed, like water flowing over quicksand. For the first time in weeks there came upon me the clear, clean memory of my self-frustrated ambition and the sense of what I d missed and missed for ever—the pride, the gusto of defending a man whom I had loved. From my boyhood I'd delighted in him both as a poet and a creature of high mettle; and for years, while I'd been laying in my biographical store, I'd cherished the belief that my skill would set his captivating qualities in a finer light than had ever yet been shed on them, and that I should break a lance too against enemies of his who still survived, humbugs, pedants, hypocrites. And how strangely, fantastically different was the thing I had done! I under the mask of Byron . . . leering, smirking, odious. . . .

What was said next I don't remember in detail. I'd accepted a second gin and Dubonnet, and I swallowed it rapidly desiring nothing better than to dull the edge of sensations now so little likely to be pleasurable. The others, with the determined politeness that covers a certain increasing lack of harmony, were continuing the discussion of the rights and wrongs of publishing revelations as destructive as Darrow implied these were. I recall Sir Harold Nicolson's challenge:

'At this rate you'll be for burning them all over again. Let's hope somebody's got two thousand guineas handy to compensate the owner.'

'At least this time we'll have the sense to read them first.' I believe this was Miss Butler. 'Can't we begin?'

'If you'd like to leave your glasses here . . .' said Murray and threw open the door of the Byron room.

It didn't on that instant have any particular significance for me that the door a few minutes before had not been closed. I was preoccupied with wishing very earnestly that I'd got my 'nerves' and my remorse over beforehand instead of being afflicted with a fit of trembling now. The two ladies went in first and I think Quennell followed and then myself.

Jocasta was standing by the marble chimney-piece. I cannot say that she was pale because she was wearing make-up nor that she was distraught because her clothes and person conveyed no hint of that, but she had a look of tenseness which must have drawn all eyes to her before they fell on the object blazing in the fire.

On the hearth lay the leather cover of the old exercise book entirely despoiled of its leaves. In the grate burning with ferocious brightness was the sheaf of pages which had drained all my talent, all my fortitude, all my powers of application during fifteen weeks I had thought I should scarcely live through. Her bag stood open at her feet, and in her hand she held a little bottle I'd seen her use when she was changing her nail varnish. The spirit lent such hungry ardour to the flames that they had already more than half devoured their morsel, and when Murray sprang forward and tried to pull out what was left with tongs, there were only charred and broken wafers to be rescued.

Addressing not me but him, Jocasta let her portentous words fall: 'I'm sorry. I burned it. It was not fit—not fit to publish.'

To this day I can't recollect what I said to her then—something, I suppose, about her having gone out of her mind, ruined me, ruined everything. She turned her face from me, but as she bent to pick up her bag, I saw a little rain of tears splash down on it.

The room was full of disappointment, consternation, anger, but it found vent only in the deeply embarrassed murmurs of those who are inhibited from discussing a crime in the presence of the criminal. Mrs. Moore's voice said with ill-feigned lightness: 'Another Byron drama! How he does conjure them up!'

'You don't know how right you are!' It was a *cri de coeur*. I wanted to tell everyone, here in this room haunted by his presence, what a fool he had made of her, what a fool he had made of me. Her tears wouldn't have stopped me. On the contrary, they provoked, they tortured me.

I can't conjecture what the scene would have turned into if Darrow hadn't ended it by announcing, not emphatically for once but in his rarer throwaway style: 'The comedy is finished. I apologise for having been the cause of wasting everybody's valuable time. If it's any consolation, I've wasted a good deal of my own.'

With that he took Jocasta by the elbow, whisked up a coat she'd left lying across the arm of a chair, and steered her unceremoniously to the door. They were at least half-way downstairs before I realised that I must follow them. I mumbled something—some confused extension of Darrow's apology, some admission of my folly in having provided no copy, and sidled out releasing no doubt the flood of question and comment which good manners had dammed up.

The light on the half-landing now struck the marble bust at a different angle, and the face appeared to be faintly and reflectively smiling. For all my urgent desire to overtake Jocasta and Darrow, on whom the front door had already closed, I was compelled to pause at the bottom of the stairs and direct one upward glance to the features that had wrought havoc in so many lives and most appallingly in mine.

Yes, whatever shadow had created the look of balefulness was gone, and even seen from below there was the glint of a smile about the lips, while the eyes, turned thoughtfully, poetically heavenwards, imparted something to the expression that was almost seraphic. Seraphic, yet with the conscious, gently mocking good nature of a man who has refrained from saying 'Quits!'

I flung myself despairingly out of the house.

Chapter Twelve

What I'd intended to do or say to Jocasta I hadn't any coherent idea of then, and have still less now. There was no opportunity of acting on whatever impulse may have possessed me because, as I came out of the house, Darrow was handing her into a taxi where Albemarle Street joins Piccadilly, and though

I called after it and broke into a run, the driver started instantly and had the lights with him.

I turned to Darrow and asked him where she'd gone. I was a little mollified by his not having accompanied her—for, notwithstanding the unmerciful blow she'd dealt me, I didn't even in that dismal crisis pretend to myself that my future relations with her were other than of infinite importance to me.

'She has to do some modelling somewhere,' he said shortly.

'Of course. I'd forgotten. Can you wonder after such a ghastly debacle? God, why did I trust her with that book?'

'Kind of reckless, weren't you? Especially seeing you had a hunch she wasn't going to care about it much.'

The sarcasm in his tone was a reminder of his own discomfiture, and I pulled myself together to conciliate him. 'I'm as much upset for your sake, Darrow, as mine. When I think of the trouble you were taking, the cables, the telephone calls to America—'

'Just what was running through my mind too!' He stared at me wryly. 'I nearly bought it, didn't I?'

'Bought it?'

'Acquired it. Nearly went back to the States with the whole thing tied up.'

'I realised it would shock her,' I groaned, 'but how could I guess she'd do anything as desperate as that?'

'How could you? What had you done to deserve it?'

Again I had the impression that he was a shade hysterical. His hands were clenched, his utterance like his movement seemed inconsequential. No one could feel more for him than I did, with my expert knowledge of what he'd missed, and since it was impossible after such a catastrophe to settle down to an evening of solitary woe, I invited him to come and have a drink with me. I would have proposed dinner but I hadn't the money to pay for it.

'I don't want to drink with you, Williams, but we're almost on the doorstep of my hotel, and I do have a few last words to get off my chest.'

It was an ungracious answer. I put it down to his distracted state, and seeing the Albemarle Street entrance to Brown's was a stone's throw from where we were standing, I went with him readily enough. He led me into the emptiest corner of one of the public rooms, where, having waved away—somewhat inhospitably, I thought—a waiter who approached us, he turned and looked me up and down in a very strange manner.

'That girl is a damn sight too good for you.' The remark, uttered with a meditative air, was impertinent, but I assumed it related, and doubtless ironically, to the high degree of moral sensibility Jocasta had so ruinously displayed.

'I know it. Hasn't she just shown that she's too good for this world?'

'I said too good for *you*.' It was with insolence that he repeated it. 'Yet she must care about you to do what she did. It was a thing way outside her ordinary scope, I'd say.'

'Care about *me*? You're right off the beam, Darrow.' Perhaps there was a touch of hysteria in my own laugh. The whole affair was so grotesque, so beyond all hope of conveying to anyone whose acquaintance with Jocasta was only a few days old.

'Why else would she do it? She wanted to save your skin and she succeeded.'

My bloodstream seemed to freeze. 'Save my skin?'

'Just that, though I don't imagine she dreamed how near you were to losing it. Maybe "save your honour" would be the polite way of putting it. You must have had some once.'

'I don't understand,' I said. I really didn't.

'She knows you're a faker, but she doesn't know I know. I kept it under my hat because I was out to get you, Williams. There couldn't have been a greater pleasure in life for me than to send you to jail. Thanks to her it can't be done now, but at least I'll give myself the satisfaction of telling you I have the lowdown on you.'

'I wish you'd explain yourself.' I was able to speak quite collectedly. After the first icy shock of encountering his hostility I'd grown numb. The drama seemed remote, and although I did want an explanation, it was almost impersonally as if I were reading the last chapter of a novel to unravel its plot, or waiting for the denouement that would bring down the curtain on a play.

'Listen, you—!' He bit back the expletive, whatever it was, but shot me instead a glance of unveiled malevolence. 'Don't hand me that line! Don't play the innocent with me! I'm wise to you now. You're a forger. What's more you're the kind of forger I *resent*.' His sense of injury drove his voice upward and made it quiver rather comically on the word. 'You hurt the standards I live by. You undermine a profession I'm proud of. You cast discredit on the merchandise of every dealer in the world who handles manuscripts, you prostitute scholarship, you plant lies and disseminate them. . . .'

'I inspire you to make long and frenzied speeches.'

'Frenzied! I'll say I'm frenzied! With my passage home postponed right on top of the Spada sale, with the sensation I went and worked up at John Murray's, with Mr. Peascod's London banker going out of his way to see me through this deal . . .'

'I never offered you any deal.'

'Williams, I told you not to hand me that line, and I'm feeling dangerous!' Possibly his vehemence affected me in spite of myself, possibly the love of justice in which, it must be evident, I'm not deficient acted as a constraint. At any rate, I held my peace. 'You never offered me any deal because you were playing safe all the way along. I'll admit I fell for it, your noble reluctance about the money angle. You put that over mighty convincingly, and it wasn't an easy thing to do. But this evening for a change it was *me* stringing *you* along. I was hell-bent on making you show your hand at last, Williams, and I did too. You were cagey, but you'd have gone as far as I needed.'

'I'm still waiting to hear what you think you've discovered.' I couldn't have been calmer. Had there existed any chance of saving the situation, I might have managed to generate some heat, some vitality, but with my creation reduced to ashes and Jocasta obviously enlightened somehow or other as to its nature, there wasn't much point in putting on an act, and I was more exhausted from the histrionics of the last few days than I'd dreamed I should be.

'Listen!' He positively hissed it at me. 'I called up Mr. Leverett this morning and went out to South Brockford a couple of hours ago to buy those Baskervilles. (You can tell that busy little green-eyed watch-dog of yours to lie down—Jocasta had an appointment with the hairdresser.) I'd no sooner rounded up what I wanted and started talking money, which takes some working up to in that house, when Mrs. Leverett brought in an unexpected visitor. For the rest of my life I'll be blessing his name, but just then he was highly unwelcome. Does Ockrington mean anything to you? The Reverend?'

'A boring sleazy character who hung round my great-aunt's house in Wales. I can't think where he comes into this.'

'You don't have to. I'm telling you. Mr. Leverett managed to remember him as an old pupil, so I got up to make myself scarce, but Mrs. Leverett was at the door signalling that she didn't want me to leave them alone together. I gather that old pupils who take to dropping out of the blue after staying away twenty years are liable to have something special in the way of nuisance value.'

'I warned Ockrington against going there. He'd brought his ridiculous petition, I suppose?'

'That was his real object—to get backing for a protest against the way the bishops are treating him—but, luckily for me, he started in with some rather corny excuses. He said he knew they were in touch with *you* and he'd mislaid your address. He was anxious to return some notes you'd left in a hotel in Wales, and as he happened to be passing and he'd always wanted to look up his dear old teacher, to recall happy associations . . . *et cetera, et cetera*. He made quite a speech.'

'Notes I'd left in a hotel!' I was completely at sea, and Darrow let me flounder there.

'The waiter kept them for you but as you didn't come in again he gave them to Ockrington to pass on. Mr. Leverett said his grand-daughter would surely be seeing you this evening and that she could take care of it, so Ockrington was obliged to hand over. After that there was a certain amount of embarrassment in the air. I didn't go, and having given those phoney reasons for stopping by, he couldn't do anything much about getting rid of me. Finally, when the small talk gave out, he was obliged to shoot his line as if I hadn't been there—how by the merest chance he'd mistakenly been mixed up in some divorce, and how the bishops were plotting to throw him out of the Church, and he knew Mr. Leverett would want to play fair and hear his side of the story. The poor old gentleman was most unhappy— said he'd never heard *any* side of the story and was there much point in telling him, and so forth. But Ockrington was all set now to go ahead. And I was going ahead too, Williams. What do you think I was doing?'

'Reading the document, whatever it was, that didn't concern you.' I wasn't genuinely indignant, only keeping up a front. I felt the detachment of a man who has been drugged.

'You know better than to say it doesn't concern me!' He seemed on the verge of growing tense again, but perhaps the realisation that he held all the cards soothed him, for he quickly relaxed. 'You couldn't call it a document—not much of a one anyhow. It was just a page of a loose-leaf book. Mr. Leverett put it on the desk where we had the Baskervilles laid out and—yes, I admit it, I took a little peek at it. You see, this Ockrington said it was evidently meant for the novel you were working on, and he gave a kind of snicker about the things that get into novels these days. Your attitude to the Byron Memoirs has been distinctly on the puritanical side, so I was a little curious as to what raw stuff you were going to try and get away with yourself. If it had been a letter I shouldn't have looked—I hope—but notes for a book, right there on the desk in front of me . . .'

'Notes for a book!' Still I reached in vain for some illuminating memory. All my notes had been destroyed, I could have sworn it.

'Shall I put you out of your misery?'

He took a small diary from his breast pocket, turned to the back pages, and read: '"The Earl of O— was reputed to be the best-natured cuckold in London, and such I found him when I held on a short lease both his house and his spouse." Do those words convey anything?'

Convey anything! They conveyed everything. The woods on the way to the Portmeirion Hotel, the particular tree I'd been leaning against when I wrote that sentence, the rage I was in because Jocasta had been to Newstead Abbey, my struggle to find the right key for my anecdote, the ambling walk among the autumnal foliage, the tide receding over the glassy sands viewed from my lunch-table, my satisfaction in having at last worked myself into the mood of fluency—and the shattering interruption by Ockrington.

What had I done? Dropped the discarded leaf in the flurry and annoyance of being disturbed by that tiresome man? It was possible. Although I'd been exceedingly careful, I should hardly have missed such a scrap nor anticipated that a waiter would deem it worth preserving for me.

Ockrington, I could guess at once, had hung on to it as a pretext for his call on Mr. Leverett. If he'd believed it was something I needed, he would have asked my Aunt Beth to forward it to me. In a few sharp instants I recalled so much and deduced so much, I hadn't the effrontery to lie. My recognition must have spoken in my eyes.

'I copied it,' he informed me with muted triumph. 'Every word including the variants and the cancellations—and the odd jottings. You may say that wasn't very ethical, but my ethics are for my customers, and you'd taken me for such a hell of a ride! There I was tucked away behind that high roll-top desk, with Ockrington preaching at Mr. Leverett and the proof right there in my hands. I'd have been a louse not to try and hit back.'

'I don't agree that it is proof,' I said with what was doubtless a melancholy suavity.

'Stop bluffing, Williams! That paper was a fragment of an author's first draft. Do you think I've handled manuscripts fourteen years for nothing? The phrase about taking a short lease of the house and the spouse—you used it in your forgery, and I hadn't forgotten it. And remember that neat little giveaway about Lady Melbourne? "Did she go to bed with him?" If those

Memoirs were genuine, why should you ask yourself that?' He paused and suddenly resumed in his high indignant note: 'That's another thing I don't like about you! Yours was a *nasty* forgery. In your highbrow way you were stooping to a pretty low level.'

'That was the last thing *you* seemed to object to.' It was the retort irresistible.

'Oh, I'll grant I was amused, but then I don't set up to be a Byron admirer. You did, and all the while you were faking confessions that couldn't have been worse if you'd had a personal spite against the man. It was a clever "alibi"—I'll hand you that—pulling the wool over our eyes with your fine talk while you were working out how much you could pep up sales by keeping it dirty.'

'That's really not true.' The impossibility of unfolding what was true enfeebled my protesting voice.

'It's true right enough and God! was I looking forward to the showdown?'

'I could see you were looking forward to something. It doesn't seem to have occurred to you that you'd have been inflicting great misery on Jocasta and her grandparents too.'

'It didn't occur to me then because, when I realised what you'd been putting over on me I was hopping mad. I could have watched you die by slow torture. Now I've had time to cool off, I don't deny it's a relief to me that she got in first with that heroic act of hers. I wish I could believe you had any idea of just how heroic it was, Williams.'

'If it was for my sake—yes.'

'For your sake! Who else's sake, for pete's sake, did she do it for?'

I humbled myself to the dust. 'But you haven't explained how she knew.'

He didn't crow over my abasement. Indeed it seemed to appease him somewhat, and he answered almost expansively.

'It appears that when she got back from the hairdresser's, Mrs. Leverett asked her to try and break up the session with Ockrington. The old gentleman had reached a state where any diversion was welcome, so as soon as she came in he led off with a flourish about these notes for your novel that Ockrington had so obligingly brought along. Whereupon she says, in her rather too truthful way, what a pity he went to so much trouble because you'd stopped writing the book. Mr. Leverett, aiming to soften that down a little, I guess, ups and tells her the notes could be something you'd want to keep all the same: so instead of dropping that page in the waste-paper basket, which I thought for a moment she was going to do, she glances over it. "It's not his novel," she says, "it's—" And she pulls herself up. Then she puts it quickly in the pocket of her dress and goes and stares out of the window.

'She was puzzled. Ockrington went off at last—he couldn't make much headway with two of us linking around—and she slipped out and left me to get down to business again. She came back later with a tray of tea, but she excused herself from staying to pour it out—said she had to get ready for her evening's work. She was more than puzzled by this time—she was worried. Once or twice I caught her looking at me out of the corner of her eye as if she was wondering whether I'd seen it or not—'

'She must have known you'd seen it.'

'No, I wasn't at the desk when she came into the room. I was warming my feet at the fire—how they live through the winter in that house I can't imagine!—and I didn't bat an eyelid. All I wanted was to spring it on you at John Murray's that the ride was over.'

'You like to play to an audience.'

'I had to make you commit yourself in front of witnesses.'

'They mightn't have enjoyed it as much as you anticipated.'

'If you're hinting that the scene wouldn't have been in the best of taste, you've got me on your side at last. But in self-defence—that sounds good coming from me to you!—I hadn't a notion Jocasta was going to be present.'

'Didn't you arrive together?'

'I thought you'd notice that. Say, you ought to see a psychiatrist about that jealousy of yours. It's a neurosis.'

I stood on my dignity and he hurried on, a shade embarrassed: 'I had to have a cab all the way on account of the pile of books I was toting, so I offered her a lift to town. She couldn't very well refuse as we were both heading for the same date, though she never mentioned it till after we'd left the house.'

'The only reason for that was to keep the secret from her grandparents. I didn't want to tell them just yet.'

'Not until you'd cleaned up.'

'It wasn't that. The fact is they'd have considered it wrong to publish. They'd have taken it the same way as she did.'

'As she pretended to. Not that she wasn't shocked right enough. You'd done your best after all to make it hair-raising. I can't figure out why you let her read it. What came over you?'

I shied away from that. 'It's funny,' I said on an impulse. 'You'll never dream what it cost me to produce that book and yet in a way I'm glad it's gone. At least, I can feel I shall be glad one day. I doubt very much whether I'd have been able to go through with it when it came to the point—the awful solidity of print.'

'I'm afraid I don't find that very credible.'

'I wouldn't have found it credible myself an hour ago, but you said something at John Murray's that gave me a turn. I had a sort of revulsion against myself.'

'I hoped you would. The way I see it is this—if Byron had written those reminiscences, they ought to be on the record whether they'd injure his reputation or not: the truth is what matters, the truth about human nature. But if you wrote them, a man of your ability using his talents to smear a great name, then you needed to have it brought home to you that you'd done a pretty slimy trick. All the cleverness you put into it only makes it so much the worse.'

They were bitter words but not bitterly spoken. My confession had purged him of his rage, and he ended his speech by trying to signal to the waiter. I didn't want to reject what would be on his part a gesture of *rapprochement*, but neither could I accept it, humiliated as I had been, so I rose with an air of valediction.

'Are you going to tell the others?' I waved my hand in the direction of John Murray's.

'I can't avoid it. There are six people, counting Sir John, who'll be haunted by this business for a long time to come. You don't suppose the story of the Memoirs being burned all over again won't leak out and grow to be a nuisance.'

'And everyone will blame Jocasta.' I got in first with that. 'Look, Darrow, ring them up at once and say you'll be back. You'll find them there still. They won't have broken up yet after such a melodrama. Give me a piece of paper and I'll write a note apologising profusely to everyone concerned and admitting it was a hoax. You can take it with you and there's an end of all arguments.'

'A hoax, eh?' He stared at me ruefully, whimsically, and finally with something of his accustomed jauntiness. 'Well, you certainly haven't gained anything by it, so we might as well let it go at that. They'll be so relieved to have their beloved Byron acquitted, maybe they'll fall for it.'

'It'll depend on how you put it over, Darrow.' I looked down at him with all the charm I could muster. It wasn't much.

'That's cool. You can't expect to come out of it with banners waving and flags flying. Even as a practical joker you won't exactly rate *persona grata*. Remember—you're still the man who cooked up something "not fit to publish" in the middle of the twentieth century. Or do I tell them Jocasta was putting on an act?'

'No,' I said, 'because you haven't convinced me that she was. Perhaps she really only glanced at that paper and noticed vaguely that it was on the subject we weren't going to discuss in front of her grandfather. Naturally she'd pull herself up and put it out of sight. She may never have given it another thought.'

'Williams, I evidently failed to make the point that she was worried.' His emphasis was impassioned. 'Our drive to Albemarle Street was positively funereal.'

'She'd have been worried in any case.' I was arguing with myself rather than him. I couldn't decide whether I preferred to believe that she'd seen through my fraudulence or that she'd braved my own and everyone else's anger to protect an idol.

'You haven't got much to go on if you didn't actually see her read what I'd written—word for word, I mean.'

'She read it all right. That dress of hers has two pockets, one on each side. She put it in the left-hand one, and when she came back with the tea, it was in the right. I saw the corner of it sticking out. Say, I'd better go call them up while you write your piece. Come along to the writing-room!'

He turned back after leaving me at a desk and said quietly— for there was someone else within earshot: 'It isn't that I want to add to your troubles, but I do think you ought to appreciate what she did for you. She's the kind of girl who might never tell you herself.'

He wasn't quite right. She didn't tell me, but she did send me back that miserable piece of paper, which came to the same thing. With it there was a brief letter which informed me that, my feelings for her having obviously changed in the last few months, I wouldn't be hurt by the breaking of our engagement.

Envoi

I HAVE written this record in my spare time at the London office of TROCO. It's a makeshift sort of room in Notting Hill Gate, over the premises occupied by Health Beverages, Ltd., the firm that markets Nokaff, the coffee substitute, and the tannin-free tea called Kosikup. The lease was obtained for a low price because the tenure is insecure; the building is to be pulled down at any time for road widening. When I took the job of London organiser—or had it thrust on me—I was under the impression that this circumstance would soon give me my get-out, but we're doing so well that the Committee is already negotiating for a lease in the new block.

Let no one tell me that success is the outcome of a will to succeed. I never wanted TROCO to survive, and I didn't think it could, but it appears that conscientious objection to taxation is a far more popular cause than I'd imagined or than my great-aunt had ever yet espoused. From the time we issued our first manifesto in *The Nudist*, *The Psychic Gazette*, *The Home Psychiatrist*, and *The Amateur Stockbroker*, we began to enrol members. Now it's largely a question of getting forms filled in and circulars sent out, and fixing engagements for our lecturers; so I often have a few hours to myself.

When I lost my job at Mrs. Rossiter's (we were never on very good terms after she suspected me of malingering), I got into pretty low water and was obliged to turn to my Aunt Beth for assistance, and after that it wasn't easy for me to shuffle out of that idiotic bargain I made with her when I was trying to get possession of a book that was already mine. I did hope to beat a retreat before I'd committed myself too far, but when Ockrington disappeared with the funds she'd raised to finance his promised campaign, I really couldn't bring myself to let her down. Besides there was the prospect of a livelihood in it, and I was extremely anxious just then to keep out of the world of books and publishers where, as Darrow had suggested, I mightn't have *persona grata* rating. Rumours about the great Byron hoax never reached the general public, but they did filter through here and there in literary circles.

I often think that if Jocasta hadn't frustrated that audacious and regrettable enterprise, I might have found myself entirely at the mercy of Ockrington, for I dare say it wouldn't have taken him long to realise the nature of my supposed 'notes for a novel' once I'd launched a book of Byron Memoirs.

By the way, he never got Mr. Leverett to start off his precious petition. For all his kind-heartedness, the old gentleman, like his grand-daughter, can turn into granite over a matter of principle; and when Ockrington persisted, he made inquiries about the case. The bishops had their way, and somewhere or other an unfrocked clergyman is living on his wits.

Aunt Beth took his defection better than one would have expected. She'd met the managing director of Health Beverages in the course of acquiring the London office, and when he told her he was struggling single-handed against the whole tea industry, not to speak of coffee, the appeal was instantaneous. She's busy at the moment translating his pamphlet against coffee-drinking into Welsh.

I used to wonder when I was working on my counterfeit what sin I could devise for Byron that Jocasta would regard as unforgivable. It never struck me that I might involve him in a mild case of forgery, yet apparently that was all that was needed. At any rate she hasn't yet forgiven it in me.

I catch an occasional elusive glimpse of her, because her grandparents have remained attached to me. They impute our broken engagement to a change of heart, a lovers misunderstanding, and they seem to hope that time will clear it up. I am less optimistic. Jocasta's star is rising. She's in the top flight now, and models of her quality often achieve brilliant marriages. Freed from the claims that I once made upon her time, she goes about much more. She can provide domestic help too for the old people. I understand her distant cousins, the Nunheatons and the Tandons, no longer consider her ineligible but are very pressing nowadays in their invitations.

A much-photographed beauty is after all a desirable asset in any circle. For my own part I could do with fewer of those pictures, which are beginning to be accompanied by items in the gossip columns: they add substantially to the difficulties of getting her out of my system. I understand so well what she meant when she said it would be hard to recover from a love affair with Byron because of having constantly to hear about him.

I haven't done any writing, except this, since the destruction of what I must continue repiningly to look upon as my *chef d'oeuvre*, but now that the shock of that episode has been deadened by time, I shall make it my aim to escape ultimately from TROCO by resuming somehow or other my literary career. The trouble is that I can't write fiction, and it takes a long while to amass the material for a biographical work. I deplore the waste of all my preparations for a full-scale book on Byron, but I've grown to feel rather out of sympathy with the subject, and without sympathy the biographer labours in vain.

Of course, there's still the excellent card index Mr. Leverett presented to me so that I might produce my little anthology about Byron and the animal kingdom. I'm toying again with that idea. It'll be rather a comedown, but the subject has at least the merit of being absolutely sexless and free from the least trace of specious romanticism.

I wonder if Jocasta still reads Byron. It seems doubtful. I'm inclined to flatter myself, fatuously perhaps, that all that enthusiasm—a good deal of it anyhow—was the consequence of trying to share something with me and, later, to wean me away from writing a bad novel.

I don't say there wasn't an element of day-dreaming in it. . . . Or was it my uneasy conscience that made me start at shadows? Or again did an unquiet spirit, not yet purged of mischief—? No, I will not, I positively shall not revert to superstition.

THE END

FURROWED MIDDLEBROW

FM1. *A Footman for the Peacock* (1940) . . . . RACHEL FERGUSON
FM2. *Evenfield* (1942) . . . . RACHEL FERGUSON
FM3. *A Harp in Lowndes Square* (1936) . . . . RACHEL FERGUSON
FM4. *A Chelsea Concerto* (1959) . . . . FRANCES FAVIELL
FM5. *The Dancing Bear* (1954) . . . . FRANCES FAVIELL
FM6. *A House on the Rhine* (1955) . . . . FRANCES FAVIELL
FM7. *Thalia* (1957) . . . . FRANCES FAVIELL
FM8. *The Fledgeling* (1958) . . . . FRANCES FAVIELL
FM9. *Bewildering Cares* (1940) . . . . WINIFRED PECK
FM10. *Tom Tiddler's Ground* (1941) . . . . URSULA ORANGE
FM11. *Begin Again* (1936) . . . . URSULA ORANGE
FM12. *Company in the Evening* (1944) . . . . URSULA ORANGE
FM13. *The Late Mrs. Prioleau* (1946) . . . . MONICA TINDALL
FM14. *Bramton Wick* (1952) . . . . ELIZABETH FAIR
FM15. *Landscape in Sunlight* (1953) . . . . ELIZABETH FAIR
FM16. *The Native Heath* (1954) . . . . ELIZABETH FAIR
FM17. *Seaview House* (1955) . . . . ELIZABETH FAIR
FM18. *A Winter Away* (1957) . . . . ELIZABETH FAIR
FM19. *The Mingham Air* (1960) . . . . ELIZABETH FAIR
FM20. *The Lark* (1922) . . . . E. NESBIT
FM21. *Smouldering Fire* (1935) . . . . D.E. STEVENSON
FM22. *Spring Magic* (1942) . . . . D.E. STEVENSON
FM23. *Mrs. Tim Carries On* (1941) . . . . D.E. STEVENSON
FM24. *Mrs. Tim Gets a Job* (1947) . . . . D.E. STEVENSON
FM25. *Mrs. Tim Flies Home* (1952) . . . . D.E. STEVENSON
FM26. *Alice* (1949) . . . . ELIZABETH ELIOT
FM27. *Henry* (1950) . . . . ELIZABETH ELIOT
FM28. *Mrs. Martell* (1953) . . . . ELIZABETH ELIOT
FM29. *Cecil* (1962) . . . . ELIZABETH ELIOT
FM30. *Nothing to Report* (1940) . . . . CAROLA OMAN
FM31. *Somewhere in England* (1943) . . . . CAROLA OMAN
FM32. *Spam Tomorrow* (1956) . . . . VERILY ANDERSON
FM33. *Peace, Perfect Peace* (1947) . . . . JOSEPHINE KAMM

FM34. *Beneath the Visiting Moon* (1940) . . . . ROMILLY CAVAN
FM35. *Table Two* (1942) . . . . MARJORIE WILENSKI
FM36. *The House Opposite* (1943) . . . . BARBARA NOBLE
FM37. *Miss Carter and the Ifrit* (1945) . . . . SUSAN ALICE KERBY
FM38. *Wine of Honour* (1945) . . . . BARBARA BEAUCHAMP
FM39. *A Game of Snakes and Ladders* (1938, 1955) . . . .
. . . . DORIS LANGLEY MOORE
FM40. *Not at Home* (1948) . . . . DORIS LANGLEY MOORE
FM41. *All Done by Kindness* (1951) . . . . DORIS LANGLEY MOORE
FM42. *My Caravaggio Style* (1959) . . . . DORIS LANGLEY MOORE
FM43. *Vittoria Cottage* (1949) . . . . D.E. STEVENSON
FM44. *Music in the Hills* (1950) . . . . D.E. STEVENSON
FM45. *Winter and Rough Weather* (1951) . . . . . . D.E. STEVENSON
FM46. *Fresh from the Country* (1960) . . . . MISS READ

Lightning Source UK Ltd.
Milton Keynes UK
UKHW012135060921
390129UK00003B/1067

9 781913 054618